*Understanding*
# MALE SEXUAL HEALTH

*Understanding*

# MALE SEXUAL HEALTH

## Dorothy Baldwin

HIPPOCRENE BOOKS
New York

For information, address:
HIPPOCRENE BOOKS, INC.
171 Madison Avenue
New York, NY 10016

*Library of Congress Cataloging-in-Publication Data is available.*

ISBN 0-87052-955-2

Printed in the United States of America.

# CONTENTS

# Introduction

Is it true that jogging can reduce sexual desire?

Should my baby have surgery for an undescended testicle? Why do some small boys keep clutching their organs?

What are male breasts, and why do they occur? Why is there a risk of losing a testicle at puberty? Why do the testicles sometimes ache?

What are the symptoms of cancer of the testicle? What is the appropriate way to deal with spots on the buttocks?

Should a man have an orgasm each time he makes love?

Why is there sometimes pain on ejaculation? What do blood spots in the ejaculate signify?

Are there proven methods to increase sexual desire?

Does Spanish Fly work as an aphrodisiac?

Are there any methods to improve failing erections?

What is the size of an average penis?

Is it normal to have a penis with a bend at the tip?

Why might an erection be slow to subside after orgasm?

Is the saying "Use it, or lose it" true?

Are weak erections due to masturbating when young? Is it damaging to ejaculate too often? How much is too often?

Can anything be done to prevent prostate problems? What are the chances of potency loss after prostate surgery?

My baby son has penile hypospadias. Is surgery necessary?

What are the advantages and disadvantages of circumcision?

Is it true that boisterous sex can cause Peyronie's disease?

What are the pros and cons of a penile implant?

The answers to these and many more questions are to be found in this book.

Research shows:

· The average male driver will not stop to ask for directions.
· He does not visit a physician unless he is seriously unwell.
· He is unaware his specialist physician is called a *urologist*.

What research does not show are the reasons for this. Many problems which afflict the male organs are *avoidable* if men take care of their health. Minor ailments of the male reproductive system can develop into major problems if they are ignored.

## It's Nothing Much, Doc

When the average man visits a physician, he hides his feelings. He says, "It's nothing much, Doc," even when the condition may be causing him grave concern. The average physician lacks training in sexual problems. Nor does he/she have a chance to gain much experience. From puberty onwards, men are the "great absence" in the physician's office.

Men suffer in a particularly distressing way when ill-health strikes. Many lack even elementary knowledge of human biology, and have no idea what is amiss. Naturally, they start to feel anxious or angry, often a mixture of both. One common response is to pull up the drawbridge and become isolated with their fears. Another is to strongly deny anything is wrong.

In this way, a minor ailment can progress to a major one, which is further aggravated by psychologic stress. When fear or pain finally force the man to the doctor's office, it is hardly surprising his behavior appears cranky. There is then the added risk that his ailment is diagnosed as psychological, when it often is not.

The goals of this book are to overcome these problems by providing information on issues of sexual health. Parents wish to know what is happening to their baby boy or growing son. Partners of men find it helps to understand the mysteries of male ill health. And men themselves will benefit from knowing how to take care of themselves.

Some articles deal with everyday problems and *how to avoid them*. Others discuss the self help options available when things go amiss. If medical intervention is required, the reasons why are clearly stated. Avoid denial. Eschew delay. When something is amiss, be prepared to seek help. In mid to late life, the main concerns are less firm erections and prostate enlargement. *95 percent of these conditions can be treated or managed if therapy is sought early enough.*

Men with an attitude problem towards physicians may consider the following research. More U.S. physicians die by suicide than road accidents, drowning and homicide combined. An estimated 12.9 percent abuse alcohol or drugs, or suffer psychiatric problems such as depression, at some time in their life (about the same incidence as the general population). There is little doubt a physician's work is highly stressful. Burn-out is common, particularly among the more sensitive, diligent and dedicated groups.

U.K. physicians get worse medical care for themselves than they give to their patients. They find it difficult to admit to health problems. One study found only 25 per cent had discussed their blood pressure with a colleague. And 40 per cent said they would definitely not seek medical help for sexual problems as they feared being thought inadequate by their peers.

This is not to attack physicians, nor to undermine due respect and admiration for their work. It is intended to reduce the attitude of awe which can be inspired in the layman and acts as a deterrent when contemplating a visit to the doctor's office. This awe can also undermine a man's ability to make health decisions for himself. It may help to remember that though most physicians are highly skilled and truly dedicated, a few are not.

Many male problems are still perceived as "closet" issues. Information concerning them lies buried beneath arcane medical terminology. Yet parents wish to know what is happening to their baby boy or growing son. Many partners of men wish to understand the mysteries of male ill health. And men themselves will benefit from knowing how to avoid sexual problems. Perhaps it is time to put aside a certain squeamishness and encourage a more open attitude toward male health.

Urology is the branch of medicine which specializes in the study and treatment of diseases of the urinary tract. The specialties include Pediatric Urology, Female Urology, Prostate Surgery, Neuro-urology, Urologic Cancer, Reconstructive Surgery, Kidney Stones, Incontinence, Sexual Dysfunction and Infertility.

Not all urologists specialize in all these areas. In fact, infertility and sexual dysfunction are recent additions to their lists. Some gynecologists (female diseases) and obstetricians (pregnancy and childbirth) have more experience. Pediatricians (general medicine in childhood) may be more familiar with infant malformation of the reproductive organs and urinary tract.

Before choosing a urologist, ask a physician if the problem is minor. It may be easily treated by a local specialist. But if the problem is major, or rare, or requires delicate microsurgery, seek the most highly-experienced urologist in town. Studies show the more often one particular type of surgery is performed, the more successful is the outcome.

If a major or rare condition is diagnosed, consider joining a self-help group. The members focus on one issue alone, and so can provide more inside information than a busy urologist with a wide-ranging practice. They have experience in coping with the condition in a positive manner which is often invaluable.

New therapies are constantly in the clinical trial stage. And there have been many medical advances in knowledge of male ailments. When sexual ill health strikes, avoid the usual manly response which is to ignore the problem and "soldier on." Though admirable in war, it is a misplaced virtue in issues of health. The problem may be one which is now easily resolved.

As far as possible, be your own physician. Many conditions which afflict the genitals are self-healing: they *will* get better by themselves. But others are severe, or highly infectious, and require urgent medical intervention. Use the text as a resource to distinguish between the two. Follow the preventive and self help programs throughout the book.

Above all, start today to give sexual health the respect and attention it deserves.

# CHAPTER 1

# The Penis

## The Great Divide

The penis is central to a man's image of himself. It is the focus of his masculinity, of his deepest concerns. Yet many men are unaware of the basic structure of the organ. This lack of information can give rise to needless concerns.

The penis and scrotum first develop as a single open tube. The lower edges form a groove which fuse together in early fetal life. This ventral groove can be seen as a "join" line on the underside of the penis. It continues on, and crosses over the scrotum like a great divide. The join can be very noticeable or the faintest of lines. There is no health significance whether it is clearly marked or not.

In childhood, the underside of the penis may not be viewed closely. If the join is first seen in adult life, it is a common cause of concern. A few men visit their physician in a state of anxiety. There is no need for concern. All is well.

## The Sliding Shaft

The penis is divided into two parts, the *shaft* and the *glans*. The longer portion is the shaft. The associated word is vagina, which is Latin for sheath. Sword and scabbard: shaft and sheath. Not much of human anatomy is so aptly named.

There is a long root to the penis deep within the pelvis. It is half the size again of the external shaft. The root acts as an anchor, and

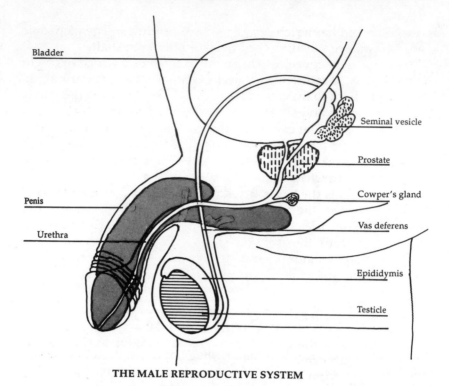

Bladder

Seminal vesicle

Prostate

Cowper's gland

Penis

Vas deferens

Urethra

Epididymis

Testicle

**THE MALE REPRODUCTIVE SYSTEM**

is a sturdy support for the extra weight of the penis at erection. Muscles around the root allow only a slight penile movement. Their main function is to assist in ejaculation.

The skin of the shaft is hairless, rather like the skin of the eyelids. It has the same elasticity and is freely movable. These factors allow the skin to slide backwards and forwards some distance. They provide a greater surface area to accommodate the organ when it is erect.

The shaft is not as sensitive as is sometimes thought. It has no extra density of nerve endings, just the normal amount. In this respect, it almost exactly matches the vagina. In fact, the shaft is slightly less sensitive than the sheath.

## The Gladsome Glans

The word *glans* comes from the Latin for "acorn." It aptly describes a baby boy's cone-shaped top. The glans is lined with mucus membranes, like the linings inside the mouth. The function of mucus is to keep the area clean and comfortably damp. The skin is very fine and has a rich supply of nerve endings. The gladsome glans is far more sensitive (and delicate) than the shaft.

The *foreskin* (prepuce) is a thick protective hood which fits right over the glans. It retracts (rolls back) a short distance for urination. It rolls right back to the *corona* at erection. The corona is the fleshy ring where glans and shaft meet. It is a Latin word which rather splendidly means "an encircling crown." Some men do not know if they still have a foreskin. An unskilled circumcisor has left so much skin behind the glans looks intact. For more information on circumcision, see Chapter 2.

The *frenulum* is the band of stringlike tissue under the glans. It is the join where the ventral groove of the penile tube fused together in fetal life. The frenulum acts as a valuable brake at erection. It stops the foreskin from rolling back too far. The frenulum has even more nerve endings than the glans. It, and the corona, are the site of maximum sensitivity on the penis.

## The "Eye" of the Storm

The opening of the glans is the *meatus*. It leads to the *urethra*, the tube for both urine and sperm. Close inspection of the meatus shows the lips form a vertical slit. Yet the urethra is horizontal, and lined with tiny ducts which open out against the stream as it passes. This arrangement is a neat simple hygiene device. Instead of urine leaving the meatus in a wide splashing spray, it is forced through the lips in a narrow spiral arc.

*Symmetry in nature is less common than may be thought.* Many a meatus is not in the center of the glans, but a few millimeters *under* the tip. Parents need not be concerned about the aesthetic effect. The position of the meatus is rarely, if ever, noticed by others. In fact, many men have this condition without being aware of it, which shows it is neither unusual, nor a reason for concern. A more extensive displacement of the meatus can occur, and parents may find this of interest. See Chapter 10.

## The Proper Study of Mankind. . .

Examine the penis at regular monthly intervals as part of Genital Self Examination (GSE). Become familiar with any freckles or moles. Blackheads or whiteheads may occur on the underside of the shaft. They clear up with appropriate genital hygiene. If wished, they can be popped out with *clean fingers*, and a *very mild* astringent dabbed on.

A *sebaceous cyst* can appear on the scrotum or the groin. It is due to blockage of the sebaceous glands. These produce an oil, *sebum*, which flows up the hair follicle to keep it lubricated. If sebum is trapped, it hardens into a yellow cheesy lump. There may be repeated attacks, or a single cyst.

Most sebaceous cysts remain small and undeveloped. They can be ignored, or popped out. But one which is rubbed by shorts can grow large and become infected. Avoid self-help. An infected cyst requires surgical excision which only takes a few moments in the physician's office. Sebaceous cysts are rare before puberty. During the monthly GSE, the important signs to check for are lumps, scaly patches and hard fibrous tissue (fibrous tissue feels inelastic, thickened and scarred). If present, they may be harmless but can be early signs of disease. Consult with a physician. If all is well, the visit is not wasted. Consultation brings that greatest of all health benefits: peace of mind.

# Penis Shape

In elementary school, they called G "Half Cock." They teased him, and would not let him join in their games. At age 21, Mr. G can still vividly recall the pain this caused. His one attempt at love-making ended in disaster. He was terrified Miss L would see that his penis was not straight.

Mr. G consulted a urologist. "I'm deformed," he said. "I'm afraid to make love. I want surgery to straighten my penis out. You cannot understand how *humiliating* my condition is."

Mr. G was examined for hypospadias. But all was well.

It is a popular fallacy that the male organ is straight. In fact, a perfectly straight penis is as rare as a perfectly straight nose. Some have bumps in the middle; these are "bottle" shapes. Others have bends at the tip; these are the "prows." And others which look straight in repose have a slight curve along their length when erect; these are "scythes." The reader may know of other interesting designs.

Teasing over penile shape starts among schoolboys. Most men can recall at least one episode from their youth. For the victim, the effects can be devastating and haunting; children tease in a more brutal way than adults remember. If there is added concern from

parents, the boy suffers further stress. It compounds his humiliation, his negative body-image and his pain.

A growing boy finds it difficult to share these sufferings. They
undermine his dignity and sense of self-worth. For a man, they can
cause catastrophic loss of self-esteem. And all this suffering is
utterly meaningless. Like so much needless hurt, it comes from
ignorance, nothing else.

A man needs to work back through the misery of the teasing. He
can re-experience each memory, then dump the lot. Keep in mind
penis shape is no more than the mark of the individual, just like
the shape of the face.

## Penis Size

Penis size is always a serious issue for men. Length and girth
measurements are of the utmost concern. From childhood onwards, all males are highly sensitive in this regard. WARNING!
No woman should be fooled by a partner who jokes of his small
size. He is *not* any less sensitive; it is likely he is more so.

Studies show the average man rates his size as "low" or "way
off what it should be." He believes his organ is size deficient, often
when it patently is not. A few men spend their entire lives under
this unhappy delusion. There is little a partner can do to assuage
this concern.

A U.S. study of body image problems found: *All the male respon-
dents, with the exception of the most extraordinarily endowed, expressed
doubts about their own sexuality based on their penile size.* It would
seem surprising if only American men express such doubts. It is
more likely these same doubts are common globally, regardless of
culture, color, creed or race.

## History Time

Male concern with penis size is not a modern phenomenon.
Back in the 14th century, Gabriele Fallopio (who first described the
fallopian tubes) typified this concern. In his instructions to parents
on how to raise sons, he sternly admonished them to "be zealous
in infancy to enlarge the penis of the boy."

Spare a thought for those poor parents! What were they supposed to do? How do you stretch a baby's penis lengthwise? And
what about *widthways*? The mind boggles at that. Fallopio's advice would be funny if it were not so absurd.

In some countries, pebbles are still tucked under the baby's foreskin to weight the penis down in the hope it will stretch. Apart from hurting the child, it does little else except to risk infection. Though skin tissue can be stretched, often to amazing lengths, the underlying structures resist these attempts.

# The Relaxed Penis

In the average adult male, the unerect penis is 4 1/2 inches long and 1 inch in diameter. *There is no such person as the average adult male.* In fact, the majority are between 3 1/4 and 4 1/2 inches long. Medical texts put any unerect penis of 2 to 6 inches as within normal range.

But is there such a state as an average unerect penis? The following can make a relaxed organ shrink by 2 inches or more:

· Very cold weather.
· Chilly baths or showers.
· A state of great exhaustion.
· A state of great excitement.
· Any mental or physical illness.
· Sexual activity which was satisfactory.
· Sexual activity which has failed.

In opposite conditions, the organ expands to its maximum. Warmth and a relaxed mental state are the factors to focus on. It is mainly in youth there is worry over unerect size. Adult men are more concerned with the non-relaxed state.

# The Erect Penis

In the average adult male, the erect penis is 6 1/4 inches long, and between 1 1/4 and 1 3/4 inches in diameter. *There is no such object as an average erect penis.* About ninety percent measure between five and seven inches long. A medical study of British men found the smallest erection was 4 3/4 inches long and the largest 9 inches. The longest *medically* recorded erection is 12 inches.

If you find an average man, shoot him!

Sensational stories in erotic magazines claim much larger sizes. The pornography industry admits the men they select to act in sex movies are not the norm.  An ongoing Australian study will soon provide a new *medical* record on size.

Shakespeare wrote "Comparisons are odorus," and his philosophy is still relevant because, at erection, there is a greater percent volume increase in the smaller penis than the larger one.  A long, low-hanging penis may lengthen a further 2 inches, whereas a small short penis can lengthen up to 3 3/4.  There is also a greater proportional girth increase in a smaller penis than a larger one.  Therefore, no man with a small unerect penis should feel inferior to a seemingly better endowed male.

## Women and Penis Size

The average vagina is between 3 and 5 inches long.  In its normal collapsed state, it is wide enough to accommodate two to three fingers.  At sexual arousal, the *inner two-thirds* increase in length a further 2 inches and widen to a full 2 inches.  This is known as the *ballooning effect*.  It is due to elevation, a natural rise of her reproductive organs when she is aroused.

The vagina has been called "endlessly accommodating."  And perhaps it is.  Because at sexual arousal the outer one-third narrows due to vaso-congestion (blood filling up the tissues), making them swollen and tight.  There is an actual gripping effect around the penis as it thrusts.  For this reason, penile girth may be less important than some men think.

If the average sizes of penis and vagina are compared, they make a perfect fit.  Yet there is a common male fantasy for tiny tight vaginas.  Only virgins have these.  If the vagina *does* feel tiny and tight in a non-virgin, the woman is not fully aroused.  She is *not* ready for penetration, regardless of penile size.

## Not Too Little. . .

Repeated childbirth can stretch the vaginal walls.  The muscles lose a degree of tone and elasticity, and the vagina feels relaxed.  A childless woman does not suffer this stretching, though she may lead an active sex life.  It is only the extreme duress of *repeated* childbirth which stretches the vaginal walls, and not in all cases.

A penis which is less-than-average in size may feel rather lost in a vagina which has stretched.  This is a common cause of concern for women in their late 30s and 40s, but only with *at least* two experiences of childbirth.  Another concern is a slight sagging at the vaginal entrance from poor surgical repair of an episiotomy, the cut used to ease the passage of childbirth.

To improve matters, experiment with different positions. In any problem of unequal size, choice of position can produce the desired effect. One option is for corrective plastic surgery to restore the vagina to its former size, but this is highly invasive. Nowadays, a stretched vagina is rare because women do exercises to regain muscle tone soon after the birth.

## Not Too Large. . .

The cervix consists of muscle which seals off the vagina at the top. It was not designed to be a barricade. Direct pounding on it would inflict pain, and thrusting would have to stop. The degree of pain can be compared to testicle pain from a sudden blow.

The ballooning effect protects women from this risk. It reduces the amount of direct pounding on the cervix, regardless of penis size. But ballooning occurs only at full sexual arousal. It does not occur otherwise. *Hence the value of foreplay.* A man with a large penis must pay special attention to this.

There is no extra density of nerve endings in the inner two-thirds of the vagina, just the average amount. So a woman's sexual pleasure does not depend on penile length. Maximum sensitivity and therefore the thrill a penetrating penis gives is confined to the outer third, the first two inches of the vagina. For these reasons, it is entirely unnecessary for any man to have doubts about his sexuality based on penile length.

## Self Help

Women with perfect figures often complain their stomachs are too large. This is because they get a fore-shortened view when looking down. In the same way, men get a distorted perspective of themselves. They get a smaller view of the penis in comparison with the breadth and girth of the abdomen and chest.

Avoid the fore-shortened, distorted perspective. Use a full-length mirror to examine organ size. Stand fully upright, with the shoulders relaxed and the abdomen drawn in. If the testicles are swollen for any reason, take this into account. It is another example of a comparably smaller view.

More men seem to have hang-ups over breast size than women over penis size. Nevertheless, "size-queens" do exist. Keep in mind hang-ups are neurotic in origin. They reflect the owner's insecurities, nothing else. It may help to realize size-queens are likely to be equally neurotic over other issues.

The *clitoris* is the female site of maximum sensitivity. Research shows that with sufficient friction, a woman will achieve orgasm if she so desires. The friction should be both rhythmic and pleasurable; it can take from 20 seconds to 20 minutes; it need not be directly on the clitoris but on the outer lips. This may occur before or during thrusting, and so is independent of organ size.

A micropenis (microphallus) is less than 2 cm. in length. It is an *extremely* rare birth defect. But at the mere mention of micropenis, a few men become convinced they have one. Check with a physician. If all is well, avoid this syndrome; avoid it at all costs. It is *denial*, an unconscious device to avoid other problems, not necessarily sexual ones. Imagining a micropenis is serious stuff, and no way to lead the good life.

## Phallacy — Fallacy

*The bigger the penis, the sexier the man*: a total fallacy. There is no relationship between penis size and the strength of the sex drive. Sexual energy comes from a complex interaction of a man's genes, his hormones, the kind of childhood he experienced, his body image and self-esteem, and his general physical and psychological health.

*The bigger the penis, the better the lover*: another fallacy. There are men with very large organs who do not satisfy their partners. And there are men with neat small organs whose partners are blissfully content. There is no relationship between penis size and love-making skills, though people who are neurotic about size insist that there is.

*The penis is the same size as the hands/feet*: again, no. Parts of the body cannot be used as a guide to penis size. Though a tall man usually has larger feet than a shorter man, this natural body equation does not work with the penis. For some unknown reason, the penis has a less constant relationship to body size than any other organ. Neither hands, feet nor any body part can be used as a predictor of penis size.

# The Glossy Glans

Tiny glands under the foreskin make a cheesy cream called *smegma*. It mainly consists of dead skin cells. Smegma is first produced at puberty, and then constantly throughout life. When fresh, it is whitish in color. It turns yellow or greenish-grey when stale. It is a valuable lubricating cream which prevents friction and keeps the glans comfortably clean and damp.

Like other body lubricants, stale smegma should be removed daily. If not, it quickly becomes a health risk. When smegma is stale, it becomes grainy in texture, the grainy texture causes friction and becomes an irritant. Irritants are carcinogens, substances which can cause cancer, and carcinogens are particularly dangerous in areas of high friction such as the glans.

A man may be more conscientious about changing the oil in his car than at washing off smegma from his penis. What can be made of this order of priority? Complete cleansing of the genitals is a daily must. This includes the circumcised penis because stale smegma collects in the skin creases of the frenulum and corona.

Young boys go through a stage of careless hygiene. They call smegma "cock-cheese" and pick at it with grubby fingers when it forms into stale little lumps. Lax hygiene is the major cause of penile infections in the teens. With appropriate hygiene, smegma is not a health risk. Parents can explain these factors to their growing sons.

# Urination

*No matter how you jump and dance,*
*The last few drops go in your pants.*

Men (and boys) rarely dry themselves after emptying the bladder. The last drops of urine are absorbed in their shorts. Fresh urine is germ-free but it does not take long for germs to breed in the warm environment of the groin. Change shorts daily, more often if they become stained; the moist heat from groin temperature causes stained underwear to smell unfresh. Pack an extra pair for a long day, or if traveling with no facilities for a shower.

Purchase underwear of loosely woven and porous fabrics. This allows air to circulate and keeps down groin temperature. Cotton and cotton mixes are affordable, easy to launder and quick to dry in a hotel room. Avoid 100 percent synthetic fibers; the fabric clings to skin and traps the natural release of heat. This can cause buttock pimples. Dab rubbing alcohol on the pimples. Talcum powder helps absorb sweat but can further clog the pores.

To avoid the last-few-drops-in-the-pants syndrome, apply upward pressure under the base of the penis. The pressure should release those last urine drops. Do it gently at first, until the correct pressure is found. It does not work for all men, nor at all times, but it might be worth a try.

# Hygiene

During the day, smegma and urine collect on the penis. If not washed off, they form a sticky greasy layer on the surface of the skin. This greasy layer is thickest at the glans. The sticky oils slide under the foreskin and form stale deposits there.

Without a foreskin, the greasy layer slides freely up the glans to the tiny crevices of the corona. They tuck into the wrinkled skin of the frenulum and form stale deposits there. When cleansing the penis, it is essential to first break down the greasy layer with plenty of soap. If not, water just flows over the oily deposits, but is unable to remove them.

## *Cleansing:*

· Start by washing the hands thoroughly.
· Avoid using body cloths as they can harbor germs.
· Work up a rich lather with warm water and plenty of soap.
· The water must be hot enough to soften and melt the grease.
· Use plenty of soap to break down the oils; to emulsify them.
· Avoid scented soaps as perfumes can cause contact dermatitis.
· Begin by washing the penis and the entire genital area.
· Then slide the foreskin right back and thoroughly wash the glans.
· Take extra care that the corona and frenulum are really clean.
· Rinse well, really well, with plenty of cool water.

# Love-Making and Hygiene

Some prostitutes ask their clients to wash before sex. (Nowadays, the brighter ones insist on a condom too.) But many partners in a relationship would not dream of asking the beloved to wash his genitals first, even when they are unfresh. It might spoil the moment. It might kill the romance.

A man can pay particular attention to genital hygiene *after* making love. He is then scrupulous in removing the pungent odor of sex from his skin. Men in this category may wish to check their priorities. Why wash after making love, and not before? Would this order of cleansing be acceptable in a partner?

Cancer of the cervix has increased in recent years. The two groups to avoid it are nuns and celibate women. Does this suggest a virus on the penis which carries a life-threatening risk? If so, is the virus more likely to be on a washed or unwashed penis? The virus is also transmitted through the male urethra, but it is first found on penile skin.

At the 1987 Singapore medical conference, Professor Wilbanks reported, "All circumstantial evidence indicates the papilloma virus, which causes cancer of the cervix, is infectious. However, there is no absolute proof of this. Male carriers of the papilloma virus are less likely to be aware of it because there is no itching, burning or pain as experienced by women." He advised men whose partners have cancer of the cervix to see a specialist in sexually transmitted disease. A particular tragedy of the virus is that many young girls are infected.

It is quicker and easier to wash a circumcised penis than an intact one. With the latter, the foreskin must be retracted to fully expose the glans. Women whose partners are circumcised get cancer of the cervix *far less often* than women whose partners are intact. What might this suggest about lax hygiene?

Medical opinion is divided as to why this female cancer is on the increase. Some physicians believe in the lax hygiene theory. Others cannot accept it due to insufficient research, and no absolute proof. However, they all agree that women should not be promiscuous. *The greater the number of partners, the greater the cancer risk.* What conclusions can be drawn from this? Until there is sufficient research and absolute proof, it may be appropriate for everyone to improve genital hygiene.

# Cancer of the Penis

Penile cancer is rare. It accounts for 0.5 percent of all male cancers in America. The figures for Europe are between 1 and 2.5

percent. Keep in mind these are percentages of all male cancers. They are *not* percentages of all men. Penile cancer is even more rare in circumcised men because the tumor cells mainly attack the foreskin.

A first symptom is a spot or sore which does not heal in two to three weeks. (*Any spot or sore anywhere which does not heal in this time might be a sign of cancer and requires prompt medical investigation*). Another first symptom is a mildly itchy foreskin, sometimes with a slight discharge. The discharge may be blood-stained and smell unpleasant. There is usually no pain with either symptom. Sometimes the glands in the groin are enlarged.

Penile cancer seems to be age related. It is extremely rare under age forty. The age of occurrence is sixty to seventy. Choice of therapy depends on many variables, including the man's general state of health. Radiation and chemotherapy are often successful. In advanced cases, it may be necessary to remove the penis to stop the cancer cells spreading.

## Advice for Older Men:

*During regular monthly GSE, pay special attention to the glans. Look for spots or sores which do not heal. Consult a physician at the first sign of alarm.*

The list of known carcinogens includes tars, soot, asbestos, chromium, tobacco smoke and strong sunlight. Penile cancer is linked with lax hygiene. One U.S. study found phimosis, a glans infection in uncircumcised males, present in 25 to 75 percent of cases. Maybe these poor men were unaware of the value of hygiene. Until all adults are fully informed, perhaps the greasy deposits from stale smegma, semen and urine can be added to the list of known carcinogens.

## The Strange Tale

Ben's uncle, being twenty, was seven years older than Ben, a real grown man. They were tossing a ball around in the yard.

"Where," Ben asked, "does the "p" word come from?"

"P for Peter?" his uncle teased. "It's American slang."

"No kidding!" It wasn't what Ben meant, but he was easily distracted. "How slang?"

"Peter was a lazy lumberjack who didn't work long, do his share.

His mates dubbed anyone like that Peter. The name caught on, in more ways than one."

"Nah! Peter means rock, a rock of moral strength."

His uncle laughed, "Yeah. Well, men also know it means to peter out." He continued teasing. "But maybe you were referring to "p" for phallus? It's a symbol. Poetry. Anything tall and pointy, soaring above humanity and reaching for the skies."

"Wow! Poetry!" Ben was impressed. Then, "Hey, you gonna quit foolin' me. Where does the *real* "p" word come from?"

"Oh, *penis*!" his uncle pretended to let light dawn. "From Latin. *Cauda.* It means a 'tail.'" His bright blue eyes suddenly turned serious. "Listen, Ben," he said. "The dog wags the tail, right? Got that clear? I never want to hear you let the tail wag the dog. Got it very clear?"

Ben got it only vaguely, and not at all clear. But he would within the next two years. He stored away his uncle's warning for future use. Strange, he mused, how many "p" words there were. He liked the phallus "p" best. Soaring above humanity! Reaching for the skies. Oh, wow!

CHAPTER 2

# Circumcision

## Circumcision

Male circumcision is the surgical removal of the foreskin. It is an issue of *culture* rather than health. It invades private areas of family, tradition and religion. Any discussion is likely to give offense. Yet today's parents may wish to weigh the pros and cons, and be aware of the health risks, before making this choice for a son.

In the 1st century, Philo, the distinguished philosopher, discussed his views on circumcision. They are brutal, and show Philo's attitude towards sexual love. He considered circumcision necessary for *"the excision of the passions."* He called the penis *"the instrument which serves these passions"* and said it should *"be mutilated, that these powerful passions be bridled."*

*Mutilated*: Philo's word! It must be deeply offensive to any circumcised man. But is his theory correct? Is the exposed glans less sensitive than the intact one? Masters and Johnson found there was no significant difference in the effect of a foreskin on sexual sensitivity before and after surgery. While no reflection on the study, the results of a newer study might be interesting now that more men are openly concerned.

And does excising the glans "tame" male passions? How do you research that? Whatever the answers, there are lessons to be learned, not only for parents, but of import to human happiness in general. Seeking some answers is the least we can do for our baby sons, our future men.

## Foreskin Facts

Until recently, the origin of the foreskin was a mystery. Embryologists now know the foreskin and glans develop from a single bud. *They are joined together at birth because neither is fully formed.* They are still developing, and continue to do so until they are ready to separate of their own accord.

*Only 4% of newborns have foreskins which have separated from the glans.* Some 50% of newborn boys have foreskins which cannot be moved back far enough to show the meatus (pee hole). Contrary to myth, a joined foreskin does *not* interfere with the ability to urinate. A baby's stream is checked soon after birth if he has not already obliged by then.

Dr. Hugh Jolly, an eminent pediatrician, wrote: "Clearly, the best thing to do about your newborn son's foreskin is nothing; leave it alone until it has separated from the glans and can be pushed back easily. You could try to do this, gently, when he is about 4 years old. During his bath is a good time to try. Don't persist if the foreskin does not go back easily; it's not an urgent matter. . . .

"Forcing back the foreskin before it goes back easily by itself is likely to tear the skin, causing bleeding. This tear heals with scarring which permanently joins the foreskin to the tip of the penis, so that correction by circumcision does become necessary. Paradoxically, therefore, ignorant management of the foreskin causes a problem where none existed."

Until the foreskin separates *in its own good time*, it protects the glans from infections. Like the clitoris, in infanthood the glans is self-cleansing. Paradoxically, it is the circumcised penis which requires extra hygiene. The tucks and wrinkles at frenulum and corona are ideal sites to harbor germs.

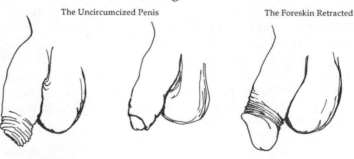

The Uncircumcized Penis          The Foreskin Retracted

# How the Deed Is Done

The following are descriptions of circumcision, Western style, as performed in modern high-tech hospitals on baby boys in their first weeks of life. Squeamish readers may not wish to read this.

## *The Clamp Method*

A ring-shaped clamp is pushed up under the baby's foreskin. The foreskin is then sliced away around the clamp. The clamp is held in place for a couple of minutes afterwards. This is to crush the raw tissue along the cut edges, and to slow down the bleeding.

## *The Guillotine*

The baby's foreskin is pulled forward right over the penis. It is then stretched as far as possible beyond the tip. The stretched foreskin is clamped firmly in the guillotine. The blade slices down and chops the foreskin off.

Both methods leave a raw area between the glans and shaft. In some cases, bleeding is profuse. The sliced-off edges slowly come together and the raw skin begins to close up. On average, it takes up to ten days for the entire wound to heal.

Jewish and Moslem parents can ask their rabbis and mullahs about the methods by which they perform the act of circumcision.

# The Cruellest Cut?

One major factor of circumcision is that it causes great pain. In most cases, the baby is not given anesthesia because it is considered too risky in the first weeks of life. The tiny mite is tied and strapped down on a special circumcision table. He lies spread-eagled and abandoned to the terrifying atmosphere of an operating room. Adults can imagine the horrifying effect of those harsh surgical lights, metallic sounds, masked faces, gleaming eyes, glittering knives. . .and intense physical pain.

— and the babe is alone. . .

— and wide awake!

— nor is he given pain relief when back in his cot.

We can only imagine how long his suffering lasts. How civilized is our brave new world, Western-style! Would an adult, with an adult's resources of courage and endurance, be expected to endure that?

The journalist Philip Boffey wrote in the New York Times: "Newborns do feel pain. Parents don't have to be told that, and many pediatricians don't either. But the contrary belief has persisted among physicians who have routinely operated on newborns with little or no anesthesia. . . . "In one survey of medical literature, 77 percent of all newborns who underwent surgery throughout the world between 1954 and 1983 to repair a serious blood vessel defect received only muscle relaxants or relaxants plus intermittent nitrous oxide. Better pain relief for infants has been possible for a long time. . . The long failure to provide anesthesia for newborns provides a salutary reminder that medical practices are sometimes based on flimsy science and erroneous beliefs, and that outside critics can bring an important perspective.

"The picture is changing. Most U.S. hospitals are believed to give anesthesia for major surgery. But some anesthesiologists persist in the old ways, and many hospitals still decline to give a local anesthetic for minor procedures such as circumcision."

## Welcome to My World

We do not know if this extraordinary welcome results in long-lasting psychologic distress. To date, there is no research or monitoring of the mental effects of circumcision. So we can only guess. And perhaps the guess is as valid as the guess that an unborn baby benefits from hearing sweet music while in utero.

The effects of heel sticks administered to newborns have been monitored. These are needles used to routinely collect blood for analysis. The baby's response to the stinging, yet mercifully swift, jab is an increase in heart and breathing rate, profuse sweating and anguished cries. Why, in the late 20th century, is there no monitoring of the effects of circumcision?

# Reasons for Circumcision

There is a well-known saying:

*Mothers demand it.*
*Doctors profit by it.*
*Babies cannot complain about it.*

The last two statements present no problem, but why do mothers demand it? (They usually care for a baby's physical well-being.)

*Religion*: About one-sixth of males globally are circumcised as religious custom. Jewish boys are done on the eighth day after birth. Muslim boys at age eight, or before their teens.

*Tradition*: The men in the family have been circumcised from way back. What was good enough for them is good enough for the baby.

*Class*: Circumcision is a middle-class issue in American and British families. In Europe, where the penis is accorded more respect, circumcision snobbery did not catch on.

*Cost*: The class issue is closely related to cost. Procedures which are expensive create their own appeal. Happy the lad from a home where meager financial resources left him intact.

*Appearance*: To Western eyes, the wrinkled end of the foreskin looks unattractive. There is a preference for the neater, more cleanly defined knob after a circumcision which is well done.

*Hygiene:* Parents have natural concerns over penile hygiene. They fear dirt can get in and fester under the foreskin.

*Aesthetics*: An intact glans appears shiny, slippery and damp. A non-intact one is matt, dull and dry. Modern thinking mistakenly relates dryness to cleanliness. So the intact glans appears dirty to those who make this mistake.

# Consider the Issues

*The Female Issue*: In the U.S., young men regularly apply for circumcision. The reason given is that the partner objects to the foreskin. These objections fall into three categories: hygiene, aes-

foreskin. These objections fall into three categories: hygiene, aesthetics and tradition. She fears the glans under the foreskin is unclean, she is taken aback by its wrinkled appearance, she dislikes the fact it is different from the men in her family. Often, her objections encompass all three.

*The Hygiene Issue*: The glans, like the mouth, is lined with mucus membranes. These keep the surfaces clean and comfortably damp. When the mouth feels dry, the natural instinct is to dampen it again. A glans which is exposed by circumcision must adapt to its dry condition.

In the past, lack of sanitation made hygiene difficult. The foreskin gained its poor reputation because it was linked with infections and unpleasant odors. Modern sanitation has done away with these problems, *providing there is good personal hygiene.*

The slippery moist skin of an intact glans matches the slippery moist skin just inside the vagina. It would seem nature intended the glans to be comfortably damp. Consider the opposite approach: Would it be acceptable if the male partner objected to the damp skin inside the vagina and suggested it be removed?

*The Aesthetic Issue*: This is an issue of perception fashioned by custom: Beauty lies in the eye of the beholder. Yet this eye can change as customs change. A partner who wishes to change an imperceptive eye may benefit from viewing the statue of David by Michelangelo.

*The Tradition Issue*: This is similar to the aesthetics issue, but it runs deeper. For many parents, tradition is honored at an unconscious level. They would feel uneasy if they acted against it. To avoid this, traditions are passed down from generation to generation without any conscious examination of their appropriate value.

In some areas, all little boys are circumcised. In others, none. A child who is in an opposite group may be teased by his peers. Parents, aware of obstacles they cannot protect a son from, try to smooth his path where they can. Be sure a boy is not victim of teasing because he is in the opposite group. Equally valid, check that he is not among the teasers.

The above reasons for circumcision can be seen as cultural, not medical. But can an act which has stood the test of time be all bad? There may be hidden wisdom in ancient customs which deserve modern respect. Why are some urologists still in favor of infant circumcision?

# Medical Reasons

## Foreskin Rips

Love-making, though not necessarily boisterous, may be over-ambitious. Under constant friction, the foreskin can suddenly rip. There may be profuse bleeding, and a mild degree of pain. There is almost always a severe degree of alarm.

Relax! Penile bleeding, like bleeding from the face, is more profuse than from other body parts. Elevate the genitals on a pillow and apply a cold pack to reduce blood flow. Keep the wound free of infection. If necessary, take pain relief. If the rip is wide or deep, it needs suturing. Consult with a physician.

*Total* rest from sexual activity is a must as healing may take some time. If the foreskin is not completely healed, thrusting will open the wound again. Reduce the risk of further rips by stopping movement the first moment the environment feels dry. A simple preventive measure is lavish use of lubrication. In most cases of lubrication mismanagement, circumcision should not be necessary. Avoid thinking it unmanly to care for the foreskin: use lubrication when it is necessary. (The section on bruising is of particular value for intact men).

## Later Problems

Foreskin problems in mid-life may be due to lack of retraction over a prolonged period of time. The foreskin then seems to lose some of its ability to stretch. When retraction occurs, it feels gritty and tight. The foreskin may partially stick, resulting in a degree of discomfort on erection.

The following is an option to consider before circumcision. The urologist, or skilled family physician, can release the tightness with a little snip and tuck. The procedure is quick and simple, and can be done in the office. Keep in mind the healing process takes longer on the penis than other body parts.

However, with repeated tightness and/or infections of the glans it is appropriate to opt for circumcision, especially in cases of diabetes. Once the foreskin is removed, there is real relief from the pain and anxiety these problems cause. In such cases, circumcision is an ideal solution.

All surgery carries a slight risk of complications. Removal of the foreskin in adult life is a more serious operation than may be understood. But keep in mind *most* surgery has perfectly satisfactory results. These warnings are only for those who regard any operation as a trivial event.

Take care of the foreskin. Lack of retraction can be due to chronic illness or disability which reduces an interest in sex. If the foreskin is not regularly retracted at erection, do so at each daily cleansing. Consult with a urologist for any unsmooth retraction which persists, or other similar discomfort.

## Cancer

Penile cancer, though rare, is more common in intact men. Cancer of the cervix is more common in the partners of intact men. These two facts alone would seem to be the final argument in favor of circumcision. But are they?

The foreskin must be removed in the first months of life. Any later, as with Muslim boys, and the exposed glans has the same cancer risk as the intact one, and the partner is as much at risk. This would seem to implicate lax hygiene. Instead of opting to circumcise our infant sons, perhaps we should teach older brothers, and sisters, the value of genital hygiene?

## Infections

*Phimosis and Paraphimosis*: Babies are rarely, if ever, born with abnormally-tight foreskins. These conditions more usually affect toddlers, older children and adults.

*Penile Infections*: A New Zealand study of 500 small boys found penile problems were five times higher in circumcised babies during the first year of life. (There is no foreskin to protect the glans). After that, the findings were reversed: there were five times more penile problems in intact small boys. Baby girls suffer more urinary tract infections than baby boys. They have a shorter urethra and germs travel more rapidly to the bladder. Yet we do not immediately jump to the conclusion that it is essential to remove some part of a small girl's anatomy. The study concluded the findings failed to support strong positions either way on the circumcision issue. "If women had no breasts, there would be no such thing as breast cancer. The presence of a foreskin, like the presence of any body part, can present problems at some time in life."

*Sexual Disease*: An Australian study showed that the incidence of sexually-transmitted diseases is higher in intact men. Herpes and gonorrhea are twice as high in intact men; syphilis and thrush are five times higher. Again, lax hygiene cannot be ruled out.

*Future Fears*: Circumcision is more complicated and unpleasant in adolescence or later life. Removing the foreskin in infancy removes this fear. The risk of female breast cancer increases with age and the surgery is unpleasant. Yet do we remove the healthy breasts of a young woman to remove the fear of mastectomy later? This analogy can be taken to absurd lengths: why not remove toe nails to avoid their ingrowing? And, to an extreme, why not remove each and every body part which might present problems at some time in life?

# The Surgical Risk

Professor Donald Smith, a distinguished urologist, wrote in the 70s: "Circumcision does prevent phimosis, paraphimosis and balanitis in adolescence and adult life. The diabetic suffers a high incidence of the latter. It is rare for the male circumcised at birth to develop penile cancer which carries a mortality rate of 33 percent. For these reasons, routine neonatal (at birth) circumcision seems indicated.

"Unfortunately, in unskilled hands the use of various mechanical devices (the ring clamp? the guillotine?) has at times caused removal of too much penile skin or even resection of a portion or all of the glans. It seems the most common cause of urethral meatal stenosis (blocked urethra due to scarring) is excoriation of the denuded meatus following circumcision."

In his book, *The Male*, Dr Sherman Silber, an eminent microsurgeon, describes what happened in a baby ward:

"The nurse noted that morning none of these five children had very much penis left. Unfortunately, this (circumcision) is a procedure considered so simple and relatively unimportant in the medical world that frequently the least experienced doctors are sent in to do it. . . . Luckily, with plastic surgery, the penises of all these children eventually healed without any deformities suffi-ciently severe to mar their later life."

One small U.S. study found only 0.2 percent of intact babies had urinary tract infections in their first year of life. Only 0.2 percent of circumcised babies had complications from the circumcision severe enough to need further surgery or blood transfusions. The decision is still unclear.

## Stop the Press!

During the week ending 11 March 1989, it was announced that safe anesthetic drugs for newborns exist. The two main ones are the narcotic fentanyl and lidocaine, locally infiltrated into the skin or used as a nerve block. At Children's Hospital National Medical Center in Washington, where criticism from parents helped bring questions about pain to the fore, anesthesia is now being used in virtually all newborn surgery.

The American Academy of Pediatrics stated there are medical benefits and advantages to circumcision. After five years of heated debate, the Academy's Task Force on Circumcision has changed from "no absolute medical indications" to a cautious advocacy on the grounds of a higher rate of penile infections in non-intact males.

The Academy concluded parents should make the decision based on a full consideration of medical benefits and risks, as well as aesthetic, religious and cultural factors. While accepting that infants undergoing circumcision "demonstrate physiological re-sponses suggesting they are experiencing pain,"the report fails to resolve the controversy over the risks and benefits of anesthesia during circumcision.

## Reversing the Trend?

The Circumcision Prevention Society produced this dubious car sticker: "Child abuse begins with circumcision." Their leaflet states: "Routine circumcision has underlyingly caused all the vio-lence in America — yes, that's right. It has produced the penal community, the homicidal psychopaths, sex offenders, child abus-ers and homosexual deviancy, not to mention celibacy, single par-ent motherhood and vagrancy." Whew! Where is the research to back-up these amazing claims?

"When we married, my husband hadn't a clue if he was intact.

People didn't talk about such things in our day. Anyway, he is circumcised. It's a botched job with ugly skin tags hanging down. He wants his foreskin back and keeps pulling on the shaft. 'How come,' he says, 'most of the world's men are intact, and we got to be the unlucky ones?' Anyway, he wants to know if pulling will help to bring his foreskin back?"

Due to the new interest in circumcision, a few non-intact men want their foreskin back. They do not want the glans exposed; they want to retrieve its protected state. Some pull lengthwise behind the corona to stretch the skin forward to cover the glans. Others ask the urologist if circumcision can be reversed. Perhaps the only comfort here is, "If it's fixed, don't mend it." Dr. X reported on the opposite phenomenon. "A few men believe a circumcision will make their sex life more sparkling. I had a patient recently who didn't need a circumcision. What he really wanted was for me to stick an extra bit on the end. A man who goes to such lengths to improve his performance really wants to be turned into a Casanova, and no physician can do that."

"One happy note on this dark landscape, the foreskin's protective function is not entirely lost. After excision, it can be used as a covering tissue in therapy for burns. In one study, 73 percent of skin ulcers treated with foreskin grafts healed completely within eight weeks, considerably faster than with alternative treatments. Foreskins grow quickly in laboratory cultures, and are easy to apply."

"Circumcision is a male issue, not the mother's or doctor's. It happens at a time when a man cannot participate in the choice. Me, I feel I was literally ripped off at birth, denied any option over my body."

"If it is acceptable to routinely circumcise little boys, why do we not routinely circumcise little girls?"

"A few young men do suffer repeated glans infections and opt for circumcision. Why are not all men allowed this free choice?"

Anthropology is the study of societies and their customs in human tribes. Discussion has been stirred up over female circumcision, and Western women have been shocked to learn the facts. When studying the issue of circumcision, be it female or male, anthropologists put both under the heading of genital mutilation.

# Parent Concern

Mr. Zed rang a medical phone-in program. "I don't want my boy docked. But he's five now and I can't move his foreskin back. I keep trying. This morning, it started to bleed."

The doctor's cheery tones grew casually studied. "Mr. Zed. Hmm. Most parents don't, ah. . . examine a child's genitals. There's no need. That's a private area of the body, wouldn't you agree?"

Mr. Zed's voice grew caring. "I'm doing my best for the boy."

"It's not, ah. . . recommended. We consider a baby's private parts *are* private, right from Day One. And your lad is five. Hmm. Well, five's a big boy, wouldn't you agree?"

Mr. Zed retorted, "We believe in the open life-style. Love, harmony, being at one with the universe, with nudity. . . ."

The physician's tone grew brisk. "My advice is take the boy to the doctor's office at once. The wound might be infected. It may need a stitch. Hmm. Boys learn privacy from their dads. It's a question of distance, of personal space, wouldn't you agree?"

The physician's cheery tones returned. "And to all you listeners out there, forget about your son's foreskin. There is no need to touch it, to keep checking. Just forget it. It may not be completely detached until puberty. In the meantime, folks, leave your baby in peace."

CHAPTER 3

# Erections

## Plumbing the Penis

The penis consists of three long tubes. Inside each tube is a network of spongy *erectile* tissue surrounded by tiny blood vessels. The two upper tubes are the *corpora cavernosa* (cave-like bodies). They become very hard at erection. The lower tube surrounds the urethra (urine tube) and continues on to form the glans. Neither the lower tube nor the glans become quite so hard at erection.

The three tubes are capable of *vasocongestion*. At erection, they swell up with extra blood. First, the urethra elongates and grows in length. Next, comes *tumescence*, during which the tubes swell up and engorge with blood. The final stage is *rigidity*. The entire penis becomes fully hard; it lifts and stands away from the body.

An erection is self-limiting. There must be a point at which tumescence stops. To enable this, each tube is wrapped separately in a coat of tough membranes. The three tubes are then wrapped together in an outer coat, called Buck's Fascia. These coats allow the penis to engorge so far and no further.

## Blood Flow

Like all parts of the body, the penis is supplied with blood from the heart. Fresh blood enters from arteries in the *pudendum* (the genital area). When the oxygen and nutrients are removed and the waste is passed out, the used blood drains into a network of veins

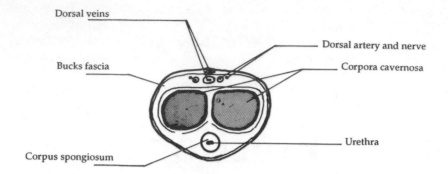

and flows back to the pudendum in a larger vein. This is normal blood flow.

When the penis is relaxed, blood enters at low pressure. It nourishes the organ as a whole. At sexual arousal, normal blood flow changes. Up to 26 times more blood is pumped in, about 4 teaspoons per minute. This extra blood enters under much higher pressure. Erection is the one time when penile blood pressure equals that of the body.

As the spongy tissues swell, they press on the veins which drain away used blood. These get squashed, though not completely. About 12 cc of blood per minute continues to flow out of the penis. So when the penis is erect, 12 cc of blood is needed to maintain the erection. And this is the amount which continues to be pumped in.

When the rate of blood *inflow* equals the rate of blood *outflow*, a steady-state is reached and the erection is maintained.

The erection process has been compared to:

· pumping up a bicycle wheel to become inflated and hard
· putting a wilting flower stem into water so it can re-erect
· turning on both faucets and plugging up the sink
· a compressed string undershirt being opened out.

These examples are not completely accurate. But they help to show more clearly what happens at tumescence.

Being permanently erect would be a hindrance in daily life. So the penis is designed to keep out extra blood when unerect. The erectile tissues collapse, becoming very small and limp. The tiny blood vessels have to be even more tightly packed to fit into an even smaller space. They do this by folding up into corkscrew shapes of truly microscopic size. These offer enormous resistance to extra blood entering the penis and causing erections at inappropriate times.

A healthy cardiovascular (blood) system is critical for the erection process. Any problem which slows down or clogs up blood flow will interfere with the ability to erect. See Chapter 13.

# Nerve Supply

A healthy nervous system is critical for erection. Engorgement cannot begin without the functioning of the *pudendal nerves* in the lower spine. At sexual arousal, they release a chemical, a neurotransmitter. This chemical relaxes the smooth (involuntary) muscles lining the tiny artery walls. Once the arteries are relaxed, their resistance is removed. The high pumping pressure forces extra blood into those folded-up, corkscrew-shaped, microscopic-sized blood vessels:

· which fills them up.
· which straightens them out and greatly expands them.
· which stretches out and greatly expands the spongy tissues.
· which then exert great pressure on the tough outer coats.
· which return the pressure into the expanded spongy tissues.
· Which results in the penis becoming fully engorged and
  rigid.

And, Hey Presto, the hydraulic mechanism of erection is complete.

The nerve centers which trigger erection are in the brain *and* lower spinal cord. They are protected by the skull and backbone. If the nerve supply is damaged, it can cause paralysis. When sexual desire is felt, the signals to release the relaxing chemical do not get through. So the penis cannot erect.

Men who enjoy risk-taking should learn how to fall safely! Always wear the recommended safety gear. Bikers in road accidents have a high risk of spinal cord injury and impotency. *Always* wear a safety helmet to protect the skull and neck.

# Which Type?

1. A *psychogenic* erection comes from the cortical centers of the brain. When these centers are stimulated, instructions to erect are transmitted down the spinal cord to the pudendal nerves. It is thought there are six variables which stimulate the brain. They are listed below with examples. Obviously these will not be to every reader's taste. But the six factors are critical. If only one does not "fit," there may be no psychogenic erection. If an erection does occur, it may be fleeting, or not rigid enough for penetration.

*Auditory*: sweet talk, throbbing music, laughter, erotic panting.

*Olfactory*: perfumes of Arabia, freshly-washed hair, skin smells.

*Gustatory*: taste of saliva, sexual fluids or body parts.

*Tactile*: feather touch, naked skin, harsh massage, fabrics.

*Imaginative*: favorite fantasies, past memories, future delights.

*Visual*: too highly individual. . . fill in the spaces.

2. A *reflexogenic* erection is a simple reflex response to touch. Tactile sensations applied directly to the penis stimulate the nerve endings here, and in the rectum and bladder. These transmit signals directly to the spinal cord. The pudendal nerves respond reflexively. This is a may, or may not, phenomenon, like the eye blink. A reflexive erection forms a self-contained *reflex arc*.

3. A *spontaneous* erection is not "willed" by the conscious mind. They happen during sleep.

Psychogenic and reflexive erections can be obtained separately, or together. They are usually combined. In ardent youth, and at other times in life, a reflexive erection may be perceived as a back-up only, an added support if a psychogenic one fails. It is an issue of individual choice.

But reflexive erections should not be over-looked. They are of particular value in certain health problems, and in potency loss due to the aging process. A few men believe it is "unmanly" or "wrong" to directly stimulate the penis. As the years pass, and a psychogenic erection becomes less easy to obtain, it may be appropriate for health reasons to concentrate on reflexive erections.

## Sex on the Brain?

The unconscious brain controls the instincts of survival: self-preservation for survival of the species. And procreation for survival of the man by passing on his genes. If there is a threat to life, self-preservation comes first. No erection can be obtained. If there is a threat to self-esteem, self-preservation also comes first. No erection is obtained because the survival instinct can protect against mental pain.

At puberty, the sex hormone *testosterone* is produced by the testicles in large amounts. Testosterone is the fuel which lights the *libido's* fires. In medical terms, the libido refers to the sex drive. From puberty almost unto the grave, testosterone keeps the sexual fires burning merrily throughout life. Sexual tension starts to build up. During sleep, the boy has spontaneous erections — not "willed" by the conscious mind. He ejaculates in sleep, or when half awake. At first, he has little control over this. His biologic clock is set for procreation and cannot be turned back. From now until old age, sexual tension is a constant. With almost clockwork regularity, it builds up and demands to be released. If release is avoided — if there is no ejaculation — he may continue to have demanding erections:

- Whether he is awake or asleep.
- Whether he is a boy or a man.
- Whether he wants them or not.
- Whether he has a partner or not.

## Mind over Matter

It would be simple if the erection process just depended upon the interaction of blood, nerves, flesh and testosterone. But man is civilized. He lives more through his higher conscious mind than his lower unconscious drives. Erection for partner sex is not a simple rutting process. Man seeks to fulfill his higher conscious needs as well as his basic procreation drives.

Some men say 95 percent of sexual desire comes from the higher conscious mind. Others strongly disagree; they insist it is 99 percent! Whatever the percentage, a man's conscious attitudes and feelings about himself, his partner, and life in general profoundly affect his ability to erect. His total well-being is involved.

In fact, the erection process is far more sensitive than the machismo image suggests. The whole of a man's character, his very soul, can be involved. Qualities such as humor, kindliness and liking one's partner count. So do selfishness, sexual priggishness and *femaphobia* (fear of women). There may be unresolved conflicts from inappropriate childhood learning. Where there is mind over matter, any one of the following can play havoc with erections:

· Impoverished self-image and self-esteem.
· Attitude to partner; partner feedback.
· Previous experience; social pressure.
· Mental stress; physical health.

In short, he can bring the whole of himself to the act of love.

## To Elevate to Office

The word erection comes from the Latin "erigere." It means to be upright; not bending forwards or downwards. Rigid. Bristling. These are powerful words, and carry great impact. A penis which engorges but does not harden cannot be considered fully erect.

And to become erect means "to raise in consideration; to exalt; to elevate to office." So it can be said the penis is raised and elevated to the office of the vagina — not the other way around. It must be exalted (fully rigid) before it can penetrate those passive defenseless walls.

The imagery is challenging, erotic in the extreme.

In reality, the penis does not always fully erect. There are times when it develops a less-than-exalted stance. And the vagina — dammit — is not quite the helpless "object" it seems. Those passive defenseless walls can prove amazingly stubborn. They refuse to yield and admit the penis unless it is rigidly erect.

## The Thrilling Paradox!

Herein lies the thrilling paradox at the heart of our sexual lives. Here is where "the irresistible force meets the immovable object." Here is the place where, "something's gotta give." (In a love relationship, it is the boundaries of the self.) Here is the perfect balance of male and female, shaft and sheath, lingam and yoni, ying and yang — whatever. Neither is complete without the other. Each is needed for the act of love. (This same perfect balance is reflected in the irresistible force of the sperm meeting and penetrating the immovable egg.)

This thrilling paradox, the challenge of the vagina to the force of the penis, adds magic and mystery to physical desire, turning our passions to ecstasy — a journey to the stars.

## The Abuse of Power

It can be seen that within sexual love there is a dimension of force. Each partner accepts this on trust, and makes accommodations for the satisfaction of the other. The result can be a delightful interplay of power give and take, winner and loser, a swopping of roles to heighten and enhance sexual love.

In some encounters, the dimension of force is abused — by either partner. Date rape and other violences, though male acts, do not entirely exclude women. Any real pressure on an unwilling partner can be perceived as sexual abuse. The boundaries of accommodation and trust have been overthrown, violated.

In malign or non-relationships, one or other person is bent on destruction. Rape and sexual torture are the most appalling of these acts. A woman who taunts a man then withholds, or ridicules his sexual prowess, intends (consciously or not) to emasculate him. In comparison to rape, her act may be perceived as a minor violation. It is not. The effects can be equally destructive and long-lasting. Though no excuse, the man may become malign in his next encounters with women.

## In Charge of the Store?

No man is unaware of the "challenge of the vagina." It keeps him, sexually-speaking, slightly on guard, slightly tense. For he can never be 100 percent certain his penis will erect. When it does, he cannot be 100 percent certain it will remain erect. And herein lies another paradox, this time at the heart of male sexual life.

A man can neither always will erection to occur, nor can he always will it to stop. There are times when he must become passive before he can take an active role. He must pause to allow both his unconscious drives and his higher conscious needs to synchronize, to mesh. If not, he may fail to erect. For this reason, no man is 100 percent in "charge of the store."

Perhaps some men care passionately about being in "control" because they do not have control where it matters the most. For no man is unaware of how stubborn the penis can be. Indeed, there are times when it behaves like newly washed hair. No matter how often or how stylishly it is coaxed, it refuses to respond as its owner would wish.

There are many parameters to erection, e.g., a partner can have more control of the penis than the man himself. This adds vulnerability to his active role. It does not matter how much worldly power he has. Wealth, status or erudition count for nothing at the critical point. If he fails at erection, he fails in his image of himself. In this respect, a man is vulnerable in a way a woman never is.

Most men ignore a brief failure. But for some, it feels deeply humiliating. Others perceive it as total disaster. They suffer horrendous self-doubt. If this happens often enough, the unconscious steps in for his self-preservation. It stops the pain of failing by stopping the erection process. The man then suffers from what is called *psychologic impotence.*

And herein lies a further paradox at the heart of male sexual life. No man wants to be impotent, whether he wishes to make love or not. So he suffers more pain from his impotency, which is there to protect him from the pain of failure. It is not as easy to be a man as some women think, nor as some men like to portray themselves.

Erection is not essential for erotic play. Indeed, some consider it distracting or at best, unnecessary. They delight in the many different routes to sexual satisfaction. They concentrate on mutual happiness. Our culture's constant stress on erection can damage many an otherwise happy relationship. Erection may or may not be related to ejaculation. Ejaculation can occur without erection.

It cannot mean much for a woman author to write words of comfort such as: "Your partner does *not* perceive erection loss as failure. Only you do — ." A man can only learn this for himself.

And anyway, not all women are understanding (Chapter 15).

## Sweet Dreams

Sleep happens in two cycles, dreams and non-dreams. During a dream cycle, the eyeballs move rapidly under the eyelids. This is *Rapid Eye Movements*, REM, and starts about 90 minutes after falling asleep. REM lasts 27 to 30 minutes, then dreaming stops.

The next period of REM sleep starts 72 to 100 minutes later. This cycle repeats itself throughout the night. When REM begins, the penis erects spontaneously and remains erect till the dream cycle ends. If awakened during REM, a man can vividly recall his dreams. In celibate men and young boys, these dreams can be erotic in content. They can be erotic in sexually active men, but not always so.

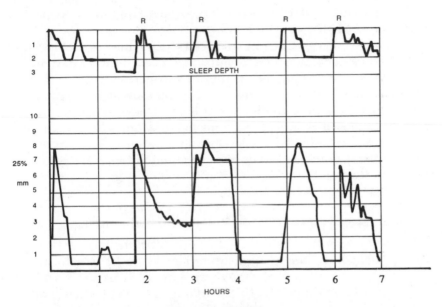

CHANGE IN PENIS SIZE

Many a man wakes in the morning with a full erection. If the dream is recalled, and it was not erotic, he thinks it is due to a full bladder. But erection on waking does not signify an extended bladder. It is NPT, the result of interrupted REM sleep.

The reasons for *nocturnal penile tumescence*, NPT, are not fully understood. They can happen during the day, particularly in non sexually active men. One theory suggests those tiny tightly-packed arteries require regular exercise. They may fill up to have a good "work-out," a thorough stretch. Another theory suggests NPT keeps the prostate healthy by promoting regular ejaculation. NPTs occur throughout life. They are infrequent in children, though parents can see their baby son erect as he sleeps. The length and frequency of each episode peaks in adolescent boys.

They gradually decrease after the age 20. Yet they continue to occur in potent men throughout life.

Any medication which contains tranquilizers, sleepers or hypnotics interferes with REM sleep, and affects the quality of NPT. With prolonged marijuana use, the dream cycles can disappear altogether. Whether this has damaging and/or long-lasting effects on NPT is not known. Nor is it known if long-term loss of NPT affects the erection process. What is known is that only 2 ounces of alcohol reduces NPT. And that 50 percent of impotent alcoholics have abnormal NPT.

A vow of celibacy does not stop NPTs. Each man learns to cope with them in whatever way is appropriate for him. An avowed celibate may choose prayer, fasting or meditation to control "the clamoring demands of the flesh." Non-celibate men are often in situations where they cannot make love. Contrary to myth, enforced (unchosen) celibacy does no harm — unless the man empowers it to. Unrelieved sexual tension does not drive him crazy. From puberty onwards, he makes accommodations. He gains relief by masturbation.

## The Solo Act

Solitary masturbation is almost a "given" in the teens. Though it may seem to be about orgasm and pleasure, it is also about ejaculation, and release of sexual tension. It is nature's way to ensure a thorough reproductive workout, with the testicles, prostate and seminal glands regularly cleared of their contents.

During adolescence, masturbation feels imperative because a boy's hormones and, in turn, his reproductive organs have not settled down. It is likely he produces an excess of semen, rather like producing an excess of sebum which causes spots. But this is not proven yet. What is known is that testosterone levels, which fuel his sex drive, peak at age 18.

One U.S. study found teenage boys think of sex every 15 minutes of every day. Though no reflection on the study, are boys this age likely to answer a sex questionnaire with "nothing but the truth?" Nor is this to question the boys' honesty. At age 15, nervous bragging is often used to conceal inexperience. But the findings help to remind parents and other concerned adults of the sheer power and raw energy of the sex drive in youth. Masturbation is ever a hot topic of debate. During the last century, obsessive hatred of it rose to a frenzied peak. Barbaric practices were used to try to stamp it out. The classic one was inserting spikes under the boy's foreskin to cause him agony when he erected at night.

Less appalling, yet equally cruel, was chaining the boy's wrists to a wall, or binding them together if he was caught in the act. Then came the gruesome warnings of insanity, epilepsy, weakened physique, shifty eyes, hairy palms, and so on. As recently as the beginning of this century, one U.S. doctor told worried parents that he would circumcise "without the benefit of anesthetic any teenage boys caught in the self-polluting act." Sadism was hidden behind a mask of concern — as it often is.

Once the idea of "self-pollution," of "masturbation as evil" caught on, a truly vicious circle began. For those self-same men, punished in youth, turned around as fathers and attacked their sons. Did they forget those urgent night erections which drove them to masturbate? Or is this an example of values passed down from generation to generation without being examined first?

The power of the imagination can be stronger than the power of facts. This is especially so where there is ignorance; for what is unknown can be perceived as very fearful. Even today, we only imperfectly understand our sexual natures. We are aware of the potential for evil as well as good. We may fear the dark and destructive side, rather than applaud the happiness.

Parents, with full responsibility for their growing sons, naturally wish to protect them in appropriate ways. See Chapter 12.

# Today

Masturbation is generally more tolerated nowadays. But a somewhat patronizing attitude has replaced the former rage. It is regarded as a "fail safe;" the sort of behavior the "disadvantaged" use as a last resort. These include the elderly, disabled and chronically sick — but no other group.

The facts, of course, are very different. Findings from many surveys indicate all men masturbate at certain periods in life, and this regardless of whether they have an available partner or not. The surveys also found most men were reluctant to admit they masturbate as they themselves regard it as a slightly shameful act. Yet in certain cases, masturbation is not only appropriate but a valuable preventive health step.

In certain disorders, deranged people masturbate openly, and to excess. This gives rise to the "pop psychology" theory of a relationship between the act and neurosis. Such muddled thinking leads to the absurd conclusion that a healthy adult male who masturbates is showing signs of being disturbed.

Masturbation is not always a second best. For some men, and for perfectly appropriate reasons, it is the preferred sexual outlet; though for other men, it is not. In general, masturbation probably accounts for more ejaculations than coitus. The issue is one of personal choice.

# Going Down

At *detumescence*, the opposite of engorgement happens. The outflow of blood becomes greater than the inflow. Eventually all the extra blood is drained from the organ. The spongy tissues collapse onto themselves. The tiny arteries fold down into their microscopic corkscrew shapes.

Detumescence happens in two stages. First, the penis shrinks rapidly to half its fully erect size. It then takes an average 10 to 15 minutes before it returns to its completely relaxed state. The timing cannot be exact. Keep in mind there is no such object as the average erection.

Detumescence occurs with satisfaction, a positive feeling of completion. It can also occur when the level of sexual arousal drops. The main reasons for this drop in arousal are emotional. There may be anxiety due to fear of failure, or interruption. There may be anger at the self, the partner or life in general. Both anxiety and anger cause mental pain, and pain from whatever cause can affect the sturdiest erection. Obviously, the erection process is sensitive to many factors, especially emotional distress.

# Priapism

In ancient tales, Priap was regarded as the god of procreation. This was because his organ was huge and permanently erect. In real life, a penis which does not detumesce is a terrifying disorder. A priapic penis is nothing to do joke about. Priapism can occur when the penis erects non-erotically, i.e., without sexual desire. The extra blood pumped in gets trapped and cannot flow out. The pain this causes ranges from moderate to severe. All men know penile pain will deflate the stoutest erection. This does not happen in a priapic penis.

In some kinds of priapism, only the two upper tubes become severely swollen and over-engorged with trapped blood. The lower tube and the glans remain unerect. As more blood is pumped in, the outer coats keep returning the pressure back to the swollen tissues. The pressure inside the penis increases and is intense.

Trapped blood can permanently damage the erection process. It forms blood clots and fibrous scar tissue builds up. In turn, these cause more blockage and more pressure. Priapism responds to medication, or irrigation of the penis, in the early stages. Otherwise, emergency surgery is essential to release the trapped blood and decompress the penis. This relieves the pain, the risk of gangrene and permanent impotence. Leukemia, sickle cell disease or damage to the spinal nerves can cause priapism. Or the penis may have been over-stimulated, but this is not proven. For men who enjoy "tough sex," *avoid penile trauma from bruising and other mismanagement.* Sometimes, priapism just happens and nobody knows why. It is a rare disorder but if it does occur — if there is pain *and* no detumescence after the usual time — go for medical help promptly. The sooner the therapy, the less damage to the erection process.

Some men have a history of naturally delayed detumescence. After ejaculation, the penis stays erect for longer than 15 to 20 minutes — the timing cannot be exact. The distinction to be clear about is the presence of pain after ejaculation or no desire. Naturally delayed detumescence does not mean lack of satisfaction. A man in this state often wishes to continue making love because the experience was pleasurable and because he stays erect. The condition remits spontaneously. The blood is released and flows back into the perineum without causing harm. Priapism and naturally delayed detumescence are very different issues. For men in the second group, there is no cause for alarm. Check detumescence times. Work out an average. Rule out specific factors which affect it, e.g., alcohol, tiredness. One option is medical investigation to check all is well. The underlying cause may be nothing to worry about. But it could be a blood flow problem which increases with time. As in other health issues, the option for preventive care would seem the appropriate choice.

## The Power of the Penis

Below is a list of erection potential at different ages. Like all average lists, it is highly variable, and not carved in stone. Yet it may be helpful while moving from one life stage to the next because nothing stays the same. All things change; some for better, some for worse. The changes are not necessarily harsh. For what is lost on the roundabouts is gained on the swings.

*Rigidity*: How many "grams force" would be needed to buckle the erect shaft? The average is a rigidity challenge in excess of 500g force. (This should *never* be tried at home!)

*Girth Increase*: Erectile capacity is measured by the increase in the circumference of the penis at the corona and the base.
*Length Increase*: Increased girth makes volume increase. Variable due to proportional difference of small/large erecting penis.

*Angle of Elevation*: How high the penis rises. This can range from almost vertical in youth to horizontal or less in late life.

*Refractory Period:* The length of time which elapses after an ejaculation before another erection can start.

*Endurance*: The length of time between erection and ejaculation. This is a learned skill. For endurance problems. See Chapter 8.

*At age 20:*
It is more a question of stopping than starting erection. Girth,rigidity and angle of elevation are maximum. Endurance is low. Refractory period can be brief — a few moments only.

*At age 30:*
Girth, rigidity and angle of elevation are the same. Endurance is improving. Refractory period can be 5 minutes, usually only on occasions of high sexual arousal.

*At age 40:*
Girth and rigidity are much the same. Angle of elevation may be slightly reduced. Endurance reaches its peak. Refractory period can be 5 to 10 minutes, sometimes half a day.

*At age 50:*
Girth and rigidity the same. Angle of elevation is horizontal. Endurance is still at its peak. Refractory period between one half and one full day; more genital stimulation is required.

*At age 60:*
If no prostate or other health problems, potential is much the same as for 50 years old. Girth and angle of elevation decline. Endurance can be high or moderate.

*At age 70 plus:*
Girth, rigidity, angle and endurance are diminished. Ejaculation may be absent. Penetration infrequent but enhanced love-making skills keeps the elderly man in the potency stakes.

The above are based on the average male in good physical health. As erection is largely "in the mind," mental health is a critical factor. Whatever the life stage, being happy and confident does wonders for erection potential. Being miserable with low self-esteem can throw a spanner in the works at any age.

## Erection: The Facts

Contrary to schoolboy myth, there is no bone in the penis. The myth probably arose from seeing mating dogs get stuck. Many male animals have a curious "lock in" effect which traps the organ in the female. This assists pregnancy function by allowing enough time for ejaculation and avoiding spillage of semen. When mating dogs are disturbed, perhaps by traffic in the street, they try to flee in opposite directions, and get stuck.

The myth of the penile bone may be responsible for that other alarming, yet equally, apocryphal myth. This is the one in which the penis gets locked in the vagina and cannot withdraw. The unfortunate couple are rushed to hospital, ambulance sirens blaring. Once there, they are separated; it is not clear how.

There is nothing inside the vagina except healthy muscle. There are no teeth, no crocodile jaws, no alligator "snatch." Yet men who are fearful of women may fear that there is. They imagine a malign "something" in the vagina waiting to harm the penis. It is a terrifying fantasy of a degree of sexual disturbance. Seek medical help promptly. The condition can be treated and cured. In rare cases of vaginal spasm, the penis would still not be trapped. The erection process is delicate and sensitive. At the first sign of trouble, it shrivels and dies. Once back to its relaxed state, the penis simply slides out — and this long before the ambulance has time to arrive. In the rare event of priapism, the woman can extricate herself by applying lubrication to the entrance of the vagina.

As recently as the 1970s, sex manuals warned bridegrooms to "keep the sight of the erect penis away from the bride during the first weeks of married life. If not, she will become extremely anxious, and be frightened the penis is too large." Today's young sophisticates may find this advice hilarious. Yet it is not as unusual as it may seem. Many young girls still harbor such frightening concerns. And are they so strange? For indeed, erections are mysterious and awesome things to behold.

# Mismanagement!

In 1985, a 34-year-old white male arrived at a U.S. hospital with a red, tender and swollen penis. He appeared to be suffering from severe penile cellulitis — inflammation of the tissues due to bacteria infection. On examination, three injection sites were found on the shaft. The patient had no previous history of mental illness. In fact, he appeared to be perfectly sane.

On close questioning, he admitted being drunk one night. He decided to test out his "theory" on how to maintain an erection by the use of expoxy glue. He began by cleaning his shaft with alcohol. Next he mixed up a solution of the glue and hardener. He then used a 19 gauge needle and a 10 cc syringe to inject the solution into his shaft. To make sure his theory was well tested, he injected the glue solution into three separate sites.

The patient remembered to clean the shaft with alcohol, but forgot to clean the needle and syringe. It took one week of six hourly shots of broad spectrum antibiotics to bring the resulting infections under control. Hot compresses were applied to the shaft to reduce the bruising and tenderness. Yet when the infections cleared up, the lumpy swellings refused to go down.

Surgery was required to remove the lumps. Vertical incisions were made along the top of the shaft. The sticky mess, pus and debris which had collected in the injection sites were cleaned out. The wounds were washed in saline solution and packed with medicated sponges. It took six weeks for the wounds to heal.

Sadly, the man has remained impotent to date. This is hardly surprising. Consider the clever and complex construction of the penis. The outer coats were brutally punctured by injections. The glue solution wreaked havoc among the delicate, corkscrew-shaped, microscopic-sized arteries.

The above is an extreme example of penile mismanagement. Yet damage due to risk-taking behavior is more common than may be thought. Avoid all types of penile experiment, any dangerous practice. Consider the complex nature of the erection process and give nature's design the respect it deserves.

# CHAPTER 4

# Care of the Penis

## The Urinary Tract

The urethra is the passageway for urine and sperm. It leads from the lips of the meatus up to the bladder. It is about 8 inches long (21 cm), and 8 to 9 mm in diameter. As the same tube is used to both urinate and ejaculate, an infection due to one activity is bound to affect the other. Infections are named by their site, with the suffix "itis" showing there is inflammation:

*Urethritis*: infection of the urethra.

*Cystitis*: infection of the bladder.

*Prostatitis*: infection of the prostate.

*Epididymitis*: infection of the epididymes.

*Orchitis*: infection of the testicles.

Urea is made of the waste products of protein metabolism. It is blisteringly strong with that familiar ammonia smell. Before leaving the kidneys, it is diluted in 95 percent water to make *urine*. Dilution stops the strong urea from damaging the delicate linings of the urinary tract.

There is salt in urine, and trace amounts of over 100 other

substances. *Urinalysis* (biochemical analysis) provides valuable health clues in regular check-ups. With urinary tract infection, it is a must. Bacteria, excess hormones, sugar, alcohol and drugs are some of the substances which can be found.

Healthy urine is *sterile*, free of germs. It drips down from the kidneys into the stretchy pouch of the *bladder*. It collects there until the level rises and stimulates special nerve endings. These send messages to the brain which translates them into the urge to urinate.

Urine which collects in the bladder is static, and static urine quickly becomes infected. If the bladder were not regularly emptied, the back-up urine pressure would seriously affect the kidneys. The renal tubules which make urea would degenerate. Kidney failure, which can be fatal, would be the result.

To avoid this, and to keep the system free of infection, the bladder has a defense mechanism called the "wash out" effect. At urination, it can almost completely empty itself. So any germs which travel up from the penis or (more rarely) down from the kidneys are regularly "washed out."

For a healthy urinary tract, drink eight glasses of water or bland fluids daily. Water improves kidney function, which increases the "wash out" effect, which reduces the risk of infection. Urinate when the urge is mild to moderate. Avoid waiting till it is overwhelming. Allow time for the bladder to completely empty itself.

"Lucien was a hypochondriac, and worried constantly over his health. He drank gallons and gallons of water each day. This excess caused a severe imbalance in his body fluids and he almost died. On recovery, the urologist found Lucien's bladder had been over-stretched. Rather like over-stretched elastic, it could no longer return to its former shape. The muscle sphincters which control urination were also damaged. Lucien was *incontinent*."

Keep urine healthy and dilute by drinking lots of liquids. Avoid excess. Moderation in all things.

# Self Help

The average bladder holds 12 to 15 ounces of urine, roughly the same volume as a can of beer or soda. The average rate of a normal healthy flow is 15 to 25 cubic centimeters a second. To check this, first gather together a measuring cup marked in cc, a stop watch, and a full bladder. Urinate for 10 seconds. Stop. The cup holds about 200 cc, sometimes more. (Keep in mind there is no such man as "average"!) However, if the contents are very noticeably less, consult with the physician.

Bladder sphincters are rings of muscle which control the outflow of urine. A small boy learns how to control them between the ages of two and four. However, and often from an early age, these muscles do not always work perfectly. At times, they can go into spasm and cause a waiting period before the flow begins. This is common and rarely a cause for concern. However, in later life, the sphincters may become weakened.

Some men find they are unable to urinate after orgasm. They may wait 10 minutes, and still be unable to go. This is perfectly normal, and due to the strong contractions of ejaculation. Expect to wait 20 to 30 minutes. The flow should start easily then. If the urge to urinate after orgasm feels overwhelming, empty the bladder before making love to avoid over-stretching it.

# Urinary Pain

The three classic symptoms of urinary tract infection are:

*Burning*: Is there a hot stinging feeling on urinating?

*Frequency*: Is the need to urinate more frequent? How often?

*Urgency*: Is the need strong? Almost beyond control?

Another symptom not always present is pus. This is an unpleasant-smelling discharge from the meatus. Visit the physician promptly. Be prepared to describe the symptoms. Older men may have other problems which signify prostate trouble. See Chapter 9. Below are "voiding history" questions which are likely to be asked:

*Hesitancy*: Does the urine flow take longer to start? How long?

*Interruption*: Does it stop and start? Come in sudden spurts?

*Reduced Force*: Is the stream weaker? Slower than before?

*Terminal Dribbling*: Is there a trickle after finishing?

*Nocturia*: Is there night waking with a strong urge to urinate? Once is usual; more often may require investigation.

*Incontinence*: Is there mild leakage?  A constant nonstop leak?

*Hematuria*: Are there flecks, clots or larger streaks of blood?

*Retention*: Is urination sometimes incomplete?  Total retention is a medical emergency.

Nocturia is very much a function of age and diet.  Younger men can try cutting down on fluid intake last thing at night.  For men over age 50, see The Prostate, Chapter 9.

# Anxiety

Chuck, age 31, had urinary pain and discharge.  "We'll take a swab of the discharge first," the doctor said.  "It could be gonor-rhea with no symptoms; you may be *asymptomatic* for the disease."

"Thanks a million!" Chuck thought.  He stood miserably in the john, waiting with specimen cup at the ready.  No matter how hard he tried, he could not urinate.  He tried whistling forlornly.  A cute-looking nurse appeared.  "Hurry there, Chuck.  We don't want to keep doctor waiting, do we?"  She smiled a cute-looking smile.

Minutes later, Chuck re-appeared, clutching the empty cup.  "I can't.  It's unnerving.  I just can't."

The cute nurse beamed.  "Hesitancy, or short-term retention.  You'll get over it.  We're going to need more specimens until the infection has cleared — *and stays clear*," she warned.

She took Chuck to a cubicle with a wash basin, and turned on the tap.  "The sound of running water is one of the simplest tech-niques to foster urination," she said.  After Chuck obliged, he asked if he could collect further specimens at home.

"Persuade me," the urologist said.  "Persuade me you know how to collect a sterile specimen."

The bladder has been called "emotionally shy."  Urinating to order is not always easy.  Anxiety can cause short-term retention.  Like Chuck's case, it is not serious, and very quickly resolved.  But prolonged urine retention (more than a day or so) frequently sig-nals severe kidney problems.  Long-term retention is a medical emergency.  Go to the physician or emergency room at once.

# Urine Specimen

Harmless plant organisms called flora live inside the urethra. If urine is directed straight into a specimen cup, these flora get flushed out at the same time. Their presence can give a false diagnosis at urinalysis. Below are directions to collect a clean *mid-stream void* specimen:

1. Wash the penis and glans thoroughly.

2. Retract the foreskin fully, if present.

3. Begin to urinate into the toilet bowl or urinal.

4. The flora are flushed out after 10 to 15 ml of voiding.

5. Without stopping the flow, move the cup into position and collect mid-stream urine until the correct cc mark is reached.

6. Stop, remove the cup and finish the stream in the urinal.

7. Avoid clutching at the rim of the cup. Germs can be present, even on clean hands, and can confuse the diagnosis.

Having two containers of urine gives a better chance at an accurate diagnosis. Instead of starting and ending in the urinal, do so in Cup 1, and urinate into Cup 2 at mid-stream. Both flows are then compared. If the bladder is infected, the white cells which fight disease will be in both specimens. If there are germs in Cup 1 and no white cells in Cup 2, the infection is in the urethra only. The diagnosis is likely to be urethritis.

## Parent Help

*For a Young Boy*: Collect two sterile containers, or boil unsterile ones for 15 minutes. Explain to the boy how and when to move the containers beneath his organ without stopping the flow. For a toddler, hold each container in turn — a groundsheet will help!

*For a Baby*: If a partner is available, use two containers. If not, one will do. Wash, rinse and dry the genitals thoroughly. Put a sterile cloth under the baby and feed him. After the feeding, place him comfortably face down in the prone position with the container under his pelvis. Massage the sides of the backbone to trigger the spinal reflex of Perez. This reflex usually starts spontaneous urination within 5 minutes.

## A Catheter

A catheter is a long hollow tube which travels 8 inches inside the urethra to the bladder. It is used to collect urine in severe illness, long-term retention or when an infection has become entrenched. To ease its passage, a sterile lubricant is smoothed over it. During insertion, there should be no pain, though there may be discomfort. Pain is a sign of something amiss. Avoid being manly. Do not "suffer in silence." Inform the nurse at once. It is natural to cover embarrassment at the procedure with jokes and other distractions. Try to avoid this. *Catheterization always carries a slight risk of infection.* A distracted nurse may be less skillful at keeping a catheter sterile during insertion.

# Urethritis

Urethritis is the generic name for urinary tract infections. The classic symptoms are burning, frequency and urgency; there may be discharge. Urethritis has many causes, some of them sexual. For this reason, information is given in Chapter 15. But it is not necessarily a sexually transmitted disease.

Urinary tract infections are not usually serious. But some are difficult to get rid of, and they are miserable things to endure. It is not only the symptoms which are upsetting. The side effects of leakage, damp shorts and odor heighten the misery.

Be prepared to cope with anxious and irritable feelings. If not, the symptoms can linger on as a stress response after the infection has cleared. Frequency, urgency and stinging pain may still be experienced, and heighten the distress.

Keep in mind the bladder and urinary tract are "emotionally shy." Relaxation techniques help calm the mind and an irritated bladder. Yoga and meditation help reduce stress. Exercise is excellent for restoring a lost sense of body control. Laughter is a universal panacea; it produces *endorphins*, the body's own pain relief. Choose a relaxation program which is enjoyable. Stay with it until all the stress symptoms have disappeared.

Take time to ensure the bladder is empty. Some men reduce fluid intake to reduce the number of painful urinations. Resist this temptation! Drink more water to dilute urine, so it stings less. If tap water is unpalatable, drink bottled waters instead. Caffeine in cola, tea and coffee is a diuretic. It increases urine volume by promoting the excretion of salts and water from the kidneys. Heavy drinkers, especially of beer, know only too well alcohol is also a diuretic. For some reason, it inflames urinary infections, and makes the symptoms worse. Avoid caffeine and alcoholic beverages until the condition clears.

If there is reason to suspect sexual disease, avoid delay in seeking medical help. Be on guard for emotional side effects. Urethritis, whether sexual in origin or not, can provoke denial. One man refuses to admit he is infected and exposes his partner to risk. Another avoids making love and risks emotional damage to the relationship. *Denial is an avoidance tactic which makes problems worse.*

Use the healing time to confront and deal with unresolved guilts. Otherwise, and once cured, impotence can occur as a guilt response. Avoid empowering it with control over happiness. For no amount of guilt, however painful, can atone for the deeper losses which impotence brings. It punishes not only the man, but the partner *and* the relationship.

Ask when it is safe to make love. It is appropriate to use condoms for a further two months because many causes of urethritis are unknown. Condoms give partner protection and reduce the risk of auto-inoculation, which is self-reinfection.

If there are no obvious symptoms, pain in the penis can be referred pain from elsewhere, e.g., a problem in the rectum can cause penile pain. So can trouble in the kidneys, the bladder or the prostate. Even an infected appendix can cause penile pain.

The pain may get worse during urination. It may get worse after (or it may get better). It may be severe all the time. Help the physician to diagnose the trouble by being clear about:

· the kind of pain — is it dull? fleeting? steady? sharp?
· the site of pain — does it spread to the abdomen? elsewhere?
· the times of pain — when it increases and when it subsides

One method to examine the penis is with physician seated, man standing. The skin is checked for color, tone, size and shape. It is palpated (felt) for lumps, lesions, rough patches, tenderness, swelling. The glans is examined for discharge or cracking skin. These can be harmless, but may be signs of infection, or tumor.

The meatus is examined for soreness, swelling, discharge or everted (turned out) lips. The groin is checked for lumps and skin discoloration. The testicles are palpated. The anus may be checked. In some cases, a prostate massage may follow.

Ask the physician to explain any findings. Listen carefully. Studies show many patients do not hear directions. They leave the office more confused than when they came. Not all physicians are skilled communicators. Ask to have medical terms repeated. Make quick notes which can be studied in leisure at home.

## Penile Injury

Penile injury is rare. The main cause is from clothing trapped in moving machinery. The hips are dragged forward, and the genitals crushed. The second main cause is from "high energy" accidents such as vehicular crashes, gun shot wounds and knife fights.

But the position of the penis makes these injuries rare because it is sheltered from harm by the torso and legs.

More usual, though still infrequent, are injuries due to personal mismanagement. After love-making, it is not uncommon for microscopic lesions to appear on penile skin. These are abrasions too tiny to be seen by the naked eye. They are harmless and self healing and in no cause for concern.

However, if sexual activity is extremely boisterous and lengthy, there is a risk of bruising. The excess friction breaks open small blood vessels under the skin. Blood and blood fluids escape and leak into the surrounding tissues. They cause the familiar black-and-blue coloring of a bruise.

Avoid penile bruising. In rare cases, it can have serious side effects. When blood vessels are damaged, there is a risk tiny scars can build up during the healing process. *Even tiny scarring can block the free flow of blood critical for erection.* Heavy scarring can cause Peyronie's disease or priapism. Regard a penile bruise as a valuable health warning for the safe limits of sexual activity.

A penile bruise is self healing. From its mottled dark hue, it turns through a range of lighter colors until it disappears. The color changes are due to the escaped blood being re-absorbed. Avoid sexual activity until the healing process is complete.

Any penile injury should be checked by a physician. Therapy for bruising is to apply a cold compress or ice pack. Chilling causes contraction of the blood vessels and slows down the rate of leakage. This reduces the amount of swelling and any tiny risk of scarring. Cold reduces sensitivity in the nerve endings, so a cold compress also brings pain relief.

A bruise on the penis takes longer to heal than a bruise elsewhere on the body. Keep this in mind to reduce concern at the longer healing time. Unless the physician indicates otherwise (for blood disorders or diabetes), apply a cold compress for speedy relief. Rest is a crucial factor in bruising — as in other cases of penile trauma. If sexual activity does not cease, there is a real risk of causing a blood clot.

## What Makes a Clot?

Mr. Y was celebrating his birthday. Things had gotten torrid between his wife and himself. He searched for new thrills. The attachment of the vacuum cleaner seemed the ticket. Mr Y put his penis into the nozzle. His wife switched on the power. Suddenly, things were less than torrid. They were downright bad.

Mr. Y went to bed nursing his severely bruised organ. Over the next days, a hard raised ridge appeared along the top of the shaft. The skin above was red, tender and sore. Mr. Y felt too embarrassed to visit the physician. He suffered in silence and prayed it would go away.

A severe bruise can result in *thrombosed penile vein*. This happens when the escaped blood develops into a blood clot, called a *thrombus*. The thrombus is usually at the corona, and very small. Nevertheless, it blocks the vein and stops blood flowing back to the body. The hard raised ridge is due to pressure from the back-up of blood.

A thrombosed penile vein can happen without apparent cause. It is not usually a medical emergency. Keep in mind the body is very good at self-healing. While the clot is broken down, other veins take over the work. However, consult with the physician to check there is no further damage.

Therapy consists of conservative management only. This means "leave things alone and they will heal by themselves." Rest speeds up the healing process. Cease all sexual activity until the condition has cleared. An analgesic recommended by the physician helps with pain relief. Apply chilly self help.

Mechanical suction devices of any kind should *not* be used on the penis. Constriction rings which tighten to maintain an erection can cause thrombosed penile vein. So do such things as twine or elastic bands used for the same purpose. The worst injuries tend to occur during solitary masturbation, when a man is alone.

## Penile Trauma

The most common trauma is trapping penile skin in a zipper. It can be very painful, even when the damage is mild. Rather than risk more pain and damage by unzipping, cut the teeth below the trapped skin with metal cutters and the zip will fall apart.

Therapy is by conservative management only. Keep the wound and surrounding area clean and free from infection. If the skin is badly ripped, visit the emergency room. The edges may need to be sutured (sewn or clipped together).

A *rupture* is a slight tearing of the tissue inside the penis. It is due to sudden force or pressure on the erect penis. Even a mild rupture is very painful. Therapy is by conservative management only, but consult a physician promptly to ensure that the damage is mild. Wear a supporter during the healing process.

One-third of penile ruptures occur during love-making. They are due to sudden shifts in position, or by awkward attempts at penetration in the female astride position. They tend to occur where there is lack of space for ease of maneuver, e.g., between the steering wheel and driving seat of a car.

Other causes of rupture include rolling over onto an erect penis, or kneading it too hard to force an erection down. Take care. The consequences of penile mismanagement can be dire.

## Fracture

If the pressure is severe, the penis can actually *fracture*. Instead of slight tearing, the internal tissues are ripped apart. There may be a crackling noise, followed by intense pain and swift detumescence. Fracture rarely occurs when making love. The main causes are high energy accidents *and* personal mismanagement such as kneading down an erection with too much force.

Penile fractures are self healing. But with both rupture and fracture, scar tissue can build up during the healing process. Scar tissue is hard, fibrous, inelastic and permanent. It blocks penile blood flow at the damaged site. When healing is complete, the penis may erect at an angle. If the angle is steep, it causes pain and interferes with love-making.

However, penile rupture and fracture are extremely rare. *Fracture of the pelvis* (hip bones) is even more rare. But it does happen. A couple may be so carried away that too much pressure is applied too suddenly on the man's hips. A pelvic fracture can crush the spinal nerves, causing impotence. Great care should be taken to avoid such fearful risks.

## Oil Those Wheels

Another cause of penile trauma is lack of lubrication. This applies particularly to boisterous lovers, and to intact men. In the former, it can cause deeper lesions on penile skin which build up scar tissue during the healing process. In the latter, it can cause painful foreskin rips. For all men, whether intact or not, *stop thrusting the moment the environment feels dry*. Lubricate the works.

A young man may feel he has somehow failed if he has to use a lubricant. And perhaps he has. But sexual passion can be intense, and excitable partners may get completely carried away. Resist thinking it "unmanly" to use lubrication. Avoid penile mismanagement by keeping a ready supply.

# Itchy Penis

Walt woke up with a hangover, and an itching penis. He drank a glass of water and settled down to scratch. Through a foggy haze of alcohol, he tried to remember the events of the previous night. As memories flooded back, he leapt out of bed.

Having reason to suspect a sexual disease, Walt examined his genitals for parasites. He searched for the tell-tale signs of scabies, fleas and pubic lice. Finding none, he called the physician for an appointment. "It's urgent," he insisted. "The itch is driving me mad."

"Hmm," the physician said, after examining Walt and hearing his tale. "The penis is vulnerable to the same skin ailments as skin elsewhere on the body. Men who have eczema or psoriasis know this only too well. If you were over age 60, I would suggest an oncologist. At that age, an itchy penis can be a sign of cancer. But your itch is due to one of two skin infections. Neither is necessarily sexual. Both are mild."

Walt gave a huge sigh of relief.

The physician continued, "The two common skin infections are *pityriasis rosea*, a virus, and *lichen planus*, a fungus. They usually start elsewhere on the body before spreading to the penis. Both look like patches of ringworm, about 20 mm across. The patches turn scaly, flaky and peeling. They become itchy. It is unlikely they appear only on the genitals. *Avoid scratching.* Apply calamine lotion to soothe the itch. A dermatologist can help, but may need to try several medications before finding one which works. If not, both conditions clear up without therapy in 2 to 3 months. Which do you choose?"

"Self-healing," Walt said. "I'll take a chance."

"You have already taken one," was the physician's wry reply.

\* \* \*

Fred consulted the doctor because his organ was itchy. Unlike Wart, he was a happily married man. The area was red and tender, with a sprinkling of tiny blisters. The physician diagnosed *contact dermatitis*, an allergic skin reaction to some substance in contact with the penis.

He said, "This calls for personal investigation. Be your own detective. Track down the possible allergens: washing powders or soaps, contraceptives, condom lubricants, deodorants, fibers in clothes, metal buckles, that sort of thing. Remove any suspects. *Avoid scratching.* Apply cool wet dressings to soothe the itch."

Fred was given a prescription for corticosteroid cream. The physician warned, "Penile skin is absorbent. Use the cream *very* sparingly. Follow the directions exactly. Avoid the temptation to over-treat: do not apply more medication to speed up the effect. Ironically, *a common cause of itch is over-treatment dermatitis.* Any local medication should always be applied sparingly."

## Hands Off

Scratching genital itch slows down the healing process. It brings more blood to the site, which raises the temperature, which further inflames the itch. This can set up an itch/scratch cycle which is difficult to break. Also, scratching opens the skin, leaving a raw "weepy" area. Wherever skin is broken open, there is a risk of *secondary infection*; other germs can get in.

The crisis period for scratching is at night. Heat, trapped by bed linen, raises the body temperature and makes the itching acute. Remove bed linen. Reduce room temperature. Lower body heat in a cool bath or shower. Avoid brisk toweling. Gently pat the area dry. Apply cool damp dressings to facilitate sleep.

Cut the finger nails short. If necessary, wear gloves in bed. It has been known for penile skin to be completely ripped during sleep. Stress is an added factor in many skin allergies and complaints. When the itching starts, focus the attention away from it and from the stress it brings. Read, watch television, practice relaxation. Do whatever fully engages the mind.

An added problem of itching is that it can bring on sexual desire. This is hardly surprising. Erections can be brought on by any stimulation, including non-erotic ones. Sexual activity is *not* recommended, though a few men swear by it. This brings only short-term relief because activity increases the inflammation. One dermatologist suggests wearing boxing gloves instead!

## Beastly Balanitis

At age 15, Junior had a red oozing patch on his foreskin. It was sore, rather than painful. He wanted to tell his mom. But he was terrified she would guess he had been masturbating. He couldn't help it. He woke up doing it in the middle of the night.

It is punishment for my sinful behavior, Junior thought. He searched the medicine cabinet for a remedy. Weeping with pain, he tried astringent. Two days later, he rubbed in Daz. But his glans hurt more, and the infection looked worse. Finally, he told his mom. "You'll have to be circumcised," she grimly announced.

The physician cleared the infection with antibiotics. He told Junior's mom to go easy on the boy. "Masturbation is not a crime. Ignorance of genital hygiene is. Instead of washing afterwards, most boys mop up the ejaculate, which makes an ideal breeding ground for germs. He has a case of over-treatment dermatitis, too.

Balanitis is inflammation of the foreskin and underlying tissues. If it attacks in youth, shocked parents fear a sexual disease. The son, if a virgin, believes those tales of infected rest-room seats. Junior's case is the more likely scenario. Many boys do not seek help. They try "cures" which inflame the glans further, and disguise the infection by over-treatment dermatitis. *Ignorance of the value of genital hygiene is the main cause of balanitis in uncircumcised teenage boys.*"

Adult men can also get balanitis. The skin may be irritated by any number of things: chemicals in synthetic fabrics, tight or damp clothing, rough blankets, any substance which affects it. Avoid scratching the sore place. Apply cold packs for self help.

If the skin is scratched or opened by other means, balanitis can set in. Check the glans and foreskin for infections, allergy;also genital hygiene. Consult with the physician promptly for an antibiotic cream by prescription only.

Men aged 30 to 50 who suffer repeated attacks may consider circumcision as one solution. For men age 60 plus, balanitis can be a symptom of something more serious: diabetes, gout or cancer. Consult with a physician promptly.

# Phimosis

Phimosis begins with an infection of the foreskin. If untreated, the infection spreads and the foreskin swells up. Eventually, the foreskin becomes so large that it cannot retract. It is swollen and tight, and cannot be moved back away from the glans.

Phimosis is the result of repeated foreskin infections such as balanitis. It is linked to neglected hygiene. Undisturbed by soap and water, a whole potpourri of germs breed merrily under the foreskin with its enclosed glans. The delicate tissues undergo a process of partial healing/ partial flare-up/ partial healing again. Scar tissue keeps building up and breaking down.

Eventually, the scar tissue becomes fibrous: hard, tough and inelastic. It contracts the meatus, pulling the infected foreskin tightly inwards. At the same time, nearby healthy tissue strives to form new scabs and becomes infected. This adds to the collection of microscopic germs breeding there: anaerobes, vibrios and spirochetes.

Some men accept the chronic irritation and the red swollen foreskin. They rarely complain of phimosis, and visit the clinic only when there is pain or odorous discharge. Antibiotics control the infection. Hot soaks may help separate the foreskin from the glans. If they fail, a small incision is made to release it. Circumcision is generally advised when the inflammation clears.

# Paraphimosis

The old tramp was worried. His penis looked alarming. It had been swollen and sore for weeks but this morning, on urinating, everything suddenly changed. The foreskin slid right back and got stuck behind the glans. He had pulled it repeatedly, but it would not budge. Now the whole organ was throbbing and turning a nasty color. He had a frightening notion that he'd gotten some kind of gangrene down there.

Fearing clinics, he visited his sister, a retired nurse.

"It's paraphimosis," she cried. "You careless thing! You let the glans get infected and scarred. Now it's so swollen and huge, no wonder the foreskin is trapped at the back." Her eyes gleamed behind her spectacles. "You're in deep trouble!" she proclaimed. He hated pleading. "Help me, Sis."

"We treated men like you at the clinic. That foreskin has squeezed the veins. They've leaked fluid into the glans, making it more swollen. Next thing, the arteries gonna get squeezed shut. And pouf! Gangrene! That's the end of you."

Her expression was grim as she donned surgical gloves. "Watch!" she ordered. "I'm squeezing the glans hard, *real* hard, for 5 minutes. That reduces its size so I can push it upwards and inwards while I push the tight ring of foreskin up, over and down." She breathed heavily with concentration. "If this doesn't work, if the foreskin won't budge, you get to choose. I release its grip by cutting nail scissors is all I've got. Or you go to hospital and I'm not picking up the tab. Or, gangrene sets in."

He tried to smile. "You were always good to me, Sis." The words choked in his throat. He started a coughing fit. The terrible hacking and rasping wracked his frame until he heard her satisfied exclamation: "Got it!" And there was his foreskin back covering the glans.

She gave him two antibiotics. He wanted to thank her. "I'll take a bath," he offered.

"Not in my house," she retorted.

Brother and sister stared bleakly at each other over the chasm of their shared childhood miseries.

"You're still the same," he said. "Reliable old Sis."

She shrugged. "Take a bath. We ought to be friends."

"I know," he mumbled. Then smiled suddenly at her.

And she smiled back, a wintry, yet somehow uplifting, smile. "It's OK, baby brother. You can stay. I'll get you well."

# The Twist in the Tail

Peyronie's disease is a strange disorder. The first symptom is a dense raised fibrous *plaque* (patch) which appears at some point along the shaft. The plaque is mainly scar tissue; it feels like a hard irregular lump on or just below the skin. A few months later, the penis starts to curve in the direction of the plaque.

The curve is more noticeable at erection because scar tissue is inelastic. It cannot stretch to allow the penis to fully engorge. The angle may be slight, or a steep 45 degree twist. The erection is firm up to the plaque. Beyond it, and the organ is soft. The plaque acts as a tether, holding the erection back.

If the angle is steep, penetration is difficult. There may be pain. Therapies such as radiation, ultrasound, cortisone shots and vitamin E do not give satisfactory results. Corrective surgery consists of cutting slits in the plaque so that it lies flat. Or the plaque is removed and replaced with a skin graft. A small *prosthesis* may be required to keep the penis straight. The main problem with surgery is that it creates scar tissue of its own. In turn, this scar tissue can create another curve. A further problem is the slight risk of damage to penile nerves. A new substance, *collagenase*, dissolves scar tissue. In clinical trials, it is injected in the plaque and gives optimal results. Collagenase is not yet accepted therapy because the side effects are not yet fully understood. To date, it is used mainly by dermatologists. Peyronie's disease is rare. It does not occur under age twenty. The more usual ages are between forty and sixty. It occurs more frequently with diabetes, rheumatoid arthritis and other fibrosing diseases. A few cases may be due to penile trauma or personal mismanagement: bruising, risky games, excessive force on sexual activity; *any injury which leaves scar tissue after the healing process*. The incidence of Peyronie's is on the increase; it is not known why.

When the plaque is first noticed, it causes great anxiety. Fears of cancer loom large in the mind. For some men, this fear stops them from seeking medical help. Avoid delay. An untreated plaque can twist the penis a full ninety degrees. Early medical intervention is a must.

A cure has not yet been found for Peyronie's disease. But in about 80 percent of cases, it will remit spontaneously. The pain stops, the hardened plaque begins to dissolve, and the penis straightens out. It can take six months or more for this to happen. Though the waiting time is not pleasant, avoid losing hope.

Some men have a natural curve on erection. These are the "scythes" and are not to be confused with Peyronie's disease.

# A Clear Passageway

"A 14-year-old boy, with repeated infections, was found to have a pencil lodged in his bladder. It had to be surgically removed."

"A 55-year-old male almost died from urine retention due to a urethral stricture caused by self-instrumentalization."

The urinary tract is lined with delicate mucus membranes which can be easily scratched, pierced and permanently scarred by self-instrumentalization. Any object put into the urethra for further sexual stimulation risks causing scar tissue, which can result in Peyronie's disease.

Paraffin oils and other fluids cause a reaction in which a large rock-hard lump of matter is formed. There is extreme pain, and the risk of retention. Bobby pins, needles, carpet tacks and air-gun pellets are some of the objects found lodged in the urethra. They get stuck in the passageway and cannot come out.

The damage done by foreign objects or fluids can be major. Self-laceration with the slivered edge of a razor blade or other sharp object is not unknown. Surgery to extract them, clear out the debris due to infection and excise scar tissue is a skilled procedure with the risk of scar tissue afterwards.

\* \* \*

"A 22 year old man inserted cocaine intra-urethrally to enhance sexual performance. His erection was priapic, and lasted three days. His condition was so frightening, an ambulance was eventually called. Blood trapped in his organ had formed clots; gangrene was advanced. The young man left the hospital minus both legs, and minus his penis."

Though it may seem trite to state the obvious: *avoid self-instrumentalization*. Keep the passageway clear.

CHAPTER 5

# The Testicles

## Testicles Are Terrific!

The word "testis" comes from the Latin for testimony or witness. In olden days, when a man took a solemn oath, he swore to tell the truth by touching his testicles. The presence of two testes bore witness to his character based on his virility. A priest could not be promoted to bishop if he had only one.

In some places, the testicles are still touched, either when swearing on oath, or for good luck. And indeed, all which is male, masculine and virile does come from the testicles. They produce *androgens*, the male hormones which *virilize* a boy — turn him into a man. They produce sperm, which can turn the man into a father. In fact, the testicles are the crucial part of the male sexual system. By comparison, the penis is merely a tool.

So the health of the testicles should merit top priority. In reality, men are far more concerned with penile health. Though this is understandable, keep in mind any trouble in the testicles can cause problems for all that is male, masculine and virile, including the penis.

The prefix "orch" comes from the Greek "orchis." The orchid was thought to resemble the testicles; or the other way around; the evidence is not clear. Whichever, the prefix "orch" is still used in medical terminology; e.g., orchitis is an infection of the testes. Testes and testicles mean exactly the same thing.

# The Scraggy Scrotum

The scrotum is a baggy pouch which covers the testicles. It is divided into two compartments by connective tissue. This acts as a fire wall, stopping inflammation in one testis from passing to the other. The skin of the scrotum is crinkled, movable and very thin. It can be hairless, or covered with single strands of darker-than-head hair.

Threaded through the skin are rows of tiny muscle fibers. These give the scrotum its crinkled, scraggy look. The muscle fibers are heat-sensitive, and act as thermo-regulators. They pull the scrotum up close to body warmth when it is cold, during exercise, love-making and strong emotions, especially fear, to protect the testes from harm.

The testicles inside the scrotum are shaped like eggs, or small oval balls. Each is divided into 250 compartments and lined with sperm-making tubes. Between these are Leydig cells, which make the all-important sex hormone *testosterone*. Both functions are under separate control from the pituitary gland in the brain.

An average adult testicle measures 1 1/2 inches long, 1 inch wide, 1 1/2 inches across. It weighs between 25 and 50 grams, depending on the man's overall size. The testes of the small, yet highly aggressive, chimpanzee weigh an average 120 grams, while those of the large, more peaceable, gorilla weigh a mere 35 grams. Whether ape data are of any significance is a matter of opinion. They are included here for interest's sake.

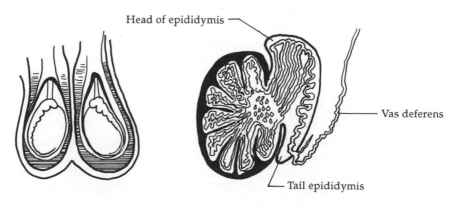

Head of epididymis

Vas deferens

Tail epididymis

THE TESTICLES             TESTIS AND EPIDYDYMIS

# Which Side to Dress?

At age 15, Virgo decided he was misshapen. His left testicle hung lower than the right, and was growing abnormally large. Each day he checked gloomily to see if the right one had caught up. He decided it was cancer. Everyone would be sorry when he died.

He stopped eating to make the growth stop. It didn't. And his Pop got mad. "Whassa matta, son? Don you wanna grow big like Pop?" Virgo blushed under his spots. He could not tell a man.

"Talk to the boy!" Pop ordered his mom, and went outside.

Virgo covered his face. "I'm gonna die soon!" he mumbled. "It's growing wrong. Down there. One side's too big." He couldn't believe it when he heard her laugh. How cruel can a parent get?

"Use your mind, Virgo. *Think*! What would happen if they both grew the same size?" his mom said. "They'd rub together and hurt. And that'd produce heat and damage the male seed." She offered to have a quick look-and-see to check if he was OK. He refused with all the outraged modesty a boy his age can show his seniors. She told him about "which side to dress." Then she said 85 percent of men had a left testicle which was both heavier and larger. She didn't know about the other 15 percent. Maybe they were the other way around. Maybe it was related to the 15 percent of left-handed men? But that was only a guess.

Virgo's fears are shared by many growing boys. To avoid this common concern at puberty, keep your son informed. Tell him what to expect.

# Out in the Cold

The average body temperature is 37 degrees Centigrade (98.6 degrees Fahrenheit). This is too hot for healthy sperm. The testicles need a temperature which is *4 degrees below* body heat, which is why the scrotum is outside the body. It provides a pleasantly cool environment in which sperm can be safely produced.

More than four degrees of heat either way can damage the production of healthy sperm. Hence those tiny muscle fibers which pull the scrotum up close to body warmth when it is cold. In hot conditions, they not only relax, but actually stretch slightly to lower the testes even further. And this increases the surface area, so heat from inside the testicles can more easily escape. Tight jockey shorts may be more comfortable than the boxer type. They give support, and show a well-groomed outline. But tight shorts interfere with this clever thermo-regulatory device. They can add to over-heating and cause fertility problems. One U.S. study into sperm counts found a 40 million decrease from a base of 100,000,000 in 1958, to 60,000,000 in 1988. The trend to lower counts was highest in men who wore jockey shorts.

## The Traveling Testes

The testes start to develop 40 days after conception. They grow inside the fetal abdomen. Near the end of the eighth month, they travel down the *inguinal canal* and through the abdomen wall. They reach their low-hanging position in the scrotum a few days before birth. A post-birth check ensures they have safely descended.

3.4 percent full-term babies are born with undescended testes. Of these, 50 percent descend in the first month of life. 30 percent of premature babies have undescended testicles; of these, 80 percent are safely down by the first month. If not, make sure the pediatrician checks that they are present and can descend. They may need to be stitched down permanently before the boy is four years old.

A blow to the scrotum is excruciatingly painful. It is felt in the testicles and in the lower abdomen. The sickening sinking feeling is at the site where the testes traveled down pre-birth, taking their nerve supply with them; they are still linked to it.

The testes can move up out of the scrotum now and then. This is called *retractile*, and is fairly common. Retractile testes usually descend and stay permanently down of their own accord before age four. However, read the next article.

## Misplaced Testes

*Cryptorchidism* means "concealed testicle." It occurs when one or both testes get stuck at some point in fetal descent. *Ectopic maldescent* means one or both have strayed from the normal path of descent. The usual place for a missing testicle is the groin. Both these conditions are often called *undescended testicles*. If the testes cannot be felt by the pediatrician, let alone brought down, make sure the baby is checked again within the first two months of life. If they are still not in the scrotum, the next check is before his first birthday. With luck, by then they will have descended of their own accord.

Keep in mind the sperm-making tubes are in the scrotum for a reason. It is now thought they can be permanently damaged by body heat while they are still growing. So the option for surgery is not really an option. Without it, the boy will become *sterile*. He cannot produce healthy sperm and so will be unable to father children.

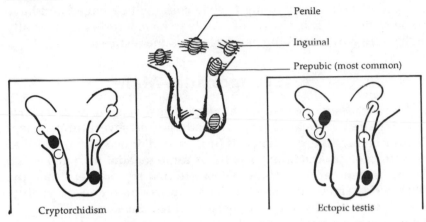

Penile

Inguinal

Prepubic (most common)

Cryptorchidism

Ectopic testis

MISPLACED TESTIS

*Orchiopexy* is surgery to bring down the testes and stitch them in the scrotum so they stay fixed. It used to be done at age four. Today, the condition is attacked more aggressively, and may be done at ages 12 to 18 months. Whatever the timing, orchiopexy is crucial before a boy's fifth birthday. By age six, there is a risk of permanent sterility.

# Hooray for One!

It is rare for both testes to be misplaced. Fortunately, the one which has safely descended can easily cope with the work of two. Nor are the Leydig cells which produce testosterone damaged by body heat. However, cancer of the testicle is 40 times more common with undescended testicles. The reasons are unclear, as only 10 percent of misplaced testes are malformed as a birth defect.

To reduce the risk of cancer, one option is to find and remove the misplaced testis rather than stitch it in the scrotum. The surgery is called *orchidectomy*, and is still fairly popular. But unless the testis is diseased beyond repair, or dead, orchidectomy may not be an acceptable choice.

The point to consider is one misplaced testicle may not be able to produce sperm, but it can produce male hormones. A boy cannot be virilized, he cannot develop into a man without these. He can take testosterone replacement therapy, TRT, but there are side effects.

No matter how much care is taken, infections and accidents do happen. The one remaining testicle could get damaged and have to be removed. It is always desirable to have a reserve, especially to have two of something as precious as the testicles.

## A Hypogonadal Man

The *gonads* are the testes. *Male hypogonadism* is the medical term for impaired testicle function. Moderate or severe impairment leads to faulty spermatogenesis (malformed or no sperm), reduced testosterone production, or both. A hypogonadal man makes too little, or none at all. Without testosterone replacement therapy, TRT, a boy cannot become virilized and has problems of fertility. He appears similar to the eunuchs of olden days.

If hypogonadism starts after puberty, the boy is already virilized. So he does not lose his masculine shape and form. He continues to look and act like a man. Yet over a period of time, his sex drive wanes. Without therapy, he eventually loses all sexual desire. A continuing course of TRT will boost his failing hormone supply, but is unlikely to restore fertility.

The causes of hypogonadism include testicular damage from birth defects, maldescent, torsion, orchitis, mumps, gonorrhea, irradiation by unprotected X-rays or nuclear plant, cancer, pituitary tumor, dysfunction of other glands such as the thyroid and adrenals, and disorders of the hypothalamus or other parts of the brain.

## Hernia

Greg took up exercise in his late 40s. He went crazy, delighting in his new smooth outline, his hard flat abdomen. He still had a tendency to paunch; it had begun in his twenties. So he spent hours hanging from the wall bars and doing abdominal workouts. One day, Greg felt a painless lump in his groin. It was very noticeable when he stood up. It disappeared when he lay down.The physician pressed under Greg's penis and said "Cough."

"Yes," she sounded satisfied. "I feel a small bulge of gut pressing here. The straining effort of the cough did it. You have an *inguinal hernia*. Now, lie down. Yes. The hernia contents have slid back into the abdomen. That's because the pull of gravity is removed when you lie down."

While Greg was dressing, the physician said, "The abdominals are great walls of muscle across your front. If they are firm and strong, they act as nature's corset for the soft organs inside. There are two weak sites in the wall at the inguinal canal where the testicles descended before birth. The wrong kind of exercise, any undue intra-abdominal pressure, can rupture these weak sites. Then a small portion of the gut (fatty tissue or bowel) can bulge through. And this is a hernia.

Surgery is the prudent option to prevent the risk of blood vessels getting pinched, and then cut off. If this happens, the contents of the hernia become strangled, deprived of blood, and gangrene sets in. Gangrene is a medical emergency. It takes only 4 to 6 hours to destroy tissue deprived of blood. If untreated, a "strangulated" hernia can be fatal. *Hernioplasty* is a surgical repair which strengthens the weak sites on the abdominal wall. The procedure is quick and simple."

Greg was undecided. He feared surgery. But he didn't like bits of his gut hanging out. . . let alone those awesome risks.

The physician said. "The little bulge can be manipulated back. It might stay put. Or it may slip down again. Wearing a truss provides comfort, support. It's your choice."

"A truss? No way! Let's go for the knife," Greg said.

A *scrotal hernia* is an inguinal hernia which has become so large and heavy that it drops down into the scrotum. It is rare the contents can be returned to the abdomen. At this advanced stage, it is more likely the hernia has become complicated. It may be so swollen it cannot be returned to its correct location. Or the swelling may result in it becoming fixed within the scrotum. Surgery removes the risk of gangrene. The man's movements, and life in general, become more comfortable.

To reduce the risk of hernia, avoid strenuous exercise which puts unnatural strain on the lower abdomen. The chief offenders are lifting heavy weights the wrong way, prolonged hanging from wall bars, repeated bouts of coughing, severe straining for a bowel movement. If carrying a heavy travel bag, use baggage with wheels attached, or trolleys. If involved in any straining effort, pain in the groin or testicle is a valuable health warning to stop.

Learn to lift heavy loads the safe way:

· Stand very close to the heavy object.
· Keep the backbone nearly straight.
· Lower the body by bending at the ankles, knees and hips.
· Use the shoulder and leg muscles to take most of the weight.

A baby born with a hydrocele is likely to have an inguinal hernia. It shows as a swelling on the lower tummy or the groin. Corrective surgery is a simple repair job. For parents who fear surgery, it might be helpful to talk with other parents, or older boys who have recently had surgery for the same condition.

## The Cooling System

Each testicle dangles freely from its own *spermatic cord*. The cord carries its life support system, the blood and nerve supply. When fresh blood enters, it is at body temperature. This is too hot for the sperm-making tubes. So a cooling device is built into the cord rather like the cooling device in a refrigerator.

The veins which carry away used blood are coiled around the arteries pumping in fresh blood. Used blood is cooler and travels more slowly. It acts as the "coolant," removing heat from the fresh blood. By the time arterial blood reaches the testicles, it is at the correct temperature.

Clever though this is, an object dangling freely from a cord can swing to and fro. It can completely twist around and strangle itself. To prevent this, there is an attachment between the epididymes (upon the twins) and the scrotal walls. There is a rare birth defect in which this attachment is missing. It can result in *torsion*; the testicle strangles to death. The likely times are in infancy and puberty. Under age 21, regard any testicular *swelling with pain* as an emergency.

## Epididymitis

If each testicle is rolled gently between the fingers and thumb, a comma-shaped lump can be felt draped over the top. This "lump" is a narrow tightly coiled-up tube. If the coils were stretched out, the tube would measure 20 feet — over three times average male height. Coiled up, it is two inches by one-half inch.

The lumps are the *epididymes*, which is Greek for "upon the twins." When sperm are made, they enter the epididymes, and are stored while they mature. They need this extra time to develop before they set out on the long journey in the race for the egg.

*Epididymitis* is an infection of the epididymes, the comma-shaped lumps which sit "upon the twins." The germs travel back through the sexual system and attack the epididymes. In youth, the infection can be due to a severe urethritis. In older men, it can be a prostate infection.

*Orchitis* is the generic name for any inflammation of the testicles. The symptoms of epididymitis and orchitis are much the same. Sometimes the names are used interchangeably. The symptoms of both are a reddened scrotum, tense swollen testicles with sudden acute pain and fever. Regard these symptoms as a surgical emergency in boys and young men because of the risk of torsion.

Ultrasound and the Doppler stethoscope help to distinguish between torsion and infection. If there is discharge from the penis, a swab culture shows if the bacteria of gonorrhea are present. Mid-stream urinalysis helps to diagnose the type of infection. Like urethritis, the infection can be non-specific; the cause is of unknown origin.

Therapy is by antibiotics and pain relief. Hospitalization is an option, depending upon the degree of infection. Bed rest is essential until the pain subsides. If at home, raise and support the swollen scrotum on a soft pad for comfort. Avoid very hot compresses to soothe the inflammation; they can damage the sperm-making tubes. Ice bags to reduce the swelling can cause chilling; ask the physician for advice on this. Wear a supporter for a few days after getting up.

Orchitis can also be the result of a sports injury, or after surgery to remove a scrotal cyst, or vasectomy. However, the main causes of both orchitis and epididymitis are infectious mononucleosis (glandular fever), chlamydia, diphtheria, scarlet fever, typhus fever, gonorrhea, syphilis and chlamydia. For information on the sexual diseases, see Chapter 15.

Not all infections are brought to the testicles via the sexual system. The other method of disease transmission is via the blood supply. And the most usual infection in this category is mumps.

# Mumps (orchitis)

The virus of mumps is highly-infectious. It attacks the parotid (saliva) glands of the face, and can travel down to infect the testes. It is unusual under age five, the early school years are the likely times. The symptoms are fever, headache and vomiting, and can be moderate or mild. Swollen glands appear on one or both sides of the face, giving a "mumpy" look. 80 percent of cases are self-healing, and recovery is speedy. But in 20 percent, the virus travels in the blood supply down to the testes. Some five days after the face swells, one or both testicles start to hurt and swell up.

*The mumps virus damages the testicles only after puberty*, and in men who were not exposed to the disease in childhood. It causes some degree of testicular atrophy in 50 percent of cases. Usually, only part of a testicle dies, and *only 30 percent of men are infected in both testes*. It is of great concern to men who have not begun their families. The degree of risk depends upon the virulence of the attack, and this can be estimated by the doctor.

Pregnant women should avoid mumps due to the risk of fetal damage. Incubation time is two to three weeks after exposure. The child is infective until the swellings disappear. Mumps vaccine, given after the first year, is contraindicated for a few toddlers: ask the family physician. The issue of whether to expose children to their infected peers is not yet resolved.

# Know Thyself

It is recommended all men become familiar with the feel of their healthy testicles. Harmless lumps can appear, and cause needless fears of tumor. Learn the external appearance of the scrotum when standing. Use a bright light to note skin color and texture. Then note the position of each testicle hanging within the scrotum.

Examine the testicles after a warm bath or shower, and lying down. Avoid erotic thoughts. Cup the scrotum in the palms of both hands. With thumb and fingers, gently roll each testicle around.

1: Become familiar with the smooth egg-shape feel of each one.

2: Squeeze gently to learn its firm, not hard, consistency.

3: Examine the epididymis and learn its consistency. It feels softer; it may be spongy and a little tender.

4: Feel the tube-shaped spermatic cord behind the testis rising up from the epididymis to learn its firm, smooth structure.

Do GSE at regular monthly intervals. Note any change in the scrotum. Examine the testicles by gentle manipulation. It should be possible to tell the back of a testis from the front. A hard, painless pea-sized nodule, any swelling on the testicle itself, is a significant finding. Do the *transillumination test.*A light shining through water gives off a translucent glow. The same light cannot pass through a tumor. In a darkened room, shine a strong flashlight behind the scrotum. If a translucent or reddish glow is seen, the lump is a harmless scrotal cyst.

## Cancer of the Testicle

Olliver Gillie, a distinguished medical journalist, wrote the following in a quality British newspaper: "Cancer of the testicle is now the most common form of cancer in men under the age of 35, and the problem is on the increase."

Now consider the actual figures. "In the United States and Europe, testicular cancer occurs in two to three per 100,000 men." The actual figures sound less alarming. Yet distinguished journalists and quality newspapers try to avoid sensationalism, they try not to exaggerate. What is the reason for such shock/horror tactics?

Most tumors of the testicle develop between the ages of 15 and 40. It is a relatively rare cancer in other age groups. It can be cured in 90 percent of cases if it is caught early. Yet studies show over 50 percent of young men wait more than six months after they notice something wrong before going to the doctor. More than six months? How tragic! Because many cancers can be completely cured if they are found early enough; in particular, testicular cancer.

The first symptoms of cancer of the testicle include:

· A rounded, obvious lump, like a nodule.
· A slight increase in the size of one testicle.
· A change in consistency; it feels harder, softer or grainier.
· A heavy, full or dragging sensation.

· A dull ache in the groin, and/or above the pubic hairline.
· A lessening of the normal extremely acute sensitivity.

If a healthy testicle is squeezed, it produces a sickening and sinking feeling. A testis which is replaced by a tumor is insensitive to pressure, and those feelings are absent.

A testicle which is replaced by a tumor seems abnormally heavy. It usually weighs more than its healthy "twin."

A testicle which atrophied early in life is smaller than its healthy "twin." A warning sign of a growing tumor is an increase in size of the atrophied testis. Because it is completely dead, the enlargement cannot be due to natural growth.

Therapy for cancer depends upon the degree of malignancy. In many cases, removal of the affected testis is the prudent option. As one healthy testis can easily do the work of two, surgery is less fearful than it might at first sound. An implant restores the scrotum to its previous appearance.

But the majority of testicular lumps do not signify cancer. They are usually scrotal cysts. The point to note clearly is that *a cancer lump is on the testicle itself*, not just within the scrotum. If a man does not know how his healthy testicles feel, how can he tell if there is size increase, change in consistency and so on?

# An Implant

If a testicle has to be removed, the space can be filled with a prosthesis. An artificial testicle is made of gel-filled silicone or rubber. It is perfectly designed to match its "twin" in size, weight and consistency. It is safe and undetectable. Though an implant may not entirely restore self-image, the fact it goes undetected greatly helps to reduce loss of self-esteem. Wear a scrotal support for two weeks on recovery. There is an embargo on love-making for three weeks, nor should orgasm be sought by solitary masturbation. Follow the surgeon's directions closely.

The embargo usually depends upon the degree of swelling and pain from the implantation. If there is no implant, love-making can be resumed as soon as it feels comfortable to do so. Though it may be highly alarming to lose one testicle, it is comforting to know the other one can easily do the work of two. If both testes have to be removed, two protheses can be implanted. Fertility is permanently lost. Hormone replacement therapy can keep alive sexual interest, but loss of both testes is a savage blow. Equally tragic, perhaps more so, is that certain kinds of testicular surgery destroy the ability to make love.  Consider counseling, as this can be a burden too great to bear without professional help.

There is hope on the horizon. . .

At the 1987 International Transplant Forum in Pittsburgh, a Chinese surgeon, Dr. Zhan Bing Yan, reported his first testicle transplant three years before in Wuhan, China.  To date, he had transplanted testes into 13 patients, including one whose wife was now expecting a baby.

Dr. Zhan said 11 patients experienced some rejection in the first three months after the implants (the body's defense system tries to get rid of the foreign matter).  In all but one case, the rejection was halted by medication.  However, further research was needed to reduce the risk of rejection before he would perform any more testes transplants.

## A Warning Tale

In 1987, the British Medical Journal reported on two cases in which the patients' initial complaint was backache.  One was a 17-year-old boy who had been treated by traction in hospital because of spinal nerve irrigation before anybody thought of looking at his testes.  This omission was even more remarkable considering the boy had had surgery for an undescended testis, and these are known to be at risk of malignant change.  Fortunately, despite spinal and lung secondaries, the boy is now well and disease-free.

The other boy, a 15-year-old, did not fare any better in the diagnosis.  First, he was referred to the orthopedic surgeons who, when he didn't improve, handed him on to the rheumatologists.  They thought he was suffering from ankylosing spondylitis, a form of arthritis.  Only when the boy became so ill that he was admitted to hospital was his scrotum examined.  Unfortunately, in spite of intensive chemotherapy, he died.

Cancer specialists insist that early detection of testicular tumors will not improve until examination of the genitals in the young male becomes routine.  Though most family physicians will check the testicles, parents need to ensure that this procedure has been carried out.

## Scrotal Cysts

A cyst is a sac or enclosed cavity filled with liquid or semi-solid matter. It is called "abnormal" medically, but only because it should not be there. Most scrotal cysts are painless and harmless. They can be inconvenient if they grow to a large size. Knowledge of these swellings allays fears of a tumor when coming across a lump.

## 1. Hydrocele

A hydrocele is a sac of water. The "water" is a clear yellowish lubricating fluid inside the scrotum. For some unknown reason, it starts to increase in volume. The cyst feels soft and watery; it is painless and harmless. Check by transillumination. Some hydroceles disappear spontaneously; the fluid is reabsorbed. Therapy is usually "conservative management only. "Hydroceles are more common in infancy and over age 40. A few can develop inside the spermatic cord.

If the cyst is large and cumbersome, the Doppler stethoscope checks it does not interfere with blood flow to the testicle. The fluid is *aspirated*, drained off with a syringe. The condition can become chronic because the sac may fill up again in a few months. Rather than regular aspiration, some men opt for surgery to stitch the sac permanently closed. However, there is a slight chance of another hydrocele developing later on.

Not all hydroceles feel soft and watery. A few are hard. The condition is rare between ages 18 and 40. If present at this age, the fluid is aspirated before the scrotum is examined. This enables better palpation to rule out cancer or a tubercular cyst.

## 2. Hematocele

This cyst contains blood with a little lubricating fluid. Check by transillumination. The blood is due to testicular trauma, an injury from a knock or blow often during sport. The blood is reabsorbed in the same way as a bruise. While this takes place, it may feel more comfortable to wear a fairly loose supporter. Wear a protector during sport.

## 3. Spermatocele

This is a painless sac containing dead sperm. The fluid around the sperm is thin, white and cloudy. Check by transillumination. The sac is freely movable, and is found above and behind the testicle. Usually, it is small and goes unnoticed. It may be discovered only on medical examination for other reasons. In rare cases, a spermatocele grows large and is mistaken for a hydrocele. Surgery is necessary only if the cyst grows to such a size it is unsightly or cumbersome.

## 4. Urocele

This sudden swelling in the scrotum is due to urine escaping from a damaged urethra. This can happen with severe pelvic trauma from road accidents or high energy machinery. Emergency surgery is required to repair the damage and drain the swelling. Antibiotics destroy infections which might be present. (Empty the bladder before driving. A full bladder can burst after sudden impact; an empty one does not.)

## 5. Variocele

This is a sac of varicose veins in the scrotum. Recent surveys find varioceles occur in 15 to 20 percent of men, usually between the ages of 15 and 45. Most, like varicose veins in the leg, are due to man's erect posture and the extra pull exerted by the force of gravity. They disappear on lying down. A few may be due to the cooling device, the veins coiled around the arterial supply.

The symptoms are a dull ache or a bloated, dragging feeling in the scrotum. The condition is harmless and does not mean love-making should cease, be less frequent or energetic. In fact, for some unknown reason, the variocele actually begins to hurt if love-making does stop. The pain subsides after sexual activity, including solitary masturbation.

The cyst lies above and behind the testicle. It feels like a bag of twisted worms inside the small swelling. It may be tender to touch. It will transilluminate. It might be implicated in a low sperm count, but this is controversial. The Doppler stethoscope is used to check the cyst does not interfere with testicular blood flow.

*Varicocelectomy* is surgery to tie off the vein. It is an option where there is pain, fertility problems, or discomfort from a large swelling. Otherwise, therapy is not required. To relieve a dull ache or pulling sensation, wear a scrotal support. This may be all that is needed and then only on days which are likely to be particularly strenuous or tiring.

# More Than Twins

In rare cases, a baby may be born with more than two testicles. The condition is called *polyorchidism*. It causes great interest, and even more folklore. One story concerns the 16th century monk with supernumerary testicles (above the usual number) who kept breaking his vow of celibacy. This was put down to his "special design" which made him "more of a man."

In fact, polyorchidism is usually associated with hernia, scrotal cysts or maldescent. In some Latin American countries, a supernumerary testicle is something to boast of, even though it may be just a scrotal hernia or a hydrocele. Only just over 50 cases of true polyorchidism have been reported in this century.

If the extra testis is healthy and functioning, there may be no reason to remove it. The decision whether to do so or not depends upon medical criteria outside the parameters of this book.

# CHAPTER 6

# Testosterone

## Hooray for Testosterone!

Hormones are powerful chemicals which act as triggers for certain functions. They are made in *endocrine* glands and travel in the blood to reach their destination. Endocrine glands include the pituitary, pancreas, adrenals, thyroid, parathyroid, ovaries and testicles. A doctor who specializes in the study of hormones is an *endocrinologist*.

Testosterone is the hormone of the libido (sex drive) in both men and women. It is the fuel which lights the fires of sex at puberty and continues to be made throughout life. It keeps the sexual fires burning merrily almost to the very grave. "Andro" is Greek for male. Male hormones are *androgens* because they support and maintain the growth of male tissues, not because they are made by men. Testosterone supports virilization for the rest of a man's life. About 95 percent is produced by the testes, 6 to 8 mg daily. The rest comes from the *adrenal glands*.

The female hormone *estrogen* is also made in the testes. Men make ten times *less* estrogen and ten times *more* testosterone than women (in her adrenals). Children of both genders make small amounts. The effects of androgens and estrogens are complex. (They interact with other hormones and systems outside the parameters of this book.)

The word "androgynous" means both male and female. It unites the reproductive organs of both genders in one structure. (The double narcissus is a flower with both male and female parts.) In this respect, testosterone, which fuels the sex drive in both men and women, unites the genders — Hooray for Testosterone!

# Hormones at Puberty

The signal to start puberty comes from the *hypothalamus* in the brain. It comes when the hypothalamus reaches a certain level of maturity. In girls, the level is weight-related; plumper girls develop earlier than their slimmer sisters. A weight relationship has not yet been established for boys. But it is likely the onset of puberty will be later in a slender boy than in a more solidly built youth.

The signal acts on the *pituitary* gland, which then makes the hormones which control sexual development. The main ones in both boys and girls are FSH, a follicle-stimulating hormone, and LH, a luteinizing hormone. Because the testes and ovaries are *gonads* (producers of seed), the hormones which stimulate them to work, FSH and LH, are called *gonadotropins*.

The pituitary sends gonadotropins into the blood stream. When they arrive at the testes, FSH stimulates the production of sperm; LH stimulates the production of testosterone and other androgens. If there are problems in either the hypothalmus or the pituitary, the complex chain starting sexual development may not begin. The boy cannot become virilized. His body remains that of a child.

It takes a year for the levels of FSH and LH to build up. Then it is all systems go. Puberty begins in earnest. The body starts to become virilized. Muscle mass develops, the genitals enlarge, pubic hair appears and so on. Consult a physician if your son has no signs of virilization by age 15. See Chapter 11.

# Quality Control

It is very important that proper control is kept over all this development. If the testicles produce too little or too much testosterone, it would have disastrous effects on virilization. So FSH and LH are produced under negative feed-back controls. Testosterone production goes rather like this:

· When testosterone rises to its correct level in the blood
· the information is fed back to the pituitary and hypothala-

mus which promptly react and stop any more LH being made
- which stops the testes producing any more testosterone.
- When the level of testosterone in the blood drops
- the information is fed back to the pituitary and hypothalamus
- which promptly re-stimulate the production of LH
- which re-stimulates the testes to make testosterone
- which causes the blood level of testosterone to rise again and so on, and so forth, throughout the man's life.

## The Right Stuff

Testosterone is sometimes called the "winner" hormone. The level in the blood rises when a problem is solved, a battle won. The relaxed or happy mood which follows winning shuts down the production of stress hormones which helped with winning. This results in a natural surge of testosterone. It can be seen that *stress hormones and testosterone work in opposition.*

If a man with normal testosterone levels is given an extra dose, his sex drive does not increase. He does not become more virile. His behavior rarely becomes more aggressive. The negative feedback control stops him from becoming sexually over-excited by reducing his own testosterone production. This is why booster shots of testosterone are of limited value for erection problems which are due to stress.

Studies of sex criminals show they do not have higher levels of testosterone. They are *not* more virilized than other men. Yet sex criminals often blame their hormones for their appalling acts. They report they cannot control their destructive urges. They are tormented by them, and live in constant fear of repeating their horrendous crimes.

It seems the perverse desire to distort the act of love into *pedophilia* (child pornography, molestation and abuse) cannot be blamed on excess testosterone. And that the brutal crimes of rape, sex torture and death come almost entirely from the mind. Chromosomes used to be blamed, but this is now proven incorrect. Until there is more research into the minds of sex criminals, one preventive measure is to remove their sex drive. The ethics of this are highly dubious. It requires the man's full knowledge, understanding and consent.

Depo-Provera is one of several synthetic female hormones

which may be used. Regular shots stop the testes from producing any testosterone. The sex drive slows down and eventually ceases. A few men report relief at no longer being plagued by their dreadful desires. But loss of testosterone produces an extreme passivity rarely found in either gender.

Testosterone is of value in the management of certain female ailments. It is given in very low, non-virilizing, doses. Though the results are not fully known, it does not seem to make a woman more aggressive, nor increase her sex drive, nor change her courtship approach to men. But great care must be taken to ensure this does not happen.

Typical range of testosterone circulating in the blood (ng/dl) is as follows:

Men 385 — 1000
Women  20 — 80
Children  20 — 80
Pubertal boys 120 — 600
Hypogonadal men 100 — 300

A man with erection problems may suspect low testosterone production. This is rare. His serum levels can be checked by an endocrinologist. If low, testosterone replacement therapy, TRT brings dramatic success. The sex drive is restored and erections regain rigidity. A safe dose is worked out, and the man is warned of the short and long-term side-effects of taking TRT.

# Steroid Abuse

The word "testosterone" comes from testes and steroid. Androgens and estrogens are *steroids*; they share the same basic structure as a group of other compounds. *Anabolic steroids* are synthetic hormones now being abused by some athletes. Testosterone enables the synthesis of nitrogen from protein to promote tissue growth and increase muscle mass. Though the health risks are known, they have not deterred those athletes determined to win at any cost.

Recent research into steroid abuse has come up with other findings. It seems testosterone is toxic to the mind as well. Due to legal fears, the number of athletes willing to help with research is not large. Yet one small study found a third of those abusing steroids reported an increase in psychiatric disorders.

At first, there was an increase in mood swings. Then, there were feelings of extreme frustration and violence. Most of the athletes experienced severe depression. About half suffered auditory hallucinations: hearing cries, sounds or voices which were not there. One man suddenly drove his car straight into a tree at 40 miles per hour as his friends watched helplessly. One estimate suggests half a billion dollars worth of steroids are bought each year in the U.S.

The mood swings of athletes, with frustration, violence and depression were thought due to the stress of competition. Further research may find some link with steroid abuse. In a different study, a group of athletes were given placebos and told they were steroids. They did not develop greater muscle mass, yet they all performed brilliantly and outshone their previous records. This is an example of the placebo effect, which is the power of the imagination over the facts.

# Klinefelter's Syndrome

Klinefelter's Syndrome is a sad yet fairly common cause of male hypogonadism and infertility. It is a genetic disorder in which there are three sex chromosomes instead of the usual two XY. In 80 percent of cases, the testes produce too little testosterone and the sperm-making tubes are damaged. The young man grows tall and thin, he lacks facial and body hair, there may be gynecomastia (male breasts).

Klinefelter's Syndrome occurs in one out of every 500 live male births. This rises to one in 100 among those who are mentally handicapped. The diagnosis is rarely made in childhood because the testes are present at birth. If the condition is mild, the young man may simply think he has a low sex drive. The sad truth may only be discovered when he and his partner consult a fertility clinic because they have not conceived a child.

If the condition is severe, puberty cannot start. Consult with the physician if your son has no signs of puberty by age 15. (See Chapter 12.) TRT is usually successful at triggering puberty and the sex drive. It does not restore fertility, nor reduce breast size. Cosmetic surgery is available to remove the breasts if they are large and cause problems of body-image.

A diagnosis of Klinefelter's Syndrome can be catastrophic for a young man in otherwise good health. Counseling helps to lower the intensity of shock and grief. An unusually passive quiet boy needs counseling before therapy. In a well-known case, TRT produced startling behavior changes. The boy had attacks of verbal aggression, which escalated into real physical violence. The dosage was further reduced to the minimum possible for sexual functioning without causing behavior disorders.

The reasons for this reaction in Klinefelter's Syndrome are not completely understood. Maybe the brain's feedback mechanism to control testosterone production was not functioning. Maybe the boy suffered brutal teasing from his peers. Once virilized, he is free of their baiting, and may pour out his repressed rage in acts of violent revenge. This latter is theory only, but helps to remind parents of the misery a boy can endure if he does not become virilized about the same time as his peers.

## Away with the Condom?

A new birth control method for men is in the trial stage. It is hoped to be the first non-permanent male contraceptive since the condom was invented 200 some years ago. 250 couples world-wide are participating in the study. The men receive shots of an anabolic steroid which stops sperm production.

The shots are a combination of testosterone and a compound which helps the hormone stay active in the body for seven to ten days. When enough is injected, the brain senses it, and signals the testes to stop sperm production. These shots of synthetic testosterone enanthate, TE, are well below the steroid dosages which some athletes take.

The problem with finding a male contraception has been the unacceptable lowering of his libido. If the trials of TE are safe and effective, the shots should be available in about ten years. There will then be a reversible option to vasectomy. It will also free women from some of the burden of birth control.

## Breast Growth

A study of 306 normal men found 36 percent had *gynecomastia*. The average breast growth was 4 cm in diameter. Another study found 60 percent aged 45 to 60 had enlarged breasts. Other studies find these data too high. But all found overweight men, and those in their 50s and 60s, are prone to this harmless yet embarrassing condition.

Gynecomastia is common at puberty and usually regresses within two years. In young men, it is almost always due to excess weight. In older men with no weight problem, it can be due to the drop in testosterone which comes with aging. It is thought this allows the small amounts of estrogens made in the testes to promote breast tissue growth.

Certain medications can promote breast growth. They interact with the natural levels of testosterone and estrogen, and upset the balance in some way. Tranquilizers, anti-depressants, alcohol marijuana and heroin are implicated in gynecomastia. If on heart medication, consult with the physician over a change of drugs. Ironically, TRT can also increase male breast size.

Gynecomastia does not seem to be cancer-related. In a ten year follow-up study of 200 men with the condition, none developed breast cancer. WARNING! Blood spotting, discharge from the nipple or a firm mass under the skin could be signs of malignancy. Visit a physician promptly if these signs appear. In rare cases, male breasts are linked with liver disease, or endocrine dysfunction. More usually, they are rarely a medical alarm. If the swellings are large, or cause problems of body-image, cosmetic surgery relieves the distress.

## Exercise Abuse

In a study of dedicated runners, 35 to 40 percent said (if they had to choose) they would rather give up sex than running. The reasons for this unusual finding were stated as the thrills of the muscle jump, the mental high, the wall, and so on. Be that as it may, whatever happened to moderation in all things?

Strenuous exercise dampens down reproduction in both sexes. Its impact on fertility seems to be reversible. One study found non-athletic women in college had 2.5 times the rate of cancers of the reproductive system and twice the rate of breast cancer as former college athletes. The lifetime risks of diabetes and non-cancerous tumors of the reproductive system were reduced.In male athletes, the hypothalamus slows down production of the gonadotropin-releasing hormone. This controls the release of FSH and LH. These stimulate the testicles to produce sperm and testosterone. Though hormone levels drop, they are usually within the normal range. The findings on sperm production are not clear.

During evolution, low reproduction during exertion was valuable for survival. If a tribe had to move suddenly, lack of child-bearing was an advantage. Today, a new problem is exercise abuse (over-exercise), which seems to cause a significant drop in serum testosterone. If a dedicated runner and lover finds his interest in the second activity waning, he can choose to take the appropriate action if he so desires.

# The Tasty Testicle

In some parts of the world, restaurant menus offer as a delicacy sheep or bull's testicles. Men believe eating such testes will increase virility. It is not the testicle itself, but the ingestion of testosterone, which is thought to do the trick.

Scientists insist testosterone cannot be obtained this way; and that eating sheep's testicles is a load of old bull. (Cooking steroids usually inactivates them.) Any substance believed to increase the sex drive can be called an *aphrodisiac*, from Aphrodite, the goddess of love and beauty in Greek mythology. A more genteel name is love potion. There are assorted thousands on the market, ranging from powdered rhinoceros horn to the juices of hot pepper and ginger, and the root of the mandrake.

Oysters have long been regarded as aphrodisiacs, perhaps because they are hermaphrodites. Having both female and male reproductive organs, they are considered to be twice as sexy. The ancients feared eating hares, weasels or hyenas in case they developed the same strange mating habits, and became sexual deviants.

In San Francisco, the authorities recently cracked down on an enterprising Chinatown merchant who was selling preparations advertised as made from gall bladders, rhino horns and the organs of male tigers. The preparations are illegal because the animals they come from are endangered species. Altogether, more than $100,000 worth of animal parts were seized. On inspection, it was found the bladders came from domestic pigs, the horns from water buffalo, the male organs belonged to cattle. But the merchant did not evade the law. He was charged with false advertising. There is no scientific proof any aphrodisiac works, whether it contains a genuine substance or not. But sexual desire is not interested in proof. It defies the laws of logic, and is only imperfectly understood. If any substance is believed to have a certain effect, the belief itself can produce the desired result.

The power of ideas is stronger than the power of facts. This is especially so in the area of sexual activity, where all men feel vulnerable and exposed at times. In matters of desire, the power of suggestion has been grossly under-estimated and under-rated.

If an aphrodisiac seems to work, passion cares nothing for logic or scientific proof!

# Druggy Things

## *Amyl Nitrite*

Amyl Nitrite is used medically for angina for treatment of heart pain. It relaxes the involuntary muscles, especially of the blood vessels. When inhaled, it acts rapidly, causing a sudden drop in blood pressure. If taken during sex, it gives a "rush;" an extra high at orgasm. It can cause headache, flushing, faintness, vomiting, blue skin color, agitation and, in large doses, shock. Severe shock requires emergency hospitalization to stabilize blood pressure and other vital functions. As a love potion, amyl nitrite can be fatal.

## *Yohimbine*

Yohimbine is extracted from bark of the yohimbine tree. It acts as an agent to enhance the release of noradrenaline by nerve endings. This increases blood pressure and blood flow, and slows the heart rate. It helps relax the tiny penile arteries to enable a reflexive erection. It is now undergoing trials as therapy for erection problems. To date, its effectiveness is inconclusive.

## *Cannabis*

Also known as pot, marijuana, hashish, grass, etc., cannabis is an illegal, non-prescription drug from the Indian hemp plant, *cannabis sativa*. Smoked or swallowed, it produces euphoria — a heightened sense of optimism, merriment and well-being. It affects perception, particularly of time and distance. It can produce mild hallucinations: sight, hearing, taste, smell and touch responses to happenings which do not actually exist.

In one study of a 100 regular users, one third noted a greater than 50 percent degree increase in sexual arousal and endurance. The other two-thirds noted no change. Cannabis, like drugs such as alcohol, cocaine, mandrax and quaaludes, tranquilizes the higher consciousness — the critical part of the mind. This reduces such things as sexual fears, guilt, shame and embarrassment.

In this respect, perhaps any drug which removes inhibitions can be called an aphrodisiac. But recent research is finding a relationship between their long-term use and reduced levels of testosterone. As yet no aphrodisiac has yet been found to replace good old, man made, natural testosterone.

## Spanish Fly!

Spanish Fly is a nasty and dangerous drug. It actually works. But in what fashion! And at what cost! Spanish Fly comes from dried beetles, mainly blister beetles found in Spain and other Southern European countries. The ingredient which triggers the erection is called *cantharides*, and is a poison. It works by drying up the delicate mucus lining inside the urethra.

Any dryness where there should be dampness causes scratchy discomfort and itchiness — like a dry patch in a sore throat. The dry urethral passage becomes raw, sore and inflamed. It is this irritation which causes the penis to erect.

The inflammation can travel to and inflame the bladder, causing frequency, urgency and pain on urination. In large doses, the toxins cause stomach pain and kidney shock. They may interfere with penile blood flow and cause an attack of priapism, but this is not proven. Very large doses kill.

Spanish Fly is a bull story. This time for real. Cantharides were first used on stud bulls which were reluctant to mate. The poor creatures, driven half mad by the itchiness, became erect and were successfully put to stud. This is how Spanish Fly won its dubious reputation as the one aphrodisiac which never fails. With a small dose, the resultant passage of semen down the urethra soothes the itchiness for a while. When the irritation flares up again, so does the erection. The man is delighted, having no idea of the eventual cost to health. Surely the urethra is prone to enough itchy problems without the added assistance of Spanish Fly.

The notion of deliberately taking a toxic substance to inflame the urethra (not to mention pain, swelling and worse) is hard to credit. Yet cantharides has not lost its appeal as an aphrodisiac. This may be because the damage appears only later, and so is not linked to its immediate cause. Beware the Spanish Fly; it is detrimental to health!

## Old Faithful

In old age, men and women continue to feel the urge to make

love. Though a woman's ovaries stop working at mid-life, they (and the adrenals) continue to produce testosterone so she does not lose her sex drive. The testicles continue to produce testosterone throughout life.

But with aging, the production of testosterone does decline. Men do not go through a distinct menopause as women do. But a few scientists now believe certain older men with highly stressful lives suffer from decline. They think these men will benefit from hormone replacement therapy, TRT, as some women benefit from ERT at menopause. But testosterone is implicated in heart attacks and prostate cancer, the two top killers of men. The issue of TRT is highly debatable. (For more information, see Chapter 14). It is important to understand that the sex drive exists in its own right. Once it is switched on, it stays switched on, even with the drop in testosterone and reduced number of erections. Avoid feeling depressed by the chart. Ngs are nanograms, and one nanogram is one thousandth of one microgram, which is one thousandth of one milligram! Keep in mind the libido exists in its own right.

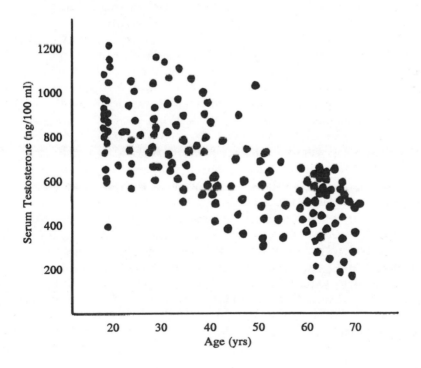

Though an older man may make love less frequently, when he does feel desire, the urge is as powerful as in youth. If he experienced great pleasures in the past, his body demands he continues to do so. Or he may decide sex is no longer a priority in life. This is an issue of personal choice.

With a painful illness, or chronic disability, desire can cease altogether. This is hardly surprising. Death of a partner may be followed by a depression. If it closes off sexual options, the continuing sex drive can be a torment of longing for the lost beloved instead of the former delight.

## Use It, or Lose It

The decline in testosterone may not be noticed until age 60 plus. It is rarely enough to curb the sex drive. Loss of rigidity at erection is usually a natural result of aging and not due to less testosterone. It may have little to do with the sex drive.

If a muscle is not exercised over prolonged time, it loses suppleness and strength. Eventually it suffers *disuse atrophy*; it withers and dies. The penis contains smooth muscle which, like heart muscle, benefits from regular exercise. NPT helps to keep the blood flow active, but this may not be enough. For the penis is not a separate part of the sexual system. It can be considered as merely the pipeline. If the pipeline stops working, the rest of the system can suffer. For example, the prostate needs regular (not necessarily frequent) but regular clear outs (ejaculations) to prevent congestion — see prostatodynia.

The "use it or lose it" syndrome does not apply to younger men. It seems they can avoid partner sex for years without risk; it is likely they masturbate. The opposite occurs in later years. The greater the age, the less full orgasmic activity, the more rapid and dramatic the risk of disuse atrophy.

Some older men believe love-making must include penetration. They think it wrong to enjoy partner sex by mutual masturbation. So they completely withdraw from love-making when erections lose rigidity, and penetration is difficult. The need to love, and to be loved, and to express that love in physical terms, is not the prerogative of youth. Couples in later life are not too old to make love if they so wish. Nor should a single man avoid solitary masturbation from feelings of guilt. *Sexual activity prevents disuse atrophy.*

# Not Too Little

In an historical sense, a *eunuch* is a castrated male, one whose testes have been deliberately removed. If it happens before puberty, he grows tall without developing male characteristics. He stays physically and sexually immature like a strange overgrown child. His sex drive is low or absent. He is infertile. A eunuch is unusually tall, with long thin limbs, narrow shoulders and broad hips. His extremities — hands, feet and skull bones — are larger than normal because the growth hormone, also controlled by the pituitary, does not receive "negative feedback control." It cannot switch off bone growth at the correct time.

At first impression, a eunuch's physique might be considered womanly. Lack of testosterone prevents the development of firm muscle mass, body hair, deeper voice and so on. The flesh stays plump, soft and hairless, the voice remains high, wrinkles appear around the eyes. But he is not womanly in any sense, particularly the sexual one. In fact, the testosterone a woman produces makes her more manly than he is.

The word "eunuch" comes from the Greek "guardian of the bed." Eunuchs, with a low or absent sex drive, were considered safe to guard the harem. But a physical caress is pleasurable in itself. And time passes slowly in a gilded cage. Many eunuchs enjoyed a far greater degree of intimate contact with the women they were guarding than their masters ever achieved.

In Imperial Rome, castrated boys were used as "voluptuates" for the "special arousal" of men. Babies of the poor were often castrated in the cradle and sold to male brothels specifically for this purpose. Some parents castrated their sons in order to use them as delectable bribes. They were offered to men in power who, in return, secured social advancements for the parents.

In Renaissance Europe, boys with exceptionally pure high voices were castrated before puberty to prevent development of the larynx. They were called *Castrati*, and their exquisitely high tones rang in wondrous echoes throughout the grand opera houses. They became rich, famous, spoiled — but that was all they became.

Most eunuchs were not castrated. Their unhappy condition was due to birth defects such as misplaced (undescended) testicles. The testes atrophied from torsion or infections such as gonorrhea and mumps. Still others had perfectly healthy but non-functioning testes due to a tumor causing pituitary disease. Other symptoms of pituitary disease are mental retardation and color blindness.

Advances in medicine avoid many of these tragic disorders. Of those which are not prevented, many are successfully treated. The word "eunuch" is no longer used. It smacks of prurience, cheap titillating thrills from lascivious gossip. It masks the appalling sorrows these terrible disorders inflict on a man.

# Not Too Much. . .

The definition of *satyr* is "an extraordinarily promiscuous man." And promiscuous means "indiscriminate, having sexual relations without regard for the restrictions of marriage or cohabitation." *Satyriasis* is "an extreme degree of heterosexual activity in men." But what is an extreme degree? By whose standards is this measured? Are satyrs promiscuous, or have they hormonal problems?

*"Man, 29, pensioned off for being oversexed."* In 1987, the West German newspaper Bild am Sonntag reported that a 29 year old carpenter from Nuremburg had been declared unfit for work because he was oversexed and unable to concentrate on his job. Medical reports showed that Wolfgang B produced 20 times the normal amount of the male hormone testosterone.

Wolfgang B went from doctor to doctor seeking help. But none was able to prescribe drugs to effectively curb his sex drive. For several years, he took tranquilizers and practiced martial arts, but nothing calmed him down. He required sex up to 10 times a day and exhausted a succession of partners, who all deserted him. Last year, he was so depressed he attempted suicide.

A medical expert quoted by the paper said being oversexed causes "constant tension, fear, shame, depression and a sense of guilt. As no doctor had the skills to curb Wolfgang B's sex drive, it would seem his condition is very rare indeed. There is yet much to be learned in the field of hormones."

# Sexual Addiction

Addiction to sexual activity is a different issue. As a concept, it is a hot topic of debate. Some psychologists believe there is no such thing. Others believe an estimated six percent of U.S. men and women are sex addicts. They are obsessed with sex, and have difficulty functioning at work, as parents, as citizens. In some cases, their behavior destroys their health.

The sex addiction theory states that the primary cause is lack of bonding. The child grows up feeling unloved and unwanted. Most addicts come from families where addiction may be overt as in drinking or gambling, or hidden as in workaholicism or fanaticism. The child absorbs these tensions and craves them in adult life.

A sex addict does not have higher levels of testosterone. The addiction is much the same as the addiction to alcohol, gambling or drugs. There is a craving for excitement, and an avoidance of the pains in daily life. Having sex soothes and comforts the craving, while distracting the mind from harsher truths. It also increases tolerance, which increases dependency, so a vicious circle is set up which is difficult to break.

Sex addicts can be helped by therapy. They learn how to reduce the craving for excitement, and to gain comfort by other means. They discover ways to control behavior and so improve the quality of their lives. The victims of sex addicts also require therapy because they suffer intimacy problems and withdraw from further emotional attachments.

Yet there is a growing school of opinion which believes that calling any destructive behavior an addiction, a disease, avoids the facts. An addiction means a person cannot control behavior and that this lack of control is usually totally separate from the rest of the person's life.

But people are active agents, not passive victims. They have choices over their behavior. Many unloved children from addictive families avoid drugs in adulthood. The reformed drinker does not have to take that first sip which will start another binge. There is a crucial moment of decision-making, of control.

People are not puppets pulled helplessly towards their doom, even if there is a family disposition towards one type of behavior. So-called sex addicts allow their obsession. They choose to lose control. Calling such behavior a disease is distracting and unhelpful. It may simply be a problem from which progress can be made and which, eventually, can be overcome. The reader may find these theories of interest.

# At Dawn's Early Light

It seems testosterone is made in 24 hourly cycles. Measurements show the levels peak by dawn's early light. Later in the morning they drop, especially after 10 a.m. This is a happy conjunction.

Sleep restores not only testosterone, but the energy required to take advantage of the rise.

Another hormone being researched in this field is *melatonin*. It stimulates the production of *melanin*, which tans and thickens the skin to protect it from harmful ultra-violet rays. Melatonin works in daylight, and might be involved in sleep patterns, mood changes and the sex drive. Perhaps this explains the popularity of holidays in the sun.

One study found the hormonal link between light and winter blues includes seasonal loss of desire. It seems that as daylight hours grow shorter, so does sexual desire in nearly five million Americans who are affected by hormonal changes. Therapy is simply to switch on all the lights, which does rather upset those romantic notions of candlelight.

Taking an average of the whole year, testosterone levels are highest in October. This is linked to the time between conception and birth, and the fact babies have poor temperature regulation. So those born in the summer do not have to expend precious energy conserving body heat. But what of babies born near the equator? This interesting research into the effects of temperature and light on testosterone production has still some way to go.

A U.K. consultant pathologist hopes to test the theory that cooler testicles produce more testosterone than warmer ones. After a control period in which the volunteers wear their own clothes and behave normally, they are split into two groups. Group A wear kilts and no undershorts. Group B concentrate on cooling their testicles by a relaxation technique known as autogenic training. The findings will certainly be interesting.

# CHAPTER 7

# Sperm

## The Numbers Game

Each *minute* of his life a man makes 50,000 sperm!

Each *hour* of his life he makes 3,000,000 sperm!

Each *day* he makes a total of 72,000,000 sperm!

These are estimates of average sperm production — give or take a few millions either way. This amazing process, this incredible feat of manufacturing, starts at puberty and continues to the grave. Compare these numbers with the woman's one solitary egg produced once each 28 days, and then only until mid-life.

But the size of sperm greatly reduces the enormity of output. If all the sperm, which had helped create all the people who have ever lived and are living now, were put together, they would just about fit into a thimble. A man's daily turnover adds up to less than a speck of sand. Obviously, sperm are invisible to the naked eye, and can be seen only with the aid of an electron microscope.

## In the Classroom

An impressed hush falls on the classroom when sperm counts are discussed. The girls first break the silence. They raise their eyes in what they hope is world-weary fashion. "Typical, men!" they say. "Over the top, as usual." The boys look superior.

The students reach for their calculators. "There are 15 boys in this class. . . and eight other classes over puberty. . . Include the teachers, 23 of them. . . four male laboratory technicians. . ." Stab, stab, stab, their fingers work the input buttons. They look up in awe at the sperm numbers produced in their school in one hour. A student remembers the media resources officers, cleaners, superintendent, site manager — and they are off again on their calculators. One student wants to estimate the numbers globally, but quickly gives up.

The lesson proceeds: "Sperm is short for *spermatozoon*, a single word. Spermatozoa is the plural. Sperm are like sheep in that you do not add "s" when talking of more than one."

"What is the point of talking about *one*?" the students cry, their heads reeling from the numbers.

"Only one sperm can fuse with the egg."

This makes things more even. The girls feel less oppressed; the boys, less superior. A few agree with the girls. "Over-kill" is the word they choose to describe sperm production. It is a tough word, stark and brutal. Naked panic appears in one girl's eyes. It is likely she is risking her future by unprotected sex.

## Talk Breaks Out

"I'll bet my dad didn't know about the numbers," says a nervous unhappy boy from a family of eleven children.

"You can bet your mother didn't either," comes back a girl's indignant retort.

And then the inevitable, "Why didn't they teach it?"

"It wasn't fair, was it? Were the teachers too shy?"

"Why didn't the parents makes the schools teach it?"

"My father says school's not the place. But he won't talk."

"Adults tells us everything else — everything, except that."

"How are we supposed to make informed choices about sex?"

"Sex Ed. is forbidden in my friend's school. That's wrong."

And one student repeats the reason they have heard so often as to why school attendance is obligatory by law — why it is not an option of choice. "Education is preparation for life, isn't it?"

All the students collapse into giggles then, because the pun was unintentional — and the dark mood lifts.

What does the reader think? Should we expect teenagers to

make *informed* life choices when the adult world withholds the facts? And the girl with panic in her eyes asks, "Can we do birth control now? Please, *please!*"

# Baby Sperm

Baby sperm are microscopic germ cells. They lie in the testes in rows, like soldiers on parade. They develop an oval-shaped head, thin neck, thicker middle and long tail — long in comparison to their microscopic size. Inside the head are the 23 chromosome threads which carry the genes which pass down family likenesses.

The tail is designed for transportation. It moves in a whip lash fashion, propelling sperm forward on the long journey to the egg. One very imaginative boy compares sperm to nuclear warfare. "Miniature warheads on Red Alert, primed for First Strike!" The girl with panic in her eyes cries, "Horrid little bugs!" Like so many other life issues, it depends upon where you are at.

# The Maternity Ward

The testicles can be compared to maternity wards. And as such, they have to be the busiest in the world. Inside each sperm making tube, activity is ceaseless. The vast production line rolls relentlessly on, with no lunch hours, no coffee breaks, no clocking off at night. As the end product rolls off the line, other sperm are half complete, still others are just starting life. Each stage of development has its own special pace and rhythm which can neither be speeded up, nor slowed down.

It takes a long time to make baby sperm — some 72 days. At the finish, they are not all perfect. Some lack tails. Some have incomplete heads. Some are so fragmented they are mere twisted blobs. This is only to be expected in any manufacturing process so vast. And, except in fertility problems, a few million misshapen sperm will not be missed either way.

# The Nursery

The epididymes can be compared to the nursery. They are the long, narrow tubes which lie coiled "upon the twins." When baby sperm are complete, they are ushered out of the testes into the epididymes. They are still too immature for the outside world. They cannot swim properly. Nor are they able to fertilize an egg.

To succeed in the race for the egg, sperm must move forward and in one direction only. Sperm motility is an important factor in male fertility. Inside the testicles, sperm can make only feeble wiggly movements. They gain motility in the first part of the epididymes. But their sense of direction is weak. They tend to swim in circles, which gets them precisely nowhere. They would fail dismally in the race for the egg.

It takes 12 days in the epididymes for sperm to mature, and to gain appropriate swimming skills. During this time, they are pushed forward along the coiled tube by tiny muscles in the thin walls. The distance they move is an amazing 20 feet. Nourishing fluids feed the sperm, help them to mature and develop full motility. Altogether, the epididymis is a highly nurturing place.

## A Short Shelf Life

It takes 72 days in the testes and 12 days in the epididymes for sperm to mature — almost 3 months. Only then are they ready for the long journey to the prostate and sex glands. Mature sperm pile up in the epididymes and are stored there — but not for long. They have a short shelf life. They remain fresh and active for less than a month. After this, they age rapidly and soon die. They are then broken down and the nutrients, mainly protein, are reabsorbed by the testicles.

A man who ejaculates once a month only might think the egg cannot be fertilized because his sperm are too old. He may think they are dying or dead. But sperm production is an unceasing process. Millions of fresh sperm arrive and travel through the epididymes all the time. Though there will be elderly sperm in the ejaculate, there are fresh ones as well, waiting to get out and start the race for the egg.

## A Long Long Trail A-Winding. . .

*Vasa deferentia* is a Latin term, meaning "to carry away from." These are two long tubes called "vas" for short, with the same outside width as a drinking straw. Yet the inner bore is narrow, a mere one-hundredth of an inch in diameter. The difference in widths comes from the thick muscle walls of the vas which propel the sperm forward in powerful spurts at pre-ejaculation.

Find the vas by clasping the top of the scrotum, placing thumb and fingers at the back. Roll the loose scrotal skin near the epididymis until the vas tube is felt. Then find the other one. These are the *vasectomy* sites where each vas is cut and tied back at male contraception. Vasectomy is a very effective method of fertility control because it stops sperm entering the vas.

The function of the vas is to carry the sperm:

· Away from the two epididymes.
· Up and out of the scrotal sacs.
· Into and up through the abdomen.
· Around the bladder in a loop.
· Down to the prostate and sex glands, in preparation for orgasm and ejaculation.

In microscopic terms, the distance now traveled by sperm is truly great. It is an amazing 12 to 15 inches, depending upon the man's overall size. Hence the thick muscles which line the vas walls, and are capable of propelling sperm forward in powerful spurts. It is indeed a long, long trail a-winding. . . .

## Sweet Semen

In the average ejaculate, there are 300,000,000 to 500,000,000 sperm. The ejaculate of the gorilla contains a mere 50,000,000. The aggressive chimpanzee again tops the list with a total of 600,000,000.

Sperm make up only 3 percent of the average ejaculate. The other 97 percent consists of fluids made in the *prostate* gland and the *seminal vesicles*. These fluids are squirted behind the sperm as it passes. So the first part of an ejaculate is richer in sperm than the last. Once the fluids combine with sperm, the mixture is *semen*.

Semen is a rich sugary fluid made of complex substances, not all of which are understood. The sugar is fructose, and the fluid has a nutritional value of 6 carbohydrates. It might provide energy for the sperm on their travels, but this is not proven. Semen is alkaline and vaginal fluids are more acid. It is thought the alkaline coats and protects the sperm inside the vagina. The prostate fluid also contains a powerful anti-bacterial agent.

Semen is ejaculated as a liquid. This quickly turns into a stringy glutinous gel. It re-liquifies 20 minutes later. This may help sperm survive in the vagina. Average ejaculate volume is 3 to 5 cc after abstaining from orgasm for three days. This varies greatly with age, fluid intake, state of health and so on.

A partner may be allergic to semen. The reaction is a skin rash (hives) or a persistent genital itch. This is very unusual. Rule out more usual infections first.

# The Exit Line

The urethra runs from the base of the bladder, through the penis to the meatus, the opening of the glans. At orgasm, semen spurts into the urethra just behind the bladder opening. The urethra is a shared passageway for urine and semen. But urine is acid-based, and acid would damage the more alkaline sperm. So urine and semen are not able to travel down the urethra at the same time.

To control this, there are two sphincters (rings of muscle) at the base of the bladder. When semen arrives, one sphincter opens to let semen into the urethra. The other clamps tightly shut so urine cannot get out. It also stops semen from accidentally backing up into the bladder. The two sphincters operate by reflex. The exit line can be used for one function only at a time.

# A Small Leak?

Before ejaculation, a drop or two of fluid bedews the tip of the penis. This fluid comes from *Cowper's glands*, and is alkaline-based. It neutralizes any traces of acid left from urination. Rather like flushing a sink after use, it cleans and flushes out the urethra to prepare it for the passage of sperm.

This fluid contains some thousands of sperm. One theory suggests these are the mega stars, determined to win the race. To avoid pregnancy, this leakage must be removed. If only one drop touches the vulva, those sperm can find their way to the egg. Removing the penis just before ejaculation is withdrawal. It is a popular self-help method of birth control among the young. It is free, simple and requires no special preparation. However, the young risk being called parents nine months later! The small drops from Cowper's glands are often to blame.

Withdrawal requires a high degree of orgasmic control which young men lack. It can cause great anxiety for both partners. Some mature and experienced couples swear by it. It is the oldest and most widely used method of birth control globally. Withdrawal provides no protection against sexual disease, and AIDS. A condom gives some. After reading the next article, parents may wish to share these facts with their sons.

# Boys' Tales

A United Nations report found U.S. teenagers have the highest pregnancy and abortion rates of any country in the developed world. During the 80s, the teen pregnancy rate was 9.8 percent compared to 3.5 percent for Europe. The abortion rate for girls aged 15 to 19 averaged 4.4 percent; double the rate for European countries.

Another U.S. study found only 2 percent of sexually active boys and 5 percent girls use condoms all the time. Over 1,000,000 teenage girls became pregnant in 1987. Some 400,000 of these pregnancies ended in abortion. Cold statistics make uncomfortable reading, yet cannot begin to portray the depth of human misery involved.

1987 was years after the news of the AIDS epidemic. So these data have alarming implications for the nation's health. Was sex education in schools ineffective? Was it absent? It is difficult to evaluate the impact of information on behavior. And the risk-taking nature of youth must be taken into account. But a belief in "boys' tales" is likely to add to the tragic figures. The following is a summary of schoolboy folklore:

- She won't get pregnant if you do it standing up.
- She won't get pregnant the first time you do it.
- She'll be safe if you tell her to pee after you come.
- She'll be safe if she jumps up and down immediately after.
- You can't start a baby if you withdraw quickly enough.
- Unprotected sex is not much of a risk.

Not much of a risk, huh? Are these boys unaware that in an average ejaculate some 300,000,000 sperm go chasing after one egg? Would they put hard-earned money on a bet like that? Somebody should tell those sperm about boys' tales. From the number of teenage pregnancies, they obviously have not heard of them!

# Survival of the Fittest

It is thought that only 200 sperm survive the journey to the oviduct. Of the remainder, some drop at the first barrier, the cervix. Others become worn out swimming through the uterus. Still others get waylaid and enter the wrong oviduct. Hardy sperm can survive 2 to 7 days in the female reproductive organs. They may need this time to become capable of fertilizing the egg.

The quality of sperm is more critical than the quantity. Motility is vital; sperm must swim forward and in one direction only. *Velocity* refers to swimming speeds; average velocity is 3 ml per minute. Faster swimmers have a better chance of reaching their destination before getting worn out. Motility and velocity are critical factors in winning the race to the egg.

The 200 survivors crowd into the *ampulla* — a wider part of the oviduct. Here, they eagerly await the arrival of the egg. If the egg is already there, they crowd frantically around it, trying to break down its tough protective coats. Wriggling in frenzy, sperm batter the outer walls, releasing chemicals to dissolve the tough coats. Finally, small holes appear in the walls and, in a flash, a few lucky sperm are inside. Of the sperm which get inside, only their microscopic heads survive. They are now up against the very last bastion, the last wall of assault. This is the tough inner membrane which protects the egg's nucleus. It is the most formidable obstacle of all.

Only one sperm can penetrate this membrane. Perhaps this is indeed the survival of the fittest. The head moves to the center and its nucleus fuses with the nucleus of the egg. Conception is total implosion, total fusion, of two nucleii. A popular fantasy regards fusion as an over-whelming and shattering micro-force.Our very identity depends upon this fusion. The chromosomes form into pairs and the blueprint for inheritance is permanently set down. The new life is a perfectly equal and democratic mix of both parents' genes.

# Fertility Problems

*Infertility* is a temporary inability to produce a child.

*Sterility* is the permanent inability to produce a child. One estimate suggests 15 percent of American and 12 percent of British couples experience fertility problems. And that in 35 percent of cases, the problem is the sperm. In a further 10 to 15 percent, there are problems with both partners. Fertility experts say there is no need for concern at lack of conception until after one full year of trying — some now think this period should be a full 18 months.

Male infertility is on the increase; it is not certain why. In 1950, the average sperm count was 40 million higher than in 1988. Excess heat may be a major cause; (dipping the testicles in hot water is a primitive method of birth control). In much the same way, tight clothing raises the temperature in the groin. A study into underwear found men who wore boxer shorts had higher sperm counts than those who wore jockey briefs.

Environmental hazards which damage the sperm-making process include exposure to X rays, radiation, lead from motor exhausts and many other pollutants. It is now thought they cause more damage than is often realized. Being outside the body, the testes are more exposed to environmental hazards than the internal organs. Keep in mind the testicles are particularly vulnerable, and avoid unnecessary risk.

# Self Help

Fertility problems are often temporary, and can be resolved by self help. During the 12 to 18 months while trying to conceive, check general health, level of stress, amount of sleep, exercise, diet, medication and substance abuse, especially cigarettes. Each is on the list of factors which can affect sperm production.

Before starting a fitness program, keep in mind it takes 72 days for sperm to mature. A recent study found men who were not under stress to perform produced higher sperm counts than those who were. Avoid performance pressure. Enjoy a relaxed intimacy in these pre-conception days. They may be the last peaceful times before a baby arrives. The following self-help tips are not based on scientific proof but may have practical value.

Direct heat: *Heat damages sperm production.* The testicles should be 4 degrees below body heat. Avoid any direct or indirect heat of the groin area. One dip in a hot tub or jacuzzi can impair fertility for up to six months. A prolonged hot bath has the same effect. One recommendation is to spray the testes with cool water daily.

Sitting: If a man were sitting naked for extended office hours, the rise in groin temperature could impair fertility. Sedentary workers can avoid sitting for long periods by moving around at intervals to lower the testicles away from body heat. In tropical climates, a bead frame fitted to the motorist's seat is a "must" to avoid a hot sweaty groin.

Clothing: Modern fashions in clothing make the problem worse. Wear loosely woven cotton boxer shorts. Eschew all garments which are tight: clinging underwear, "spray-on" jeans and other closely fitting constricting trousers. At home, and where possible, wear a wrap-around sarong. Consider the Scottish kilt, the African cloth, the Indian dhoti, the Roman toga.

Weight: Attempt to reduce a weight problem. Excess flesh at the buttocks, inner thighs and lower abdomen not only keep the groin hot, they actually raise the temperature. If obesity is advanced, seek professional help. If mild, and weight loss is slow, try a water-cooled jock strap available from the fertility clinic.

Lubricants: Check the use of lubricants. Some commercial products actually block sperm. A Canadian study found many infertile couples who substituted egg white for their normal lubricant were successful in conceiving. It is thought egg white might be an appropriate lubricant because it is protein and does not kill sperm cells. Saliva is also thought to block sperm.

Caffeine: Excess caffeine may be a problem. It is thought to interfere with sperm metabolism and sperm formation. This is more likely with a heavy coffee drinker — 4 to 8 cups a day. There is a low, but definite, correlation between excess caffeine and impaired sperm function. Reduce (or weaken) the volume of coffee, tea and cola drinks containing caffeine. Substitute fruit drinks, herbal teas or bland drinks.

Making love: Find the partner's exact ovulation dates. The family doctor, gynecologist or family planning clinic will help with this. Then, some 7 days after menstruation ceases, make love frequently. Use the split ejaculate method until ovulation occurs.

Keep in mind the first part of the ejaculate is richest in sperm. The penis must be deep inside the vagina just before ejaculation. Withdraw immediately after the first spurt. This releases the highest concentration of sperm close to the cervix. It keeps out dilute semen and stops the ejaculate from spilling out. The woman stays still with legs raised for an hour. The split ejaculate is not entirely proven but it is worth trying for a few months.

If these self-help techniques fail after 18 months, consider professional medical help.

# The Fertility Clinic

A medical history is taken to rule out risk factors such as misplaced testes, torsion, mumps and sexual disease. The first investigative test is semen analysis. It checks sperm count, shape and motility, and total semen volume. A man may regard even the suspicion of infertility as a tremendous assault on his masculinity. *Potency* and *fertility* are two very different things.

A semen specimen can be collected in privacy at home. Abstain from ejaculation for 2 to 5 days, the time varies from clinic to clinic. Abstinence allows sperm to build up in the epididymes and gives the best chance of a good specimen. During the period of abstinence keep fit and relaxed, eat well, drink plenty of fluids, reduce coffee and alcohol intake.

Prepare to provide a specimen of the ejaculate. Wash the hands, penis and glans thoroughly first. Ejaculate into a sterile container by solitary masturbation only. It must not be by withdrawal, nor from the contents of a condom. Avoid using lubricants to aid masturbation as they may destroy sperm. Collect the entire ejaculate. If only one drop is missed, total volume measurement will be incorrect. As there are more sperm in the first part of the ejaculate, total sperm count will be inaccurate too. Cover the specimen and keep it at body heat. Dispatch to the clinic or laboratory as soon as possible.

# Semen Analysis

## Sperm Count

There are at least 30,000,000 sperm per milliliter in 2 ml of semen. This can range from 28 to 225 million per ml. There is no general agreement on the lower limit for fertility. Some experts believe there is a fighting chance at 20 to 10 million per ml, if sperm have good shape and excellent motility.

## Sperm Shape

In an average ejaculate, there are always misshapen sperm. These may be tapering or round, giant heads or pin heads, two heads or two tails, and so on. The greater the number of abnormal shapes, the less chance of fertility. Average semen contains almost 90 percent normal sperm. This can rise to 99 percent and drop to 66 percent. For semen to be considered fertile, there need to be at least 60 to 65 percent normal shaped sperm.

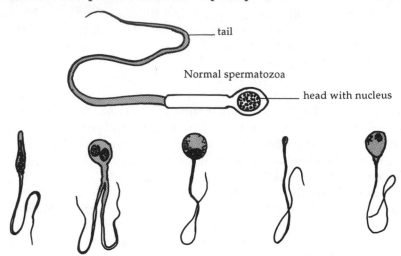

Abnormal spermatozoa

## Sperm Motility

When semen is first ejaculated, sperm are fairly motionless. They can reach the uterus in 30 seconds, but this is due to the powerful ejaculation spurt and to female muscle spasms which pull the sperm upwards. They then become motile, travelling at about 3 millimeters per minute. If 70 percent of sperm are motile, there is no problem. Less than 50 percent can mean their sluggishness reduces the chance of reaching the egg.

## Semen Volume

Adequate semen volume is between 2 and 5 cc. If there is too little, the semen is concentrated and thick; sperm are not well-protected from acid vaginal fluids. If too much, the semen is over-dilute and sperm are more likely to spill out of the vagina.

# It Ain't Necessarily So!

Sperm behave differently in a laboratory test tube. They only survive two to six hours. Many of these estimates are informed guesses. If the results are poor, avoid being downcast. Stress at producing a specimen, and fears of infertility, can be the cause. Laboratory human error includes mishandling, miscounting or mislabeling. Have two or three analyses over six to eight weeks, with one from another laboratory. Only when the results are consistently poor is there need to consider further steps.

There is a rare birth defect of blockage in the sperm-making tubes. The germ cells begin to make sperm, but most get blocked from maturing. Skilled fertility specialists can now recover a few mature sperm to fertilize the egg outside the woman's body. Globally, only two have been successful to date.

The study of male infertility has a long way to go. Avoid clinics not medically run, or approved. Rather than undergo removal of varioceles (which does not seem to help) and testicular biopsy, one choice is to opt for AID or GIFT right away. The procedures are a drain on emotional and financial resources. The success rate for live births is now one in five. Whatever the choice, try to avoid feeling less manly. Eschew sad and depressing thoughts. They lower self-image and self-esteem, which adds to stress. Stay hopeful. Keep trying. Also keep in mind men with hopelessly low sperm counts have thrilled the experts, their partners and themselves by becoming fathers.

# Sperm Tales

## *"You can use up all your sperm"*

Boys who masturbate frequently worry about this myth. And it is believed by a surprising number of older men. Though most males know sperm are made throughout life, it is a difficult myth to dislodge. It arose before the invention of the microscope, i.e., before sperm could be seen. Semen was then thought to be part of the blood fluids which had to be preserved at all costs.

This particular myth is so strong that there are cults where the faithful ejaculate into cups, and drink the semen. By this means, they believe they preserve their precious blood fluids, the vital forces which keep them healthy and strong. Other cults train their disciples not to ejaculate; neither when making love, nor in solitary masturbation.

Abstinence appears to have little effect on sperm quality. A recent survey studied specimens of semen produced after 12 hours and again after 120 hours. The sperm count, shape and motility were not altered by abstinence. However, a very long period of abstinence does produce less high quality sperm.

## "You lose body strength when you ejaculate."

This myth is a close relation of the previous one. For years, sports trainers and coaches have instructed athletes to abstain from sex 4 to 5 days before an important event. A recent study from Colorado State University tested a group of athletes a) when they had abstained for 5 days, b) within 24 hours of making love.

After each ejaculation, the athletes were measured for stamina, exertion, agility, reaction time, balance, muscle power and other factors for high performance skills. The study found "no significantly measurable difference" in either case.

## "You can damage yourself if you don't ejaculate."

This myth probably comes from the ache which can be felt in the testes, the indelicately named "blue balls" syndrome. A young man, with too high hopes on a date, can experience this ache. He imagines it comes from the build-up of pressure of his unrelased ejaculate with their millions of sperm. But repeated ejaculations over a short space of time produces the same ache.

Before ejaculation, a great deal of extra blood is pumped to the testes. These aches can be due to unrelieved *vaso-congestion*: the extra blood has no chance to drain away if sexual arousal remains high. Or they can be due to over-exercise. Rather like aching muscles, the genitals develop aches if they are over-exercised by repeated ejaculations over a short space of time.

## "You stop making sperm when you are old."

By age 70, sperm production does drop. But in one study, sperm were found in the ejaculate of 48 percent of men aged 80 to 90. It is now believed sperm from older men are not as healthy as in youth. There is a slight increase in disorders of the chromosomes or the genes which can result in birth defects. The level of risk is unclear as the majority of men do not wish to become fathers at this stage in life.

CHAPTER 8

# Orgasm

## The Big O!

Orgasm can occur without ejaculation. And ejaculation can occur without orgasm. Basically, orgasm is a nervous system response and ejaculation is a reproductive one. There may, or may not, be erection and/or sexual satisfaction with both.

But erection, orgasm and ejaculation usually follow in one sequence. Sexual tension increases with rhythmic friction. The penis thrusts deeply so the frenulum and corona receive maximum friction, maximum sensation. Like a latent sneeze which has been building up, the persistency of the irritation factor becomes explosive. As orgasm nears, the rhythm changes. Thrusting may be short and deep or stop altogether if no further sensations are required.

At pre-orgasm, rhythmic friction rarely fails. The entire body may be involved and the mind is switched off. At pre-erection, rhythmic friction can succeed or fail, depending on the 6 variables, and such factors as sexual need, sufficient time and so on, e.g., sudden noise can kill an erection but may have little effect at pre-orgasm.

The big "O" is not always so big. It can range from physical and emotional pleasure of such exquisite intensity that it seems unendurable to sensations which feel little more than a sneeze. The breadth and depth of sensation does not necessarily reflect upon the man, his partner or the situation. Orgasm is as variable as human life.

## On Your Mark!

There are two stages to male orgasm: emission and ejaculation. They follow each other so quickly they can be difficult to tell apart. In youth, each stage is clearly separate but may not be noticed if orgasm is quickly over. In older men, they mellow and blend into one stage. The one-stage climax generally lasts longer than the youthful two stage.

The word *emission* may be confusing as it is also used for wet dreams, sometimes called nocturnal emissions. Yet its meaning is appropriate here because the emission stage begins when sperm are pumped out from the epididymes along the vas to combine with semen for ejaculation.

The urinary tract lengthens by 3 and widens by 2. Massive waves of pleasurable reflex contractions ripple throughout the sexual system. They are triggered by the spinal nerve reflexes which switch on when the orgasmic threshold is reached, when sexual tension peaks. The longer a man takes before reaching his orgasmic threshold, the more sperm will be pumped out and gather in the *bulbous urethra*, a small bulb which acts as a temporary holding site.

The holding bulb swells. The pressure triggers the bladder exit reflex to close. The prostate and seminal glands contract and pump fluid behind sperm in powerful rhythmic spurts. All this happens in 1 to 4 seconds. The sensations are of impending ejaculation. It is the point of no return. There is a blissful sense of inevitability. On your mark. . . !

## GO! GO! GO!

The second stage is *ejaculation*. The spinal reflex triggers ejaculation muscles around the root of the penis. These muscles together with waves of contractions from the holding bulb squeeze to a beat of 0.8 second intervals; the same beat as female orgasm. More prostate fluids are pumped into the holding bulb at each contraction. The shaft helps propel semen out of the penis in 3 to 10 ejaculatory spurts. This number varies considerably with age, health, time since last ejaculation and so on.

The ejaculation muscles are powerful enough to propel semen

some distance from the body. The furthest medically recorded is 30 cm. The sensations at ejaculation come from both stages of climax: the powerful waves of contraction throughout the reproductive system and the actual spurting at ejaculation.

The second stage can be delayed in order to have so-called multiple orgasms. This requires practice. Some men can do it by mind control alone. Others require external pressure on the perineum just before the orgasmic threshold is reached.

The entire body and mind can be involved in orgasm. No other activity produces such intense excitement followed by such total release. Orgasms vary enormously in the pleasure they bring. The first one can feel the best because there is more liquid in the ejaculate so the sensations last longer and feel more pleasurably intense.

## Changes at Orgasm

The *shaft* of the penis, being fully engorged with blood, reaches maximum rigidity, length and width just before orgasm.

The *glans* does not become as rigid as the shaft. It is larger than its relaxed state, and may darken due to vasocongestion.

The *meatus* (urethra opening) widens its lips, and is moistened with fluid from Cowper's Glands.

The *testicles* enlarge 50 to 100 percent their normal size. They rise and rotate so the lower surfaces are in firm contact with the body.

*Blood pressure* rises from an average systolic 100-120 to 220.

*Heart rate* increases from an average 60 to 80 beats per minute to 100 to 150 — and can rise to 180.

*Breathing rate* It becomes fast and shallow, and can speed up to three times its normal resting rate.

*Body muscles* are held in such a state of high tension that the slightest touch produces an instant quivering response.

*Body language* includes face contorting into a rictus — a glaring grimace. The hands may claw, the toes curl, the feet arch.

*Mental faculties* appear to be "gone," as if nonexistent, so deeply are they buried beneath orgasm's spell.

*Nipples* swell, harden and become erect in 60 percent of men.

A *sex flush,* or rosy hue, starts at the nipples and spreads over the chest, back and buttocks in 25 percent of men.

*Sneezing* attacks can occur due to nasal vasocongestion.

*Perspiration* occurs in one-third of men after orgasm. The entire body may be drenched in dew, or just the hands and feet.

## Orgasm and Health

Orgasm can be a powerful muscle relaxant. Its effects can be ten times as strong as the effects of valium and other tranquilizers. After illness, orgasm can assist on the road back to health. Some physicians believe it is the best prescription for easing mild back pain and so allowing a completely relaxed night's sleep.

Orgasm is of specific value for prostate health because the gland, like a stuffed-up nose, benefits from a thorough cleaning out. Regular ejaculation avoids *prostate congestion,* a painful condition which mimics prostatitis. It may also help delay urine leakage problems in later life, but this is not proven yet.

Orgasm can be excellent aerobic activity. Blood pressure, heart and breathing rate have a thorough workout without the bother of donning a track suit. The benefits to mental health can be invaluable: profound emotional release, closer partner attachment, an increase in mutual love, support and self-esteem.

When a top athlete exercises, his blood pressure, heart and breathing rate rise only slightly. Yet they rise steeply at the explosive force of orgasm. The rise is not due to physical effort, nor to advanced sexual techniques which demand a high energy output. The rise comes directly from the orgasm itself, from the build-up of tremendous sexual tension until climax is reached. If recovering from heart disease, it is not necessary to fear the effort of thrusting will damage a weakened heart. Though this fear is understandable, it can kill the ability to erect, and so deny the health benefits to be gained from orgasm.

After a debilitating illness, a man may abstain for longer than necessary because he cannot tolerate the image of himself as frail. He may dislike the idea of having to limit his movements. Though advanced sexual athletics are unwise, it should not be necessary to limit thrusting time. Choose positions which demand the least physical effort. These include partner up and astride, or man standing as she kneels face down. Relax. Enjoy.

Love-making puts about the same degree of demand on the heart as walking briskly, or climbing two flights of stairs. One rule of thumb: If a man can walk on a treadmill at more than two miles per hour at a 10 percent grade without any significant increase in his blood pressure or adverse changes in his electrocardiogram, his exercise capacity should be sufficient to allow for safe love-making with the usual partner. Consult with the physician on this.

A heart attack, any illness due to the aging process, can be deeply depressing. Fight these feelings. Slowly. Take recovery day by day. Enjoy the waiting period by indulging in erotic fantasy. Set a date for love-making to resume. Then plan for it in the same way as when young and planning to charm a new and exciting date. Give health reassurances if a partner is anxious. If there is no partner, plan for masturbation as a special treat. Bathe, shave, don attractive clothes, attend to hair and nails. Move out of the sick room with its memories of pain. Order flowers and wine. In short, arrange for a splendid occasion. No rest or medication is quite so restorative as the sense of virility which comes from pre-planning the act of love.

## The Party's Over?

Detumescence happens in two stages. First, the penis shrinks rapidly to half its fully erect size. The second stage can take 10 minutes or more. During this period, both penis and testicles reduce to their usual size, the muscle fibers of the scrotum relax and the testes gradually descend.

Detumescence can be halted at the first stage. A full or partial erection can be maintained if stimulation remains high. But in some men, the penis develops an acute hyper-sensitivity. The slightest touch is unbearable until detumescence is complete.

After ejaculation, there is a waiting period until the prostate and seminal glands refill with fluids. The *refractory period* is the time after one ejaculation and before another can be achieved. This differs widely. It gets longer over one period of repeated ejaculations.

The more mature the man, the longer he can make love without ejaculating. Elderly men can make love regularly and have a splendid time with no ejaculate at all. This is perfectly normal, with no damaging health effects. As love-making does not have to include penetration, so it does not have to end with ejaculation.

However, if there is a consistent lack of orgasm which gives anxiety or pain, consult with the urologist.

# Ejaculation Pain

Orgasm is a strange and primitive sensation. The experience is unique to each individual, which makes it difficult to share. There can be times when the pleasure threshold is raised to an exquisite extreme. The intense sensations build to an agonizingly explosive force which borders on the knife edge of pain. This is called the pleasure/pain syndrome.

The pain part of the syndrome can be clearly seen at orgasm. The facial muscles contort to a rictus of agony. The clawing of hands and feet equally express pain. The entire body language shows the fine line between pleasure and pain. A child watching parents imagines they are torturing each other. Lock the door.

There may be times when pain only is experienced. In these cases, neuro-physicists believe parts of the brain translate the pleasure/pain syndrome incorrectly. The fine line shifts, and the pleasure part is translated as pain only. If this happens rarely, it is nothing to worry about. If frequent, consult a urologist.

Pain after ejaculation is a different phenomenon, and fairly common. Usually, it is more a discomfort than pain, a heaviness or cramps felt in the lower abdomen. It is due to the powerful muscle contractions involved in orgasm, and is a normal response to the tremendous effort involved. The pain should soon subside with rest after ejaculation. If the pain persists, see Chapter 9.

# Blood in the Ejaculate

Blood can show in the ejaculate as bright red streaks, or darker specks like coffee grounds. It may be due to the explosive force of orgasm breaking open a small blood vessel in either partner. It can be mistaken for menstrual blood. Check by masturbation. If it occurs rarely, the condition is self-healing.

But if blood appears in the ejaculate more than two or three times, consult with a urologist. The condition might be a sign of chronic urethritis. Check for the symptoms. If present, the germs are causing a low-grade prostate infection. In very rare cases, blood in the ejaculate can signify prostate or bladder cancer.

# Ejaculatory Control

Many men suffer major concerns over timing; they ejaculate too soon or too late. The issue is too soon or too late for what? For whom? A man is primed to ejaculate within in a few seconds of arousal. Yet if he does what is natural, he is called a premature ejaculator. Why is a woman not called orgasmically retarded instead?

It can be perceived that the labels "premature" and "retarded" ejaculation are judgment calls. They are a throw-back to the notion that a woman's satisfaction is independent of her actions and feelings, but dependent upon the man. It is tied to the misperception that "sex is what men *do to women*" rather than "sex is what men *do with women.*"

Ejaculatory control is not inborn. It has to be learned, and requires a degree of maturity most young men lack. But all-age men can lose control at times, which it is hardly surprising, for they take upon themselves the tricky and delicate task of controlling their own excitement while helping to stimulate their partner to greater heights. This can add a dimension of stress and distress. Premature and retarded ejaculation are now called stressors. They do indeed exist, and can cause great distress depending upon the degree to which a man longs to gain control. These stressors are still considered serious dysfunctions by some sex therapists, but are simply a matter of learning new skills.

# Stress

Orgasm and ejaculation are about letting go, losing control. From an early age, children learn the body's desires can be wayward and the mind should stay in control. Ejaculation distress can arise if this early learning is too harshly taught. The pain the child suffers builds a taboo in the unconscious. The taboo can become translated into an adult fear of losing control.

There are other reasons too, but the basic taboo is a belief the mind should remain on watch over the body's behavior. Indeed, everyday life and social interaction would be impossible without any such criteria. Many people with normal childhoods find it difficult to let go, to lose control and experience complete satisfaction. There is nothing bad or repressed about this. With love, time and practice, the condition eventually wears off.

Aiming for mutual orgasm is inappropriate. It is demanding on the man, and requires a high degree of control plus knowledge of the partner's orgasmic threshold. As the mind is "gone" at orgasm, aiming for mutual ones would seem of little value. Many men gain more pleasure from watching their partner climax first.

# Trigger Happy?

*Premature ejaculation* is defined as consistently climaxing before wishing to do so. Whether ejaculation occurs before penetration, immediately at penetration, or after only a few thrusts, is of no significance. The fact a man cannot control ejaculation and wishes to do so is the cause of distress.

One U.S. survey estimates 75 percent of men ejaculate less than two minutes after penetration. The British call "premming" the French disease; the French call it the British malaise. The most popular theory about the cause of premming is hasty teen sex, rushed for fear of discovery, which sets a pattern in adult life. But would this theory hold up in countries with different attitudes to early sexual activity? Other theories include:

· Unresolved guilts over teenage masturbation.
· Humiliating experience of failures at first attempts.
· Being hurried by, or guilts from using, a prostitute.
· Dislike, or secret fears, of current partner.
· Femaphobia, fear of women in general.
· Fear of interruption, lack of privacy.
· Fear of pregnancy, or some reprisal such as sexual disease.
· Inappropriate childhood learning.
· Low self-image and self-esteem.
· Concern for personal pleasure only.

However, some 30 percent of "premmers" have a physical problem. This may be a highly irritable uretha, an inflamed and "trigger-happy" prostate, or some infection at the base of the bladder.

The man can usually tell if the cause is physical or psycho not, visit the doctor before trying self help.

# Self Help

The simplest and easiest advise includes:

1. Make love a second and third time.
2. Have a few drinks.
3. Change love-making positions.
4. Grow older!

Premming happens because a man cannot recognize he is nearing ejaculation and cannot act in order to delay his orgasm. It is due to lack of appropriate focus, nothing else. If the condition causes misery, act now to overcome it. Once premming becomes entrenched, there is a risk the unconscious steps in and creates psychologic impotence to avoid the pain of future premming.

Before starting the program, practice stopping urine flow in mid-stream. Focus on the sensations felt. Re-start the flow, then stop again. Squeeze the muscles of the back passage tight. Focus again. Become familiar with focusing on all these sensations. Continue to learn proper focus during the following exercises. Ask these two simple questions: Do I, or don't I, recognize the signs when I am coming? What sensations must I focus on to learn proper control?

The answers can be gained from solitary masturbation. Allow for plenty of time and privacy. Focus solely and totally on the task. Believe that control can be learned. Expect some degree of failure at first. Above all, give top priority to the exercises.

1. Become erect and highly aroused. Focus on the sensations deep within the pelvis before the crucial pre-emission stage. Once this stage is recognized, use the *squeeze technique.* Two fingers on the frenulum, thumb opposite at the corona — and squeeze, squeeze hard. Not only will the urge to ejaculate stop, but the erection itself may disappear.

2. If this fails and ejaculation occurs, the squeezing was not hard enough, or lacked real intent. Avoid being downcast. Allow for refractory time, or wait until later, and repeat the entire exercise again. Then continue as below.

3. Again, stimulate the penis to reach pre-emission. Stop, and repeat the squeeze technique. Use this "stop start" method five times, then ejaculate. Practice makes perfect. Repeat, over some days, weeks or months until full control is achieved. It is about unlearning fear of failure, so it may take some while.

4. A man may insist he is focusing, which he usually is. But the focus is in the wrong place. It is on the negative learning problem — the knowledge of having failed so often he is bound to fail again. Which he then does, which reinforces the condition.

5. Men used to be told to distract their minds from feelings of imminent ejaculation by focusing on money or work. This is a mistake. Focus must be solely and totally on the deep physical sensations. Once these are familiar, the focus then becomes when to control them — and nothing else.

## Partner Prem

Some men have full masturbatory control, but lose it with a partner. In this case, she can control the exercise, manipulating the penis outside the vagina until the pre-emission stage. Then give the nod or word for her to begin the squeeze technique. When ejaculatory control is gained, try penetration. She must be able to get at the penis quickly; astride on top is appropriate. If underneath, the man's focus is split between recognizing the pre-emission stage and preparing to withdraw. Help to arouse her first. If penetration is difficult, there is a risk of thrusting, with subsequent loss of control. Use plenty of lubrication to avoid this.

Keep in mind rhythm-and-friction trigger ejaculation. *Avoid thrusting*. After penetration, lie still. Either person can begin moving in a short while, very slowly at first. She watches for his signal to remove the penis and begin the squeeze technique. Aim to repeat the exercise five times before ejaculation. If this is not possible, avoid being downcast. With sufficient practice, the squeeze technique is highly effective.

(A partner who has been subject to premming may be reluctant to help. This is understandable. Partners of prems often suffer too. Or there may be a power struggle between the couple. In this case, consider seeking help from a sex behavior therapist).

Some men regard the squeeze technique with horror. They stop and cool down by use of ice or a cold washcloth. Then they start the process over again. Over a few months, they notice a longer and longer period between initial excitation and ejaculation.

# Gun Shy?

*Retarded ejaculation* is defined as "ejaculation which happens too late, or not at all." The condition is less common than premming. Nor does it damage the relationship so much, especially at first. A delayer may find he easily ejaculates on his own, often after love-making. The condition begins and ends with partner sex.

All men delay at times and for the same reasons as they prem. A young man rarely does, unless his particular taboo is especially strong. In elderly men, not ejaculating over many love-making sessions is a normal part of the aging process. A mature man who fails to ejaculate is not a delayer.

Fear of pregnancy is a major factor in delay. If withdrawal was used as a method of birth control, the stress of timing it right probably affected control. The lone responsibility of holding back can develop an unconscious dread of ejaculating, especially if an unwanted pregnancy occurred in the past.

The pregnancy taboo results from the best of intentions, and can be appreciated by both partners as such. But once delay sets in, avoid thrusting too long in the hope of unblocking the taboo. There may be times when this is successful. At other times, semen dribbles out with no satisfying explosion of release. To avoid this becoming chronic, work through the next article. If the pregnancy problem remains, seek contraceptive advice first.

# Self Help

Dr. Kegel, a gynecologist, drew up a program of exercises to help women strengthen the pelvic muscles stretched at childbirth. They are known as *Kegels*, and used with problems of bladder control. Yet Kegels can be successful therapy for stressors, both delay and premming. (And they may help to avoid urine leakage problems in later life.)

Kegels strengthen the muscles at the penile root, and improve blood flow to the pelvic area. They help focus sensation prior to ejaculation. Many men with perfect control do Kegels regularly to get stronger and keener sensations at orgasm.

Week 1. Squeeze the muscles of the back passage tight. Then relax them. Do this 15 times, twice daily, for a week.

Weeks 2 and 3. Gradually build up to 65 squeezes, twice daily. Squeezing can be done anywhere, even waiting in line.

Weeks 4 and 6. Hold the squeeze to a count of three — then relax. Build up gradually from 15 times twice daily to 65 squeezes, twice a day.

Note the word "gradually." Avoid extra squeezes. The muscles get sore, and require rest. Kegels then have to be resumed at week 1 again. It usually takes 6 weeks before improvement is noticed.

# Theory Land!

One theory suggests men with ejaculatory distress are acting out a power game. Coming too soon, or too late, are ways of using a partner, which is meant to abuse her, not always unconsciously. Such men are said to be cold, controlling, unrelaxed. They hold unexamined and inappropriately high values. The over-powering need to be in control prevents them from being intimate.

But theories are theories and open to debate. It is hardly surprising a man who loses control may have a passion to control other areas of life. Keep in mind these can be acutely painful conditions; they can cripple self-esteem. The coldness may result from the distressor, not the other way around.

Yet the theory may be worth checking, for distressors can damage the nicest of men. Why make life sadder by empowering one condition to create an added emotional one? After checking the self, check the relationship: is it really close? In what ways could it be more satisfying, more effective? (And because being uptight slows down the effects of self help, learn to relax!)

Some men with naturally gentle natures are in manipulative relationships and cannot cope with conflict. The stressor may be unconsciously encouraged by a partner as a way of controlling him. Here it is she who is playing the power game, not he. Consider professional therapy. Deeper unhappiness and the risk of psychologic impotence can result from leaving things as they are.

# Disability

Sadly, horrendous things do happen in life. They are not just the provenance of nightmares. An accident at work, or on the highway, or a crippling disease, can strike at random. A man may suffer spinal injury or neurological disease. Sudden diabetes is a cruel enemy which can rob a young man of his power to erect.

In some accidents, mutilation of the penis can be so severe that amputation is necessary. Rest assured that no urologist will do this unless the extent of damage is beyond repair, and the penis cannot be saved. Amputation prevents gangrene and saves life. Very advanced penile cancer is another reason for amputation. It is critical to understand:

*A man can have an orgasm without an erection.*
*A man can have an orgasm without the use of a penis.*

It is equally critical for both partners to understand:

*A woman can have an orgasm without penetration.*
*A woman can have an orgasm without a penis.*

The human spirit is wondrous in its courage and resolution. It can adapt to almost anything, if it so desires. Loss of penis, or permanent loss of erection ability, is a savage assault on a man's self-esteem. His first reactions may be equally violent and destructive. A seemingly quiet and depressive state can be just as emotionally damaging as a raging bitter response.

Keep in mind the healing process can be speeded up by orgasm if so desired. Use pornography, erotica, anything which works. Persist in the effort. Terrible grief over the loss is bound to break through at times. Weep. Do not shut out mourning. Then go for orgasm again. Give it a best shot.

In a loving relationship, the partner can take control. Seduce him. Act like a red hot momma. Shock him out of grief and pain by relighting his sexual fires. Turn his emotional energies away from his broken body and the sick room, and back to where happiness lies.

He may need plenty of stimulation. Dress, or undress, in a highly erotic fashion. Use stocking tops, black suspenders, peek-a-boo bras, scarlet nighties, frothy lace, leather gear, whips —

whatever excites him. Consider a vibrator or dildo for him to activate. He needs to master, to dominate, to know he can satisfy his beloved and himself again.

Avoid concern over his feelings. He is still a man, a real man, and will find your particular brand of "medication" irresistible. Continue to enchant him until he has an orgasm. Then tell him to be ready for another session later on. Emotional healing begins when he is ready to take control of the action. Instead of a broken and bitter future, a man without a functional penis can act like a man.

# Loss of Penis

*Phalloplasty* is the construction of an artificial penis. It requires the skills of a very experienced urologist and plastic surgeon. It is a painful procedure; tissue from the groin or abdomen help build up the structure. An artificial penis which erects has not yet been created.

Penile self-mutilation, though rare, is not unknown. Such behavior can appeal to transsexuals, religious fanatics and the mentally deranged. Clinical medical studies find there is a close relationship between genital self-mutilation and the following:

- Impoverished childhood experience
- Submissive, masochistic relationships with women
- Domineering mother aged 35 to 50 at son's birth
- Absence of father leading to abnormal feminine identity
- Weak, vacillating, bullying father leading to symbolic and then actual repudiation of the penis.

*Ah, parents! If only we knew the power of our role,*
*and the pain and damage we inadvertently cause!*

Jealous partners, in a fit of fury, have been known to amputate the penis. Whatever the degree of provocation, this is a terrible assault. It may seem trite to state the obvious, that no behavior merits such appalling violation. The penis is crucial to a man's identity, the focus of all he regards as masculine and male.

# Re-Attachment

If the penis is accidentally amputated, stay alert. Wrap it in a bag to prevent freezer burn, and place it in the fridge. Total replant surgery is possible by highly skilled microsurgeons in this difficult and delicate task. Western physicians report the time lapse between injury and re-attachment should be less than six hours. Any later, and the ability to urinate, experience penile sensations, erect and ejaculate may be lost.

In 1986, the official Chinese news agency Xinhua reported the case of a Pakistani whose penis was crushed in an industrial accident. Local surgeons lacked the skills to sew it back on. So the man, together with his crushed organ, flew to Shanghai to consult the leading authority on plastic microsurgery. A surgical team at Shanghai's No. 2 Medical University used some of the man's skin and a piece of his rib to construct a new penis from the crushed organ. It was then successfully sewn on. Within two weeks, the man "regained the function of his penis," the Xinhua report said.

Since 1982, surgeons in the same unit have performed fifty similar operations on Chinese and foreign patients. All but one reported the surgery a success. Most of the men have been able to father children. A photograph of a baby girl born to an ex-patient is available as proof.

## Penis Transplant

In 1987, the Bangkok newspapers in Thailand reported the first penis transplant surgery in medical history. A soldier was rushed to hospital minus his penis. It had been cut off by his jealous wife, and could not be found. In the hospital, a Thai man was being prepared for a sex change operation.

The seven-hour transplant operation was performed by a panel of three surgeons specializing in microsurgery at the Police Hospital of Bangkok. A week later, the donor left the hospital after his sex change operation in a "satisfactory condition." The unfaithful soldier returned home with his newly transplanted penis later. There is no news of what happened after that.

The report stated previous transplants failed due to tissue incompatibility. It concluded: "It was an amazing stroke of good luck that the two men were of the same tissue type."

CHAPTER 9

# The Prostate

## Tony's Story

Tony was driving his parents home after a visit. Not two hours out of the city, and his dad asked for a stop. Tony couldn't pull off the freeway. By the time he spotted a rest room and his dad got out, an odd smell was drifting through the car.

"Bleached your hair again?" he asked Sonia.

She dug him in the ribs. "It's your dad, you dolt."

He didn't get it. "Smells like the kids' diapers."

"Sssh! They're coming back." Sonia hissed.

Tony watched his parents return to the car. Douglas, his Dad, still had that spritely walk he remembered so well. He really loved the old guy. How old was he, anyway, . . . 64? 67? Not old by today's standards. . . and finally, the penny dropped. The rest room and the car smell. Tony's eyes filled with sudden tears. He grabbed Sonia's hand, and squeezed it, hard.

Later, he quizzed his mother. "It's prostate trouble, isn't it? How long has it been going on?"

"You know your dad," she smiled to erase her anxious frown. "He'll never admit anything is wrong."

"I'll take care of things. Get information." He kissed the top of her head. "Pass that on to dad for me, will you?"

In bed that night, Tony cradled Sonia in his arms. His eyes were wet again. "That beautiful old man," he said.

"Not so old," she grinned. "Nicely mature. He's neat. I'd fancy him myself if I wasn't married to his son."

## Site of the Prostate

Tony was reading from a medical book. "The prostate lies directly below the bladder and surrounds the first part of the urethra. It enlarges after age 50 and presses on the bladder and urethra. This is the reason for leakage problems in later life."

"Why is the bladder upstream, then?" Tony asked. "And why does the pee tube run through the prostate if it causes trouble?"

"Design fault," Sonia replied. "Women know all about them."

"Nature's not so clever, huh!" Tony snorted, and read on."Any swelling of the prostate upsets urine control because it presses on the bladder and the urethra running through it. This can cause *incontinence*, ranging from mild urine leakage to total loss of control. A very enlarged prostate automatically causes urinating problems in an otherwise healthy man."

"That means dad is OK. Thank heavens!" Tony breathed a sigh of relief. But he could not tolerate the thought it might happen to him. He turned the page.

"For most of his life, a man is unaware he has a prostate. With exercise programs, e.g., Kegels, he can learn to distinguish the two stages of climax. Such exercise may help delay prostate enlargement, though this is not proven. But some men are prepared to try them to avoid leakage problems before they begin.

"What on earth are Kegels?" Tony asked Sonia.

"Wonderful things," she murmured sleepily. "Got my muscles back again after the birth of the twins."

## Voiding Problems

*When the hair becomes grey and thin, ordinarily — I dare say, invariably — the prostate increases in volume.*
         — Sir Benjamin Brodie, 1820.

At birth, the prostate is a tiny heart-shaped blob. At puberty, it grows to the size of a walnut and produces prostatic fluids from dimples rather like those on a golf ball. At age 50, the cells start to over-produce, and the prostate starts to enlarge. Over the next 20 years, it continues to grow and can reach the size of a lemon, even a grapefruit. The extra tissue becomes harder, tougher, more fi-brosed.

From age 60 plus, the enlarging prostate can press on the urethra which runs through it, and the bladder which is above it. The pressure causes leakage problems common to older men. The condition is *benign prostatic hyperplasia*, BPH (benign means non-malignant; hyperplasia means increase in cell growth). BPH is not a disease. It is an annoying complication of the aging process.

At about the same time, the bladder sphincters which control urine flow can start to lose tone and strength. From an early age, these muscles do not always work well. At times, they can go into spasm and cause a waiting period before urination starts. In later life, weakened sphincters add to the problems of BPH.

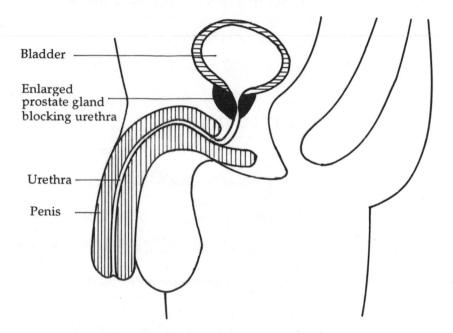

Bladder

Enlarged prostate gland blocking urethra

Urethra

Penis

The symptoms of BPH and/or weak sphincters are:

- Decrease in size and force of urine stream.
- Hesitancy when starting voiding.
- Straining to begin or continue.
- Stop-start action of stream.
- Lack of a defined stream finish.
- Leakage of drops after stream ends.

There may be frequency and urgency. Nocturia can be up to five times each night. Hesitancy can take thirty seconds or longer. Annoying or distressing though these symptoms are, *there is no pain with BPH.*

BPH is more common in Western cultures. Post mortems on men aged 40 plus found an 80.1 percent overall incidence of enlarged prostate. This increased to a maximum 95.5 percent at age 70 plus. Though the data may sound depressing, they can be seen as comforting. From the number of healthy, happy and active older men, it seems BPH does not significantly alter the quality of life, providing the condition is well managed.

It is not known what causes prostate cells to grow. It does not happen if the testicles are non-functioning, so testosterone is implicated. Interesting research into the effects of diet and body temperature is in progress. It is now thought, though not proven, that preventive health steps when younger may slow down the progress of BPH.

Tony decided to buy a copy of the book for himself.

# BPH Self Help

Tony telephoned his father. "I'm sending you a book. It's worth a read, or a quick flick through."

"Quick flick, my eye!" grunted Douglas, when the book arrived. Nevertheless, he settled down to read.

"Regular ejaculation keeps the prostate and seminal glands healthy. It may slow down the hardening process, but this is not proven. Weak bladder sphincters are helped by exercise. Kegels are excellent. If BPH problems have begun, it is not too late to strengthen these sphincters. Practice stopping the flow in midstream. Do this very slowly at first. Sudden effort can cause sudden weakening and do more harm than good.

Attitude of mind is all-important. Where one man finds getting up to urinate at night an outrage, another accepts it calmly, philosophically, as a natural part of the aging process. Avoid anger or frustration with BPH. The urinary system, like the blood system, reacts negatively to tension and stress.

Keep extra shorts handy, just in case. If repeated visits to the rest room cause embarrassment, make "urgent telephone calls" instead. One theory suggests the company of an older partner is less stressful than a younger one, e.g., the need not to stray too far from a rest room can irritate a younger partner. And this can add tension, which increases the stress, which increases the urge to make those visits — just in case. The best way to conquer BPH is to:

1. Stay active *mentally*. Engaging the mind in real mental challenge distracts it from the annoying effects of BPH.

2. Stay active *socially*. Giving help to agencies caring for people with problems reduces the size of BPH distress.

3. Stay active *emotionally*. Loving others unconditionally is the path to receiving unconditional love.

4. Stay active *physically*. Kegels might help in disability, or some limit to general mobility.

5. Stay active *sexually*. The prostate functions best with regular ejaculation, in whatever form this takes.

## Incontinence

Some 6 percent of American men under age 65 are incontinent. Between 1 and 2 percent live in nursing homes, though they are still relatively young. It seems families can cope with feeding, bathing and dressing problems, but not with incontinence. The percentage of incontinent men rises steeply with increasing age.

## Sexual Interest

A few older men with BPH experience an increase in sexual desire. This may seem surprising as the level of testosterone drops. In part, this is due to pressure from the enlarged prostate causing sensations rather like those at ejaculation. "Though the spirit is willing, the flesh has not altered its pre-BPH state."

"Huh! That's all they know," Douglas smiled proudly. He had enjoyed the information so far. The next article looked grim.

## Special BPH Problems

BPH ranges from mild to moderate to severe. Many men sail through the later years with only mild BPH. But for some, the condition can deteriorate rapidly. Be on guard against the following. If any one occurs, consult with a urologist at once.

*Pain on Urination*: As the prostate enlarges, increased pressure on the urethra causes tiny scarring at each urination. Like a vicious circle, scarring narrows the urethra more, which causes more scarring. This interferes with the bladder's wash out effect; it only partially empties, and the retained urine becomes infected. The resulting cystitis causes urinating pain.

*Incontinence*: To add to the vicious circle, the bladder over-stretches to hold the retained urine. Over-stretched bladder tissue can be compared to frayed elastic fiber. The bladder walls weaken and lose the ability to fully contract. Eventually, the result is total incontinence.

*Total Retention*: The urethra can become so scarred it completely closes. Urine is retained and becomes infected. The pressure in the bladder causes back-up pressure and potentially lethal kidney damage. *Total retention is a medical emergency!* The urine must be siphoned off before the kidneys suffer permanent damage.

*Blood in Urine*: Consult with a urologist if blood appears in urine or the ejaculate.

## BPH Surgery

BPH surgery used to be a wretched procedure. Both the operation and the recovery time were long and painful. Many men were left impotent. Today, *transurethral resection* of the prostate, TURP, is quick and effective, and restores a man to his former self.

A *rectoscope* is a tube with a tiny electrified wire loop at the end. It is snaked by catheter into the penis and up the urinary tract to the prostate. The loop trims away the extra tissue, leaving the prostate intact. The trimmed tissue is analyzed for malignancy. The procedure is painless, avoids an incision and leaves no scar to heal.

TURP takes about an hour. A meal can be eaten that evening, or the next day. A catheter remains in the bladder for two days to allow for recovery. Once the catheter is removed, the man goes home. It takes a few weeks for mild leakage to completely stop.

TURP does not affect the quality of love-making. If erections were satisfactory before, they remain so afterwards. The testicles are unaffected. But the bladder sphincter is usually sliced off by TURP. So at orgasm, there is no ejaculate. But the sensations of a dry orgasm feel just as pleasurable, just as intense.

At emission, sperm are pumped along the vas as usual. But at ejaculation, semen is spurted backwards into the bladder. This is *retrograde ejaculation* (not to be confused with retarded ejaculation). It results in sterility. Being unable to father a child is rarely a problem at this age. But if it is, consider artificial insemination. One minor side-effect is that the urine looks cloudy and the aim of stream may need relearning.

TURP has an appreciably high incidence of side effects. According to some U.S. studies, 6 percent (25,000 men a year) become impotent. Another 2,000 to 4,000 become incontinent. And within 10 years, 10 percent need further surgery because the prostate tissue has enlarged again, and the BPH symptoms have returned.

Upsetting though these data may seem, compare them with the following. In 1989, the nation's 7,700 urologists performed more than 400,000 TURP. Consider how many men escape side effects. The total cost of the 1989 TURP surgery was just under $3 billion. Medicare alone paid well over $1 billion for some 250,000 procedures. In some cases, however, the enlarged tissue is too hardened and fibrous for TURP, and a radical prostatectomy is required. This involves the removal of the entire prostate.

Douglas felt the cold hand of panic grip and squeeze his heart. He was fit, healthy, spry. He did not want the knife. Ten years ago, he saw what the operation did to a friend. It had turned a decent active guy into an impotent sack of a man. He felt an over-powering need to make love with Beth. He would finish the chapter later, when he felt calm.

# New Therapy

At the first sign of leakage, some men give up hope. They opt for instant surgery; they go straight for the knife. Yet there are other less invasive techniques to tackle BPH.

1. *Physiotherapy*: Try the program of exercises devised specially to improve control. Or, try Kegels at home.

2. *Medication*: There are drugs to increase sphincter resistance

to BPH pressure; drugs to shrink an enlarged prostate; drugs to relax prostatic muscle. All these are in the trial stage.

3. *Incision*: Also in the trial stage is a technique whereby a small incision enlarges the bladder neck to improve the flow.

4. *Ultrasound*: This trial method bombards the enlarged tissue, turning it to pulp which can then be sucked out by aspirator.

5. *Microwaves*: By this trial method, microwaves are used to heat and shrink the enlarged tissue.

6. *Wait and See*: In a few cases, after a prostate examination, the condition improves or stabilizes; it is not known why.

Some urologists do not recommend these options, many of which are in the trial stage. The risk of urine retention with back-up pressure damaging the kidneys may be too high. The choice of therapy depends upon how advanced the BPH is, and the degree of discomfort from the symptoms. Read the following.

7. *Balloon Angioplasty*: This involves using a catheter to insert a small balloon into the penis. X-rays help to position the balloon at the site where the urethra is squeezed. The balloon is inflated and forces the urethra open. The entire procedure takes 30 minutes and can be done in the physician's office. A catheter is left in place for a few days. Many urologists first do a prostate biopsy to exclude cancer. Balloon angioplasty is not recommended for advanced BPH.

A similar technique involves inserting a prosthesis into the rectum. A probe places the balloon close to the prostate. When inflated, the balloon forces the prostate away from the bladder. This relieves the pressure, which relieves the problems. Again, it is a simple procedure and can be done in the office. Balloon angioplasty seems to be the most promising therapy. To date, only 2,000 men have chosen it. Yet it is safe, avoids pain, hospitalization and high medical costs. It does not cause retrograde ejaculation. Between 50 percent and 88 percent men experience instant relief from BPH symptoms.

As yet, the main disadvantage is long-term success rates. Some men are free of BPH symptoms three years later. But it is not clear if this will apply to all men. The alternatives have to be weighed, and the risk of repeat therapy accepted or rejected.

"Hey," Douglas beamed at Beth. "I might avoid surgery."

# Choices

The choice to opt for surgery and end BPH has its attractions. Men who lack the diligence to continue with exercises, or those who do not wish to alter their lifestyle, may go straight for TURP. Some physicians consider surgery an artificial solution, and it involves a degree of risk, no matter how small.

Modern thinking is to try less invasive techniques first. Ask the urologist about exercise, medication, balloon techniques and so on, plus their success rates. Do they depend upon a change in lifestyle or behavior? If so, are these changes acceptable? Choice is a highly personal matter. What suits one man may be totally unacceptable to another. Investigate all the available therapies to make an informed choice.

Douglas had made his choice. There was no doubt in his mind. "Don't tell Tony I've seen the urologist," he said, as Beth drove him home after the office appointment. "I don't want him to know I've gotta kiddy's balloon shoved up my —."

"Shush!" She ruffled the grey hair on the back of his neck. "My very handsome husband. I shall love you just the same."

In the peaceful silence which descends when a car engine is switched off, Douglas reached for Beth's hand. "Damn good doctor!" he murmured. "Damn good wife! I'm a lucky man!"

# Care of the Prostate

Other prostate problems include cancer, infection and congestion. Some physicians strongly recommend regular check-ups for men over age 40. Other are less keen if there are no symptoms of disease. For the individual man, the decision is one of personal choice.

## Regular Check-Ups

The prostate can be palpated (felt) through the rectum. The usual positions for palpation are bending over the examination table, toes pointing inwards; or lying sideways, knees to chest. Digital examination is by insertion of a gloved finger. An ultrasound probe may be used. The probe is slightly more reliable but less comfortable than digital examination.

Valuable information can be gained from prostate size. Is it enlarged? By how much and in what sites? Further information can be gained from its consistency. Does it feel mushy, lumpy or hard? In patches, in nodules or all over? If so, what are the reasons?

## Prostate Massage

The massage consists of digital stroking pressure which "milks" out prostatic fluids. Be prepared to hold a sterile culture tube in place during the massage. The fluids are examined for the presence of bacteria; the analysis is an important diagnostic tool. A prostate massage brings instant relief from the pain of congestion. However, it should not be done over-vigorously.

In conditions such as suspected tumor or acute infection, it is actually dangerous to massage the prostate. Even mild pressure can spread the malignant cells or bacteria into the body. *Epididymitis* is a common example of infection spread by prostate massage. Most physicians are aware of these risks, but not all.

If the body temperature is raised, it signifies infection. If there is bone pain, it might signify cancer. Prostate massage is inappropriate in either case. Check these symptoms are absent before consenting to a massage.

## Blood Tests

The "tumor marking" test provides a simple way to detect prostate disease, including cancer. It measures the concentration of a special type of protein normally present in blood in small amounts. It shows if therapy for prostate cancer is effective, or if the cancer has moved to other parts of the body.

## Diet

Reduce the amount of saturated fats in the diet. Over-consumption might be linked to prostate cancer because fats can change the interaction of hormones. Men with non-functioning testicles do not produce testosterone, and rarely suffer prostate cancer. Carrots provide beta carotene, thought to be an anti-cancer food.

Tony's eyes traveled down to the title of the next article. "I'm not reading that!" he told Sonia. "Forget it!"
She took the book and read aloud to him.

# Where the Sun Doesn't Shine

A colo-rectal examination gives clues to problems not caused by the prostate. The anus sphincters are checked for tone. They could be weak due to neurological disease. Urination problems can be due to fissure, a break in skin lining, or hemorrhoids, often called piles. The rectum is checked for fistula, which is an opening due to a burst abscess or ulcer. If lumps or polyps are found, these are investigated for signs of tumor. In fact, the purpose of a regular colorectal examination is the early detection and removal of a cancer growth. "If everyone over 50 had check-ups for colorectal cancer, the cure rate could be as high as 75 percent," according to the president of the American Cancer Society. The examination may be by ultrasound, or by *colonoscopy* — a long tube with a telescopic lens which allows the colon to be viewed, and can reach further than a digital examination.

No prostate investigation is painful. But neither is it exactly comfortable. An added embarrassment is the over-powering urge to open the bowels. One option is to use a suppository the night before. There is security in knowing the bowel is empty. A small comfort, but every little bit helps.

Tony almost lost courage. Sonia gave him the necessary prod. "If you have those tests, I'll get my varicose veins done."

# Acute Prostatitis

Prostatitis is an infection of the prostate and is usually a complication of urethritis. It is not contagious, or inherited, or a sign of cancer. It can attack suddenly in youth. Avoid delay in the hope the infection will clear by itself. Early therapy stops the germs from becoming entrenched in the prostate, causing a chronic disabling disease which is difficult to dislodge.

The symptoms of pain, fever and shivering are added to burning, frequency, urgency and nocturia. But unlike urethritis, pain is not limited to the penis. It hurts deep in the abdomen. It can hurt to ejaculate or open the bowels. There may be blood in the urine, which shows as a pinkish stream. In severe cases, there is urine retention. When the symptoms appear, take body temperature to check for fever. The temperature can rise to 39 C (102 F), a sure sign of infection. The main distinction between prostatitis and a condition called prostatodynia is fever.

Antibiotics and bed rest are effective within a few days. Tranquilizers and anti-spasm drugs may be used to calm an acutely irritated prostate. Sitz baths bring soothing relief. Ask about fluid intake. Copious amounts can overstretch a bladder already swollen from infection. Avoid caffeine in cola, tea and coffee. Abstain from alcohol and sexual activity for the next six weeks. Sit in hard rather than soft chairs whenever possible.

# Chronic Prostatitis

Symptoms of urethritis have been present for a long time. They have been ignored or the disease was not fully cleared. There is low back pain, aching in the bowel, a dragging in the groin. On sitting down or standing up, it can hurt slightly. There may be mild fever, or a general feeling of not being entirely well. A prostate massage and urinalysis may be required. Two urine specimens are taken just before the massage, and one just after. Drink copious amounts of water, and resist urinating two hours before examination to keep the bladder full:

- Void 10 cc of urine into a sterile culture cup.
- Void 200 cc into urinal — about half the volume in bladder.
- Void a second 10 cc urine in a second culture cup. Stop.
- Bend over, holding the prostate culture tube.
- Collect fluid from the prostate massage which is now performed.
- Void into a third sterile culture cup.
- Finish off by voiding in urinal.

Move cups under the stream so flow does not stop. Voiding is held back for massage only. Specimen one flushes out germs from the urethra, specimen two germs from the bladder, specimen three germs from the prostate. If bacterial counts are 10 times higher in specimen three than one and two, the diagnosis is chronic prostatitis.

Hospitalization and more than one antibiotic may be tried if chronic prostatitis is difficult to dislodge. Try to be patient. The infection may be deep within the prostate. If the condition continues to causes misery, if it seriously reduces the quality of life, surgery may be an acceptable option.

# Hallo, Sailor!

*Prostatodynia* is something of a mystery. It mimics the symptoms of prostatitis, with frequency, burning and urgency. But it is not the same thing. There is no fever as no bacteria are present. So it may be called non-bacterial, or non-specific, prostatitis. Prostatodynia is common amongst sailors. In marine circles, it is affectionately called "sailors disease." But any traveler can get it, so can a man who is sea-sick at the mere thought of a boat. It is linked with an irregular sex life — no ejaculation over a prolonged time followed by a period of high sexual activity. In this case, it is due to congestion. It rarely occurs if renewed sexual activity is average, not high. It may be partly responsible for pain after ejaculation.

Even more curious, only some men with irregular sex lives get prostatodynia. It is thought they hold back at ejaculation (stay erotically aroused) for longer than is appropriate. They learn to expect pain on urination and/or ejaculation, and do not suspect a partner of passing on sexual disease. Some do not bother with therapy. They continue, or abstain, from sex until the condition clears, usually in one to two weeks.

However, and especially with the first attack, it is understandable to be very concerned. When the symptoms appear, take the temperature to rule out prostatitis. If ejaculation has been avoided for some time, or if there has been a prolonged period of erotic play with no climax, masturbate to orgasm now. One option is to see a doctor in order to rule out prostatitis.

It seems storing ejaculatory fluids for prolonged periods of time is not good for prostate health. So regular ejaculation is a way to avoid prostate congestion. This does not mean an excess of sexual activity. It is not how often ejaculation occurs, but how regularly and completely the fluids are emptied out.

The risk of prostatodynia has health implications for the chronically ill or disabled, for men who spend long periods away from a partner, and for prisoners in jail. But the risk applies only to those who would have been very sexually active otherwise. And not all men are; from choice or temperament, or both.

If the health value of regular ejaculation were more widely known, might it soften society's attitude towards masturbation?

Might it help remove those feelings of shame or disgust attached to the act? And what implications might it have for men tempted to commit crimes, and trying to resist?

Recent research indicates other factors can trigger this mysterious condition: allergies, chlamydia, viruses and yeasts. *Truckers beware!* An injury to the buttocks, or discomfort from a long journey on a badly sprung seat, are implicated. Highly-spiced foods and strong doses of caffeine may also be involved.

## Sailor Therapy

Medical therapy for prostatodynia is limited. Antibiotics do not work, though a broad spectrum type will mop up other organisms which might be affecting the prostate. Tranquilizers and/or anti-spasm drugs help calm an acutely irritated condition. *However, a prostate massage brings immediate relief.*

Even if denied, lack of ejaculation may be suspected. It can be difficult to admit to abstinence, perhaps from mistaken pride. With retention, called *incomplete ejaculation,* not all the fluid contents are pumped out. This can also cause congestion. A prostate massage brings immediate relief.

If medical therapy is not a viable option, yet there is pain, follow the conservative therapy for prostatitis. Bed rest calms the inflammation. Sexual activity aggravates it. Wait until the pain subsides. If the symptoms are mild and cause little discomfort, maybe sailors know best as far as therapy goes.

As a preventive health step, avoid ejaculatory abstinence. If with a partner, increase the incidence of love-making; for younger men, up to four times a week. When traveling or without a partner, masturbate to orgasm at regular intervals. Avoid haste. Allow sufficient time for full and complete ejaculation.

## Cancer of the Prostate

Prostate cancer is the second most fatal male cancer. Lung cancer is the first. In the U.S. alone, there are 100,000 new cases each year, and 30,000 deaths. Its incidence increases with age, and is most common in the 60 to 80 age group. One in 11 men will suffer from the disease and it is on the increase; nobody knows why.

One theory suggests environmental causes, e.g., Japanese men living in Japan have a low rate of prostate cancer. If they move to Hawaii, this low rate soars, though it stays below the rate for the native population. A recent British study suggests lack of regular ejaculation increases the risk.

Black men in the U.S have the highest rate in the world. This only happened in the last few decades. A dietary factor may be over-consumption of saturated fats, which have the ability to change hormones in the body. Eat carrots for beta-carotene, which now seem to be an anti-cancer food.

Millions of men over age 50 have tiny cancer lumps in the prostate which are harmless and inactive (dormant). They appear benign. They do not grow. Death from natural causes occurs in the natural time span. Medical opinion is divided over whether to remove these inactive lumps or not. There is a risk surgery will activate dormant cells which then start to grow. Prostate cancer can be treated and cured if it is detected early enough. It would seem a prudent option to have regular colo-rectal examinations.

# Cancer Therapy

Malignant prostate cancer occurs mainly over age 60. Unhappily, in many cases, there are no obvious first signs. Pain comes on suddenly, in weeks rather than months. It hurts just above the pubic hairline, in the groin, or lower spine. Pain can spread to the legs. Until recently, the disease was rarely diagnosed until it was advanced, and little could be done. Regular colo-rectal check-ups now avoid this unhappy state.

## Radical Prostatectomy

This is surgical removal of the entire prostate and seminal glands. The operation saves life, but the side effects can be severe. Impotence usually follows in men over age 70. In younger men, potency generally returns within a year. At age 40 plus, 90 percent of men become potent again. At age 50 plus, it is 80 percent. At age 60 plus, 60 percent. Sadly, within all-age groups, 2.5 percent to 5 percent of men suffer some degree of incontinence.

## Radiation Therapy

There are a variety of ways in which radiation therapy is used. These depend upon the man's general health and how far the tumor has progressed. One type of radiotherapy is external beam radiation. The beam can be sharply focused on the tumor which avoids damage to nearby tissues. The course is spread over six to seven weeks. High doses of rads are involved. Only 50 percent of all-age men become impotent. But there is a chance radiation therapy does not destroy all the tumor cells.

## *Hormone Therapy*

If the female hormone estrogen is given, it stops testosterone production. Estrogen therapy can be an effective way to make the tumor regress. But the high doses put a strain on blood circulation. They increase the risk of blood clots in the heart or brain. Some surgeons recommend castration; both testicles are removed to stop further hormone production. Though this may seem unacceptable, it is an appropriate choice in very grave illness.

It is hoped new drugs in the trial stage will have the same effects as estrogen. They involve chemical castration without affecting blood circulation. They act by stopping the pituitary from producing luteinizing hormone which blocks the production of testosterone. And it is hoped a new combination therapy may be effective for milder cases. This is a very brief overview. If prostate cancer is diagnosed, ring 1-800-4-CANCER of the Cancer Information Service for more detailed information. Or send for free booklets by the Department of Health and Human Services, Public Health Service and National Institutes of Health.

# Gully's Luck

"I don't believe you," Gully said. "I've been lucky all my life."

The urologist winced. "I'm afraid your luck has not held up. There's no doubt it is cancer of the prostate."

"What are my chances?" Gully asked. "Am I going to die?"

"Choice of therapy depends on the degree of invading cells. Even when widespread, prostatic cancer responds well to therapy. If the tumor is small or local, the survival rate is equal to that of the general male population in your age group. Physical condition and normal life expectancy are taken into account. Also the quality of life after therapy. . . ."

"You mean you wanna neuter me," Gully growled.

The urologist continued, "At first hearing, the side effects can sound as bad as the tumor itself. But all therapies have a good rate of success. You should be in better physical shape. Cut out smoking. Drinking. Take exercise. You know the routine."

"Yes, yes. Take the joy out of life." Gully grinned. "Let me tell you, Doc. I've a stout heart and a stubborn mind. If this thing can be beaten by will power, I'm your man."

It wasn't easy. There were days when Gully was too weak to throw his weight around. There were times when he felt too sick to crack a joke. The worst time was when they said the surgery had made him impotent.

"Butchers," he snapped. "If you can take it away, you can damn well replace it."

And they did. As soon as he was strong and fit again, Gully was given a penile implant.

# CHAPTER 10

# The Baby

## In the Beginning

For the first five weeks of life, the reproductive organs are the same for both genders. They have the basic ingredients to become male or female. There is a raised genital ridge, which can develop into a penis or clitoris. There are raised folds which can develop into the scrotum or labia (vaginal lips).

Both develop a complete internal duct system. Special tissues on these ducts can develop into testicles or ovaries. A baby boy inherits programming for maleness on the Y chromosome of his father's sperm. During weeks five to eleven, the tissues on the ducts are instructed to become testicles.

At the same time, the genital ridge grows lengthwise to form an open penile tube. The raised folds migrate to the base of the penis to form an open scrotum. The open edges of the penile tube and scrotum join together in early fetal life. This "join" is like the safe zipping up of the genitals. Hypospadias is a rare birth defect in which this "join" is not complete.

Your baby's inheritance for maleness is his *genetic sex*. From conception, and throughout life till death, the instructions for virilization (maleness) cannot be changed. The XY chromosomes are in each body cell. When old cells die and are replaced by new ones, the XY chromosomes reform in the new nucleus.

## Eve Came First

When the testicles are made, they start producing male hormones. This happens some fifteen weeks after conception. The male hormones are sent to the brain stem. From here, they take over and control the growth of the sex organs. By three months, this is almost complete. Your baby boy is capable of spontaneous erections at about one hundred five days of fetal life.

Once the male hormones take over, his *biological sex* is set. This is *hormone gender*. It is also called his *genital sex* because this is how he will perceive himself after birth. The bits which are not needed are *vestigial*. They remain tiny and undeveloped. Men have vestigial blobs of what could have been the uterus and vagina by the prostate. Women have vestigial blobs of the testicles and prostate by the ovaries.

An added and important function of the male hormones is to suppress the female-making tissue from developing. This does not happen in baby girls; all embryos are originally programmed to be female. If something goes amiss, if the testicles are malformed or produce insufficient hormones, the fetus would develop into a baby girl. As far as nature is concerned, Eve came first.

This is a simplistic overview of embryonic development. More information can be found in books on early human development.

# It's a Boy!

"I can see that!" Jane said proudly. "Look at his testicles! They are red, puffy and sort of swollen-looking."

The midwife said, "Your hormones are circulating in Marvin's blood. They'll be flushed out soon. Within the next week or so."

Stan waited until the midwife left. "His penis looks tiny," he whispered. "Do you think he's, you know, all right?"

"It's a question of comparison," Jane said stoutly. "Wait till the swelling in his testicles dies down. Then his penis will look bigger. In proper proportion."

It is natural for parents to be concerned with penis size. Keep in mind the swollen testicles make the organ appear small. Avoid judging on comparative size. Avoid judging when the penis is relaxed. Your baby will have erections in the bath, at diaper changes and so on. Wait until then.

Parental concern with size can communicate itself, even to a tiny child. This concern can be buried in his unconscious, and emerge in adulthood with unhappy consequences. A whole life can be spent under the mistaken delusion that the penis is too small based on early parental concern. Try to avoid this.

# Micropenis

There is a condition called *micropenis* (microphallus) in which the penis is less than 2 cm in length. It is an extremely rare birth defect and the cause is unknown. The baby may be perfectly healthy otherwise. If the penis is properly formed with a clearly defined glans and shaft, the defect is an issue of size, not of shape.

More often, there is some malfunction of the sex hormones or testicles. There may be disorders of the chromosomes. Have your baby checked promptly. One medical option is to apply a mild testosterone cream to the micropenis for three to six months. It usually produces a moderate growth in size. If this fails, oral testosterone replacement therapy can be taken for three months.

A plastic *prosthesis* (artificial substitute) allows the boy to urinate standing up. It is of great psychologic value. At puberty, natural testosterone made by the newly working testes usually provokes an increase in penis size. If not, testosterone replacement therapy may solve the problem once puberty ends.

A difficult issue for some parents, whether or not to have their baby boy circumcised, is discussed in Chapter 2.

# Baby Swellings

Many baby boys are born with tiny swollen breasts. A whitish fluid may ooze from them. The fluid used to be called witch's milk, and was thought to have magical properties. The breasts and testicles are glands (unlike the penis), so they react to maternal hormones still in the blood. Avoid squeezing the breasts as it stimulates the milk flow. Both milk and breasts disappear within a few days.

Jane noticed a swelling on Marvin's shaft. The nurse said, "No problem! There can be more than one. We don't know what causes them. They are painless, and don't interfere with peeing. They usually disappear in the first weeks of life."

Jane took Marvin to Dr. Spink. He was disinterested. "We wrap the swelling in ice-cold dressings until it disappears. Or draw off the fluid by syringe. Neither therapy is pleasant for Marvin. Why not wait and see if it reabsorbs spontaneously? The self-healing process sorts out most minor problems in time."

"But," Dr. Spink warned, "If it gets bigger, do not try ice-cold therapy yourself.  Sudden cold induces shock and can be fatal in infants.  Come back for a further check next week."

## The Traveling Testes

The testicles start to develop forty days after conception, about the time a woman misses her second period.  They grow inside the fetal abdomen.  About four to six weeks before birth, they travel down the *inguinal canal* and through the abdomen wall.  They reach their low-hanging position in the scrotum a few days before birth.  A post-birth check ensures the testicles have descended.Undescended testicles occur in 3.4 percent of full-term babies.  About 50 percent of these descend during the first month of life.  Some 30 percent of premature babies have undescended testicles.  About 80 percent of these travel down before the first month.  If your baby's testicles are not in the scrotum by age 3 months, make sure they are checked again before his first birthday.  By age 18 months, there is a risk of infertility.  When Marvin started to walk, Jane noticed his testes move up and down out of the scrotum.  It happened when he coughed or cried.  This is called *retractile* or migratory testicles, a fairly common condition.  They usually descend  and stay permanently down of their own accord before puberty.

To be on the safe side, Jane asked Dr. Spink if retractile testes could be damaged in the same way as undescended ones?  Did Marvin need surgery?

"To be honest, I'm not sure," Dr. Spink said.

"What would you do if Marvin was your son?" Jane asked.

"Opt for orchiopexy," he replied.  "To be on the safe side."

## The Tender Testicles

A blow to the testicles is excruciatingly painful.  The pain is felt low in the abdomen, together with a sinking and sickening feeling.  The location of these feelings is where the testes grew in fetal life.  When they traveled down before birth, they took their nerve supply with them, and are still linked to it.

The testicles are outside the body, so are more vulnerable to accidental blows.  When boys play rough and tumble games, they rarely hurt one another in this area.  Perhaps they have an unconscious awareness of a shared vulnerability.  Small girls can inadvertently jump or stand on the testes and cause great pain.

When this happens, and the girl is admonished, she feels shame and confusion. But she also feels outrage; why did no one tell her boys are vulnerable down there? A child's picture book of simple anatomy can help resolve this problem.

# Baby Balanitis

*Balanitis* is a bacterial infection of the foreskin. If untreated, the bacteria spread and infect the entire glans. The area becomes red, swollen and tender. It is sore rather than painful. There may be discharge, pus produced at the infection site.

Balanitis is more common in circumcised babies in the first year of life as there is no foreskin to protect the newly exposed glans. Parents who opt for circumcision should be aware of this. Balanitis often follows diaper rash. Clean the genitals in a warm bath which helps loosen encrusted feces, or rinse away liquid ones. It avoids the risk of harsh wiping on delicate skin to remove traces of soiling.

A baby with a sore glans can be sweet-tempered during the day, but restless and unhappy at night. The physician will prescribe a mild antibiotic cream. To speed the healing process, leave off the diaper when possible.

# A Meatal Ulcer

Repeated infections of the glans, such as balanitis, can spread into the meatus (opening for urine). A meatal ulcer is an open sore inside the urethra (urine tube). The symptoms are crusts of pus, or spots of blood, around the meatus. The baby screams when he urinates. The pain is not due to a tight foreskin, as may be thought. It is due to hot urine which scalds the raw ulcerated tissue as it passes.

The healing process takes longer on movable body parts. Each time a protective scab forms, it can break open on movement. At urination, the penis moves slightly. Repeated breaking and re-forming of a scab can cause scarring which narrows the urethra. The narrower it gets, the more frequently the ulcer breaks open, the more pain the baby suffers each time he urinates.

To avoid this, take your baby to the doctor at the first sign of infection. A rod covered in antibiotic cream is put into the urethra. It holds the tube open to stop further narrowing, and gives the ulcer time to heal. The cream coats the ulcer, and protects it from hot urine. Surgery may be avoided in this way.

# Urethral Stricture

A few babies are born with *urethral stricture*. It is a birth defect in which the urethra is too narrow, or closed off. If untreated, the urethra would swell up under urine pressure, and death from *uremia* would result. This does not happen. The ability to urinate is checked soon after birth in the unlikely event the baby has not already obliged!

*Stricture can be a complication of poor circumcision.* If too much skin is left behind, it can adhere to the glans during the healing process. Or if the ragged edges of the wound do not heal well, infection can set in. Chaffing by diapers aggravates the condition. Scarring builds up and the urethra becomes blocked.

If surgery is required, a *meatotomy* opens the meatus wider. The debris of infection is cleared out. Parents are shown how to keep the meatus open so it does not heal by closing in on itself. A sterile tube is gently inserted into the meatus once a day for two weeks, and at longer intervals for a further two weeks. The wound should then heal with a satisfactorily wide opening. None of this is the least bit pleasant for the baby boy.

# Parent Help

Parents naturally feel alarmed when a beloved baby has penile problems. They suffer appalling emotions. They may demand to know nothing else is wrong. To calm parental anxieties, an *endoscopy* may be done. A tiny telescope is inserted in the penis to examine the urethra. A *biopsy* cuts tissue from the lining for analysis. It is a terrifying procedure for the baby, and very painful too.

Babies do not care one jot for parental worries. Nor do they appreciate the urologist's skill. They scream and struggle and refuse to lie still if an adult is hurting them. Their natural — and healthy — response is to try to stop the pain.

There is a serious risk of further harm in trying to treat a struggling baby. To avoid this, most hospitals "mummify" the infant first. He is encased in a tiny strait jacket so he cannot wriggle about. Parents who insist on further tests may be unaware of this mummifying procedure.

Keep in mind that, *medically speaking, no doctor can be 100 percent sure about anything*! And that when parents panic, urologists will give in; they will suggest further tests. Learn to trust in your baby's powers of self-healing. Painful procedures on an infant, if unnecessary, are a high price to pay for adult peace of mind. When the tests involve the genitals, the price can be higher. Unconscious dreads and fears can be the result, and cause sexual problems in adult life.

## An Older Child

If an older child requires genital therapy, find out exactly what is involved. One U.S. doctor says the only children frightened of a syringe are those with pre-knowledge that it hurts. When giving a shot, he neither mentions pain nor avoids the truth. The child is told to be ready for a sting, and to sit on his hands — just in case they fly up in surprise when the sting comes.

A child has less tolerance to pain than an adult. Asking him to participate reduces his fear. Prewarn warn your boy if therapy involves pain. Stay with him. Not all parents have a tender, intuitive attitude to a child's pain. It cannot be expected all physicians and nurses have the magic touch. Procedures which are quickest over may be considered the best route. Research shows they rarely are.

Two U.K studies found a single hospital admission of more than a week, or repeated short admissions before age five, are related to an increase in behavior disorders from age ten through the teens. Some hospital admissions are not really necessary. Ask if surgery can be on an out-patient basis, or stay with your son.

To a child's mind, pain inflicted by an adult, and which comes without warning, seems deliberate and terrifying. It can traumatize him. When hospitalized, he lives in constant terror of the next attack. Basic trust in parents is seriously undermined: why have they left him alone in this terrifying place? When basic trust is damaged, it can cause long-lasting problems at home.

## Hypospadias

Glandular hypospadias is a birth defect in which the urethra does not grow down to the tip of the glans. The meatus is some millimeters below the tip, "hypo" meaning "under." The shortened urethra acts like a bow-string, contracting one side of the penis and pulling it slightly inwards. The curve is usually downwards, and is called *chordee*.

Glandular hypospadias usually gives a boy no trouble. His father can explain how to take care when directing his stream. This is of value before the child attends preschool as urine can splash backwards onto his, or others, shoes. Take care when explaining this to a boy. There is a risk he may secretly worry or boast to his peers, and then become the butt of their jokes.

Some urologists call the condition *balanitic hypospadias*. It was thought to occur in approximately one in six hundred live male births. However, the incidence is on the increase; it is not known why. Perhaps early records were not well kept.

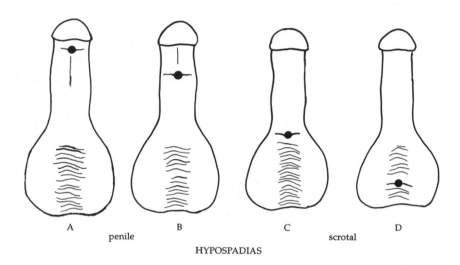

A               B               C               D
        penile                          scrotal
              HYPOSPADIAS

## *Penile Hypospadias*

When the meatal opening is on the shaft, it is called *penile hypospadias*. The degree of chordee may be pronounced. There may be tough fibrous tissue which is inelastic with no stretch or give near the urethra. The whole penis may be bent under, making urination difficult. There is pain on erection, and problems of penetration in adulthood.

Corrective surgery is available at age four or six, but the time varies widely. On no account should the baby be circumcised. The foreskin is essential to build up the penis, and will be removed during surgery. The urethra is reconstructed to extend to the tip. The chordee is resected so the penis straightens out.

## *Scrotal or Perineal Hypospadias.*

The penis may be attached to the scrotum, or the scrotum split in two. The testes may be undescended. In first degree hypospadias, the entire ventral groove of the genital join may be wide open. This serious condition requires the dedicated skills of a very experienced urologist and plastic surgeon to put things right. Some of the most worrying questions for parents are:

· Will our baby become a man?
· Will he suffer teasing at school?
· Will he be able to make love normally?
· Will he be able to give us grandchildren?

The answers depend upon the degree of defect. Urologists and plastic surgeons do their best to build a serviceable penis. Parents may gain some comfort from Professor Donald Smith's very sympathetic approach:

"Adequate surgical correction demands, above all, straightening of the shaft so that normal intercourse is possible. This must be followed by formation of a urethra which extends to or near the tip of the glans so that semen can be deposited deep in the vagina. For psychologic reasons, it is best that corrective surgery be completed before school age."

# Epispadias

"Epi" means "above." *Epispadias* is the opposite of hypospadias. The opening of the urethra is somewhere on the top side of the penis, and chordee is upwards. Epispadias is a serious defect. There may be damage to the bladder sphincters — the rings of muscle for urine control. A great deal of corrective surgery is needed, especially if the damage extends to the lower abdomen wall.

After surgery, some 50 percent of children remain incontinent and they lack bladder control. At first, this news can be shattering for parents. Counseling is available for the boy and the family. The child needs all the encouragement and love available to help him lead as normal a life as possible.

Fortunately, epispadias is a rarer birth defect: 1 case to 10 of hypospadias. Until the cause is known and preventable, the main hope lies in the surgeons' skills. They do their best in a tough battle to defeat nature at its worst. The microsurgery involved is very complex, and some results are startlingly good. Avoid despair. Your baby may belong in the fortunate group.

## Two of a Kind

Once in 5.5 million births, a baby is born with two organs. This is called *diphallic male genitalia.* One penis may be rudimentary, and the other well-formed. Or both may be equally well-formed. The urologist checks the structure of each to discover which has the better urinary tract. Typically, only one penis will have a urethra which is working well. The other organ is then removed. An equally rare birth defect is the development of the penis behind the testicles. An experienced microsurgeon can remove and reposition the penis in its correct place.

A baby born with testicles but no penis is usually raised as a girl. The testes are removed and an artificial vagina created. At puberty, estrogen therapy develops female secondary sexual characteristics: breasts, wider hips, rounder shape and so on.

The decision to remove the testes and raise the child as female may seem highly debatable. There are bound to be those who strongly disagree. To date, no artificial penis has been designed with full functioning ability. Whatever one's attitude, the issue does highlight the extent to which the penis is regarded as central to male self-image and self-esteem.

## Hermaphrodite

There are many ancient legends of babies born with both male and female organs. A favorite one tells of how Zeus decided to create the perfect godperson. S/he would be complete in every way. S/he had the ability to make love and self reproduce. Zeus called this fabulous creature Hermaphrodite.

Hermaphrodite grew so wondrous in every aspect that s/he became exceeding proud. Haughty and overbearing in complete self-fulfillment, s/he had no need to reach out to others for love. In lofty isolation, Hermaphrodite spent idle years in blissful self love. This annoyed Zeus. He was saddened and finally outraged. Taking up his mighty sword, with one terrible stroke he split Hermaphrodite in twain.

Then there were two godpersons: Hermes and Aphrodite. Each was a perfect man and a perfect woman. Perfect in every aspect, except each was no longer complete. Now each needed the other. Each knew the torments of loneliness. . . .

And so it has been, from that day forward. Hermes searching for his Aphrodite. Flesh of his flesh, the lost half of himself. And so it will be, from now until forever. Men and women forever incomplete, forever alone. Searching for wholeness by reaching out for love. Searching. . . forever searching. . . .

A true hermaphrodite is born with one (or more) testicle and one (or more) ovary which are functioning. In extremely rare cases, there is a clearly defined penis and a clearly defined vagina. More usually, there are indistinct parts of each. The presence of undefined genitals is an instant medical alert.

It is the functioning of both testicle and ovary which makes for a true hermaphrodite. This is not noticed until puberty, when a child presumed male may begin to grow breasts or experience monthly bleeding. However, the presence at birth of both penis and vagina, or their indistinct parts, is noticed immediately. A chromosome test verifies the baby's genetic sex. But in true hermaphroditism, there are mixed particles of both male and female chromosomes. Fortunately, the condition is extremely rare.

## What is Intersex?

A few babies are born in an unfinished stage of sexual development. It is their outer sex organs, the genitals, which are not clearly formed. The babies are not true hermaphrodites. Close inspection and, if necessary, a chromosome test shows their real gender. In 75 percent of cases, it is a girl with an extended clitoris which is mistaken for a penis. This inherited condition occurs in 1 in 25,000 births and is passed on by both parents. More rarely, it is a boy with a very small penis and undescended testicles. The internal sex organs are usually clearly formed.

Such babies are called pseudo, or false, hermaphrodites. The problem may be an inability of the adrenal glands to produce cortisone, while producing extra amounts of a hormone which has the ability to virilize girls, but does not affect boys.

A chromosome test shows true genetic gender. The level of both male and female hormones in the blood are checked. Once these factors are known, corrective surgery can help put things right. Afterwards, it likely that the child will lead a perfectly normal life.

If a baby lacks clearly defined genitals, it is crucial for his psychologic well-being that his true gender is discovered promptly. A boy's sexuality includes genetic sex, biological or genital sex, reproductive status, gender identity and body image together with the appropriate sexual responses, behaviors and values he has absorbed and been taught since infancy.

All these factors are powerful forces. They do not act in isolation, but are interdependent. They interact in a highly complex manner from early fetal life until puberty and profoundly affect his psychosexual orientation. If mistakenly raised as a girl, a boy has problems of thinking himself into maleness at puberty. Early medical intervention prevents these tragic cases. (Perhaps it should be stated here research has not yet found any link between homosexual, transsexual or other psychosexual behaviors and chromosome disorders or other genetic problems.)

## Let It Be. . .

This true tale happened some years ago. Empathetic parents should now avert their eyes.

"Maude was soaping her babies in the bath when the door bell rang. Thinking her darlings safe in two inches of water, she went to answer the door. On her return, she found her one-year-old baby daughter had drowned. Her three-year-old son was sitting in a gory mess, clutching a rusty razor blade in one plump little fist. Wanting to please his mother who had threatened to cut off his penis to stop him pulling on it, and to show he was a good boy, he had almost managed to completely severe it. . ."

Never tell a small boy his penis will drop off/ shrivel up/ be chopped off and so on. It may be said as a joke, but more usually threatened as punishment. It may be said in an attempt to stop the child pulling on his organ, especially in public places.

These kind of threats are not only dangerous; they are counterproductive. They force the child to clutch his precious penis even harder, and pull on it even more to make sure it is still there. It is the same behavior as that of an adult who keeps checking wallet or purse in areas where pick-pockets are rife. When there is risk of danger or loss, the natural response is to clutch ever more tightly.

Most children play with their genitals. It is now considered unusual if they do not! And little boys are especially proud of their "willie" sticking out. One of the things parents learn to accept about children is that if they can embarrass you in public, then they certainly will!

164

Two simple suggestions for such child management are: 1) If unacceptable behavior is ignored, it soon loses its appeal. 2) If scolded or fussed over, it develops into an attention-grabber.

A boy who cannot stop handling his penis may be suffering from inappropriate stimulation. A bored child will find ways to excite himself and the penis is handy. An over-excited child will find ways to calm himself down. The penis is used as a soothing or exciting mechanism, according to psychologic need.

Consider altering the level of stimulation. Is there enough unconditional love? Harsh or constant criticism can cause penis clutching. So can inconsistent care behavior which is acceptable one day should not be unacceptable the next. The confusion this causes makes a child clutch himself for psychologic support. When these factors are adjusted, the penis ceases to be the focus of needs.

CHAPTER 11

# Puberty

## Changes at Puberty

*Puberty* is the transition period from physical and sexual immaturity to maturation. The young boy's body becomes *virilized*, and turns into a man. The process takes an average of three years, usually between the ages of 12 and 15. By the end of puberty, the reproductive organs are functioning, and the boy is capable of fathering a child.

*Adolescence* follows puberty, and can be perceived as a "catching up" process. Though the boy becomes an adult in the reproductive sense at age 15, he lacks the skills of maturity in other respects. Adolescence is concerned with his intellectual, social and emotional maturation. It is thought to continue until the late teens, or early twenties. Not all changes at puberty are pleasant. Many men can recall at least one change they disliked, and which caused distress. Worries over body image are not uncommon. Loss of self-esteem can lead to acute shyness, even depression. Added to this, there is the competition factor between age mates.

Both boy and parents benefit from knowing that puberty and adolescence are the most widely variable stages in life. Averages for maturation are given in this chapter, but do not mean very much. Natural human variation results in some boys developing earlier than others. Schoolboy teasing over this can be cruel.

At puberty, a boy's behavior is usually juvenile. So parents may be unaware of his worries and fears. Studies show many boys have problems of body image at puberty. For a few, these are warning signs of psychosexual difficulties in adult life. A boy who is given appropriate information together with reassurance and approval in his early teens may sail through puberty on a fairly even keel.

Research shows boys have little or no interest in preventive health. They visit the physician's office only if they are injured or very sick, or need a certificate to join, or abstain from, sports. They rarely make appointments. If they do, they may not show up. Teen boys are the "great absent" from the health care scene, closely followed by their dads.

Yet it is during these years boys form patterns of diet, exercise and seeking medical help which will influence their health for the rest of their life. This chapter is for parents who require information on the changes at puberty. It might also be considered appropriate for the boy himself to read.

## The Growth Spurt

Puberty starts with a growth spurt, a sudden height increase due to rapid skeletal (bone) development. There is more than one spurt during puberty. Each follows a distinct pattern of order:

The head, feet and hands begin enlarging to adult size.
Next, the arm and leg bones grow longer and stronger.
Last, the trunk begins to develop to full male size.

It is not unusual for a boy to grow 1 1/2 inches in eight weeks. The bones become harder, more solid and less flexible. Under pressure, they fracture rather than bend. Height increase may continue until age 18, or more. A boy who begins puberty later than his peers may worry over his short stature. He gains comfort by knowing height at age 15 is no indicator of final adult height.

Bones grow at different times, e.g., the hand bones start to enlarge four months before the lower arms. There is a slight loss of symmetry — hands appear too large for arms until the limb bones catch up. Movements become clumsy; objects tend to break and body collisions occur when a "gangly" teen is around.

Each accident reinforces a painful sense of awkwardness. Scoldings or jokes make the condition worse. Explain what is happening with re-assurances that this stage soon passes. Exercise improves co-ordination. Encourage a reluctant boy by telling him young athletes rarely suffer from this lack of physical grace.

# Body Strength

From ages 12 to 16, a boy's heart weight nearly doubles, and the heart rate slows down. There is an increase in blood pressure, volume and red blood cell count. Body temperature falls. Lung capacity increases, and the breathing rate slows down. Muscle stamina and strength almost double. Athletic ability soars due to increased production of the male sex hormone testosterone. It enables the synthesis of nitrogen from protein into greater muscle mass.

Appropriate diet is essential for health at any life stage. It is of particular value at puberty. Slender boys can appear to "outgrow their strength." Their movements seem listless and restless at the same time. They are easily fatigued. Some suffer "growing pains," which are night aches in the limb muscles and bones. Avoid over-exercise. Increase fluid intake and relaxation time. Keep the limbs warm at night.

Proteins, the body building foods, are essential during the growth spurt. Vegetarians, especially vegans, need large amounts of a wide variety of plant proteins for nutritional balance. Whatever his size, a boy's appetite should be hearty. A rule of thumb is that it should be be equal to, or larger than, a man's. If the appetite is poor, he may need "babying" with favorite foods for a while. Or he could be filling up on low nutrition snacks. Make sure mealtimes are calm and unhurried. Avoid reprimands. If he dines alone, suggest he reads or otherwise engages the mind, to stop eating from becoming boring.

The teens are the "make or break" years for posture. Muscle and bone develop rapidly to support the emerging adult frame. A tall boy may stoop until he adjusts to sudden height increase. He may slouch or bury his neck in his shoulders. There is a slight risk of poor body alignment in adulthood. Nagging over posture is counter-productive as the boy shields himself from the painful words by hunching over further. Adult example is the appropriate teacher. Exercise also works.

The benefits of sleep may be under-valued at this age. Ten hours are recommended, though not always achieved. Motivate a reluctant youth to get to bed at a reasonable hour by explaining that the growth hormone works best during sleep. All boys long to be tall.

In late adolescence, a strong and final boost occurs to the building of a powerful frame and the strength of bones. Heavy drinking during this period affects this. Weaker bones and a less powerful frame may not be noticeable now, but can be responsible for osteoporosis in later years. Avoid excess alcohol in the late teens.

# Skin Changes

The peaches-and-cream complexion of childhood disappears in the teens. The skin becomes thicker and slightly coarse in texture. Testosterone is responsible, as it is for the oily skin of adult men. It causes greater sebum production in the sebaceous glands. Overactivity of these glands is common at puberty, and causes acne.

Acne is inflammation of the sebaceous glands. It is thought the thickening skin plugs the pores, and sebum cannot escape. The trapped sebum hardens and darkens, forming a blackhead. Or it becomes a sore and angry-looking lump which spreads and leaks fluid under the skin. The usual places are the forehead, cheeks and chin. It can spread to the shoulders, chest and back.

Over 50 percent of boys suffer at least one attack between ages 14 and 18. For mild cases, wash regularly, dab weak antiseptic on leaking spots and, perhaps, remove the more unsightly blackheads. Increase fluid intake. Work and play outdoors when possible. Mild acne usually clears by the early 20s. Severe acne can cause infected cysts and permanent scars. The physician may prescribe antibiotics, Retin A or Acutane. Teens often share medications, so warn your son Acutane can cause birth defects in pregnant girls.

Acne is a major source of teen embarrassment. A boy, already uncertain of his role, can be extremely self-conscious. He imagines everyone is staring in horror at his poor blemished face. Reassure him others do not notice his spots half as much as he fears.

# Body Odor

In mid puberty, *apocrine glands* in the armpits and groin begin working. They produce a thicker heavier sweat with a musty body smell. It is a special individual odor, and not unattractive when fresh. But when stale, bacteria quickly breed on the sweat and the odor becomes offensive.

From puberty and throughout life, the feet are another source of heavy sweating in males. Unlike body odor, the smell is unpleasant even when fresh. Toenail hygiene is often overlooked. The nails grow long and unkempt, and odorous debris collects underneath. Daily washing, dusting with talc, change of socks and a weekly home pedicure will keep the feet smelling sweet. Going barefoot when possible is excellent therapy for growing feet.

Some adults regard apocrine sweat as a *pheromone*, a sexual attractant. From insects to apes, animals secrete pheromones in order to attract mates. To date, there is no evidence human apocrine sweat has the same effect. Nevertheless, there is an expanding market for smell attractants. These claims may or may not be suspect: the contents appear to do no harm.

# Fungus Infection

*Tinea* is a fungus infection of the skin, common in teen boys. The fungus grows in a ring, hence its nickname "ringworm," though it has nothing to do with worms. Tinea is highly contagious. It spreads rapidly in warm weather. There are frequent outbreaks in schools, colleges and sports clubs during the summer months. The fungus spores are too small to be seen with the naked eye. They pass by contact, especially shared use of towels, shoes and combs. They are picked up on bare feet from gymnasia floors, and the wooden slats in locker rooms and swimming pools.

The most common form of tinea is *athlete's foot*. It starts between the toes, and often spreads to the heels. The infected patches turn white and soggy when damp. They peel off, leaving a red raw area underneath. Anti-fungal powders and creams are usually non-prescription. Follow the directions exactly. Remember to dust inside footwear with anti-fungal powder. Athlete's foot does not live up to its name. It infects "couch potatoes" as well as highly active boys.

Tinea, the inelegantly named "jock itch," grows on the inside upper leg. A typical patch grows 5 to 7 cm across, and can be very itchy. Due to its position, it looks alarming. However, it is not serious. Apply anti-fungal medication directly on the patch. Wash hands thoroughly afterwards because tinea can spread to the finger nails. Dust anti-fungal powder liberally inside trouser legs, pajamas and shorts. If the patch enlarges or spreads, consult with the physician for oral medication.

*Nail-biters beware*! Tinea spreads rapidly along the bitten edge of a cuticle and under the nail itself. An infection here is painful as well as itchy, and can be difficult to treat. If severe, the whole nail lifts and separates from the underlying tissue, and may have to be removed.

When facial hair first appears, tiny spots can develop on the cheeks and chin. These are not acne, and soon subside. Take care to avoid pulling the skin taut, and shaving the face too close. This causes the hair to spring back into its follicle. On regrowth, it travels under the skin and forms a septic bump.

There is a great thrill in having a first shave. It takes a little while and a few experiments to decide which type of razor best suits the skin. Whatever the choice, keep shaving equipment scrupulously clean. Tinea fungus can infect the skin under newly growing facial hair. Wipe surface of an electric razor with anti-fungal cream or use disposable razors until the infection clears. (Tinea of the scalp is more likely before puberty.)

## Adam's Apple

Towards the end of puberty, the larynx (voice box) enlarges. The vocal cords increase in both thickness and length. This results in the "voice breaking" process. The higher pitched tones of childhood are slowly replaced by the deeper bass sounds of the adult male. It takes three to nine months for the larynx to grow to adult size. During this time, there is a switching back and forth between a piping childhood pitch and the deeper adult tones. To make matters worse, there are times when only high squeaks are emitted as the growing cords adjust to their new size.

The enlarged larynx is popularly called the Adam's apple. On a slender neck, it looks painfully prominent for a while. But the squeaking and prominence do not last for long. When thicker neck muscles of the adult man develop, the Adam's apple becomes less noticeable by comparison. The voice breaking process can be annoying. But it is over in a few months, and it is interesting to guess what depths of tones will emerge.

## Breast Growth

*Gynecomastia* are male breasts. They occur in half of all pubertal boys. The swellings may be slight, or fairly pronounced. They are due to the rising levels of testosterone and estrogen reacting with normal breast tissue. The swellings disappear within one or two years. If not, consult with the physician.

Gynecomastia is a major source of embarrassment in the early teens. The boy may refuse to participate in sports if he has to remove his shirt. Communal showers are a torment; keep in mind

172

peer teasing can be cruel. On such days, episodes of truanting or hypochondria (imagined ill-health) are the usual escape routes. The boy may implore surgery to correct his unhappy state.

Gynecomastia is more common in plump boys. Weight reduction brings health benefits as well as aesthetic ones. A note to his teacher may allow him to wear his shirt during exercise, and to shower at home. When shopping for clothes, avoid T shirts and narrow sweaters. Choose loosely fitting shirts of bulky material which help to disguise his shape. A smart coat or bomber jacket boosts self confidence which encourages the boy to "walk tall."

# Genital Development

On average, the genitals take three years to develop to adult size and function. Being oval-shaped, the testicles can be measured by volume increase. Before puberty, they are 1 to 3 ml. In adults, 12 to 25 ml. Rather like the growth spurt, genital development occurs in a distinct pattern of order. The stages are numbered:

1. The testicles and scrotum begin to enlarge. The scrotal skin reddens and changes in texture.

2. Sparse pubic hair starts to grow at the base of the penis. This may cause a few small spots to appear.

3. The penis begins to enlarge both in length and girth. The testes and scrotum continue to grow.

4. Pubic hair develops color. It becomes darker and coarser and covers a wider area.

5. There is a further size increase in the penis and testicles. The glans is now fully developed and distinct.

6. Pubic hair is adult in character and distribution. Upper lip, armpit and body hair appear.

7. Sperm production reaches the appropriate level for nocturnal emissions to start.

8. There is a sudden increase in body strength and the genitals reach complete adult size and shape.

Stage 1 begins at age 11.8 years, with a time spread of just over a year either way. Stage 8 is reached at 14.11 years, with a time spread of 1.1 years. The maximum growth spurt occurs during Stage 3. But keep in mind puberty is the most widely variable of all life stages. Though the average maturation period is 3 years, it can range from 1 to 5 years in a perfectly healthy boy. The prostate and seminal glands also develop to adult size and begin working. At the end of a puberty, all parts of the boy's sexual system is fully functioning. It has reached the same sexual maturity as that of an adult man.

# Torsion

Torsion arises from a birth defect in which the testicles hang free in the scrotum. If a testis dangles freely, it can twist around on its cord. This twisting is called *torsion*. It can destroy the testicle. Though torsion is fairly rare, all parents of pubertal boys should be aware of the symptoms.

When the cord twists, the blood vessels inside are squeezed tight. Hot fresh blood still enters as it is pumped in under pressure. But the cooler used blood, which flows more slowly, is trapped and cannot get out. The testicle quickly swells up. No more blood can get in or out. There is pain, usually sudden and severe. There may be nausea and vomiting. The lower abdomen may hurt. "Swelling-with-pain" always requires urgent investigation.

*Torsion is a surgical emergency.* At detorsion, the testicle is untwisted and stitched firmly in the scrotum. It is a simple 10 minute procedure. The time factor is critical. If the cord is not untwisted four to six hours after the symptoms begin, the testicle starts to atrophy, to wither and die. Slowly yet surely, the life is strangled out of it. Recovery is possible in the next 12 to 24 hours. After this, the chances of life are slim. After 48 hours, an *orchidectomy* is required to remove the dead testicle.

Torsion is usually unilateral, on one side only. But when one testis has twisted, the other is at risk. At detorsion, both testicles should be stitched in place. Be sure this is done. It used to be thought torsion occurred mainly in newborns. In older boys, the testes become swollen and hurt for many reasons, and the correct diagnosis was often overlooked. New technology helps diagnosis by use of ultrasound and the Doppler stethoscope. If blood is heard swooshing in and out of the testis, the problem is not torsion.

It is now known 65 percent of torsion cases happen between ages 12 and 18. It can also occur in the early 20s. More rarely, at a later age.

A few boys have a history of mild "swelling-with-pain" which remits spontaneously. Parents may think it of no real concern. Beware! Avoid waiting for the pain "to get better by itself." If the swelling is bilateral and surgery is delayed, the boy cannot mature into manhood — a tragedy beyond words.

Note the swelling-with-pain combination. This is the key for alarm bells to ring. Infections such as mumps can cause the same symptoms. Avoid parental diagnosis. Under age 21, always suspect torsion. Take the boy to the emergency room at once.

It is not unknown for a boy who thinks masturbation evil to believe the symptoms are due to his actions. He then endures the pain until it becomes excruciating, by which time it may be too late. Should a boy be told of the risk of torsion? Will he become anxious? Parents can estimate the degree of information; a sensitive youth need only know to report swelling with pain in the testicles at once.

# Dreams

As sexual maturity develops, the prostate and seminal glands fill with fluids. Sexual tension begins. The first experience a boy may have of release is ejaculation during sleep. These ejaculations are "wet dreams," or *nocturnal emissions*. The boy wakes to find the bed damp; or to find he is masturbating in a half-dream state. Once the pleasure of orgasm subsides, he feels relaxed and secure in his manhood. If he was taught to regard masturbation as evil, he suffers self-loathing and guilt.

The "sex object" of his erotic dreams may be a person in the public eye — an actress or sports star. It could be much nearer home — a sister, mother, school teacher, friend. If in the latter group, the boy is shocked and frightened by what appears to be wildly inappropriate content of his erotic dreams. It is unlikely he will discuss this with parents. It is usually an invasion of privacy for parents to pry.

He needs reassurance over the nature of dreams, and their all-too-frequent astonishing contents. He benefits from knowing the libido translates his admiration of certain adults into a fantasy of physical desire. He may consider himself wicked and unnatural, not understanding that all humans have fantasy lives which are unreal. A well-informed book or a conversation of dreams and fantasies in his presence often helps to allay fears.

# The Solo Act

For boys, the word "masturbation" has a curious ring. They tend to confuse it with "menstruation" in health class at school. Both are long, difficult to spell and even harder to pronounce. For bolder youth, the temptation to write "master baiting" is not easily overcome!

Masturbation is almost a given in the teens. The levels of testosterone circulating in the blood peaks at age 18. Spontaneous erections can occur at any hour of the day or night. They can happen at highly inconvenient times. Deprived of an outlet for sexual tension, the boy masturbates or is awakened by nocturnal emissions — wet dreams at night.

Many dads find it difficult to discuss sexual matters with their sons. Boys find it equally difficult to broach these topics with older kin. Erections and masturbation are private matters, after all. The questions which most concern a boy, but which he is most unlikely to ask, are:

- Is it abnormal?
- Can other people tell?
- Does it use up all my sperm?
- Will it harm my ability to make love as a man?
- Am I doing it too often? How much is enough?

# Parent Help

Parents and other concerned adults can try the same approach as they would for teenage spots. For spots, a boy needs to know:

- Why he is getting them.
- Why they are a normal part of the teens.
- Why he should keep his skin clean.
- Why people do not notice them half as much as he thinks.
- Why his skin will not behave like this once his hormones settle down, i.e., when he is a man.

Substitute erections for spots. It may help to hint the bath or shower is a useful place. It is warm, clean and private, and no one can tell. A mention that adults make love 2.5 times a week, and that his hormones will settle down, helps a sensible boy understand there is moderation in all things.

Girls of this age are generally unaware of the phenomena of spontaneous erections. They delight in showing off their newly-developing charms. If a boy erects, they think he deliberately willed this state. They do not understand he has little control at this age. Being naive themselves, they believe his unwilled erections are due solely to their charms. A few then imagine they have unlimited sexual power.

A boy can feel humiliated by this treatment. He perceives it as deliberate "sexploitation." He feels angry and embarrassed at the tell-tale bulge in his pants. It is a psychic assault to be at the mercy of a schoolgirl he may not even like. To add insult to injury, the girl has greater skills of maturity than he.

To regain self-esteem, the boy may mutter coarse insults just within her hearing. Or he spreads improbable tales of her unbridled sexual behavior behind her back. Every schoolboy knows the most wounding of insults: "prick teaser," "slag," "cunt." Most school girls hear them at some time in the teens.

Bewildered and hurt, the girls fight back with the only weapons they have. They flash their charms further; they taunt more daringly by gesture and touch. This results in more unwanted erections, anger and embarrassment. Some boys develop femaphobia (girl hatred), a sorry state of affairs at any life stage.

Not all girls behave in this manner. But the spirited ones do. Though they know it is inappropriate, they do not understand why. If daughters are told of spontaneous erections, they can make informed choices over their subsequent behavior. They can opt to deserve the schoolboy insults, or not. While information may not remove all the socio-sexual problems of puberty, it may help reduce some of the gender battles, confusion and hurt.

## Homosexual Fears

Puberty begins and ends two years earlier for girls than boys. The male maximum growth spurt does not begin until age fourteen. So a fourteen-year-old girl is usually taller and more mature than her male age mate. From the mid-teens, her growth slows down while his shoots up. By age sixteen, he has outstripped her in height, weight and strength.

Before age sixteen, the disparity in growth does not make for relaxed relationships between the genders. Boys dislike being looked down upon, literally, by girls. As intellectual, emotional and social skills follow the same maturation pattern, some boys resent what they perceive as a superior attitude from their female age mates.

Same-sex friends are perfectly natural in the teens, as at any age. Due to the maturation disparity, there is a special security in them. They are rarely signs of emerging homosexual behavior. A homosexual boy may be aware of same-sex orientation long before puberty. As a small child, he does not understand this awareness but recognizes that he is somehow different at a much earlier age.

Many heterosexual boys experiment with homosexual practices at summer school, scout camp and so on. Even at home and under close supervision, boys experiment with mutual masturbation. These activities do not create homosexuals, nor do they interfere with the development of adult heterosexual desire. Same-sex friends are a normal part of the maturation process, whether intimacy occurs or not.

According to one survey, two-thirds of America's 11 million teenage boys have had sexual intercourse with a girl. The first time for most was around age 15. The boys said peer pressure was responsible for early frequent sex without real relationships. Be that as it may, another survey found 50 percent of boys retained their virginity until age 17.

Yet another study found parents provide major encouragement for boys "to get involved." It seems parents of both genders show concern over a son's appeal to girls. Unconsciously, they want him to be sexually active to prove he is manly. Consciously, they want him to wait. Where does this unspoken parental pressure come from if not from needless fears of homosexuality?

Homophobia is a deep and irrational fear of homosexuals. It is prejudice so extreme that many otherwise enlightened parents cannot cope with it. The concerns of this book are not to tackle prejudice. But those who are interested may find the following article of some use.

# A Homosexual Son

What creates homosexuality is not understood. One theory suggests it starts in fetal life. In some five percent of cases, brain clusters are not sufficiently masculinized during the sixth month. This could be due to an enzyme not triggering sufficient testoster-

one production. Or there is an androgen-sensitivity, so
oping fetus lacks sufficient male hormones.

The baby boy is perceived as more passive than the
child. This can set up a vicious circle within his envi
Adult expectations of male behavior are assertion and aggression.
If he fails to meet these criteria, the stress on him to conform can
be painful, and damaging to his psychologic growth.

In some cases, the boy is isolated with his parents, an only child.
In others, the punishments he receives are too harsh or otherwise
inappropriate for his temperament. He suffers low self-image and
self-esteem from peer group bullying at school. It is not surprising
he develops a fear of intimacy. On a desperate search for self-ap-
proval, he avoids the critical aspect of the opposite sex.

Parents can accept the fact that a son has no choice over his
temperament. He is himself, a blessing to those who raise and love
him, and may become a truly sensitive man. This theory does not
answer all questions, only a few. But it does explain why homosexuality has been a constant down through the ages. The issue of
homosexual development will be discussed in more detail in the
author's next book *How to Raise a Son Successfully*.

## Not Too Early. . .

*Precocious puberty* is very early sexual maturity. It is generally
considered precocious if sexual development begins before age 10.
Most early developers are healthy and normal, and the reason is
constitutional. Check male history on both sides of the family for
an inherited disposition towards early sexual maturity. If present,
share this information with the boy.

It is unusual for precocious puberty to cause precocious sexual
activity. Parents and other concerned adults can be free from this
fear. But a boy who matures earlier than his age mates feels
isolated from them. Sex information helps him understand what
is going on. If not, such things as wet dreams or breast growth can
cause strange alarms and fears. The stress of these will further
isolate him from his peers.

Problems of adjustment arise because the boy looks more mature than he actually is. Adults can easily forget his mental, social
and emotional skills do not keep pace with physical precocity. The
boy may be given responsibilities or tasks he is not mature enough
to cope with. Emotionally, he is expected to "act like a man" when
what he really needs is re-assurance and hugs. Children, espe-

cially siblings, may cruelly tease his clumsy movements, lofty height, prominent Adam's Apple and so on.

At school, a bright boy benefits from being in a higher grade. A less academic youth can join older boys for exercise and sport. This enables him to interact with children his own size without knocking them down. He is freed from "unfair" advantage due to greater height and muscle mass, and keeps his enjoyment of physical activity keenly alive.

In rare cases, precocious puberty is due to endocrine or brain disorders. There are usually signs of other serious things amiss; consult with the physician. (Precocious puberty is eight times more common in girls, and starts at age eight. It is directly related to body weight, so plump little girls suffer on both counts: they feel "different" and "fat." Information, love, approval and sensible management help to reduce anxiety and distress.)

## Not Too Late. . .

There is no general agreement over the age for *delayed puberty*. The two medical indicators are: no increase in testicle size by age 14 and no growth spurt by age 16. Until then, the boy is considered a "late" developer. Like precocious puberty, it is an inherited disposition, and no cause for concern. But by age 15, if neither indicator is present, consult the physician. Delayed puberty can be more of a handicap than precocity. Contact sports and athletic ability are highly valued at this age. A late developer is small, lacks muscle mass and body strength. His larger age mates perceive him a hindrance on the team. He is the youth found lurking in the background, pretending not to care when he is always picked last.

The pain of this means enjoyment of sport is quickly lost. Nor is it always in the boy's best interest to insist upon his unwilling participation. Encourage solo activities: gymnastics, swimming, lifting weights and so on. These develop his physical skills under more comfortable conditions without distress, and so help to boost his body-image and self-esteem.

It is less easy to resolve the problems of interaction with girls. Having developed two years earlier, they make him appear more immature than he actually is. They may spurn his company, or treat him as the classroom pet. These are tremendous assaults on his dignity, his body image, and his self-esteem.

A follow-up study of late developers found at age 33 they had lower status jobs than the early maturers. They married at later ages, had fewer children and earned less money. Parental empathy produces a gentle tact and sensitivity which helps him through this difficult time. Praise, reassurance and hugs boost self-image, and prevent damage to his self-esteem.

## But Just Right. . .

The tendency to start puberty early or late is inherited; it runs in families. In almost all cases, the boy is maturing at the right time for him. In general, black children mature before white, those in hot climates before those in cooler zones, those whose parents are in skilled rather than unskilled occupations. As weight is now known to be the trigger which stimulates puberty in girls, it may well be the same factor in boys.

Ignore parental pride at early development. It is not always as desirable as it might seem. Recent studies show certain female cancers occur more often in girls who start puberty young, another reason to watch prepubertal weight and, if necessary, correct the diet.

On a social level, early developers attract a great deal of hero worship from their peers. Boys are extremely competitive over height, muscle mass and physical prowess. The boy who receives too much hero worship can grow complacent and arrogant. If girls shower him with admiration, such easy conquests make his attitude towards them patronizing, even cruel. An added problem of overindulgent parents can result in laziness, under-achievement at school and neglect of inner life.

At school, a tall boy who is gentle-natured may be picked as a target for fights. These challenges come from age mates bruised by their own lack of height. It is an unhappy state of affairs for tall boys. They stand erect like great oaks, stolid and mute, battered by smaller yet highly punishing fists. Unaware of the pain of being short, tall boys are bewildered by the hostility they (unconsciously) call forth. If the fights are suppressed, the boy is still likely to be made something of an outcast. Explain these facts to a tall gentle-natured son to avoid his becoming something of a recluse.

## Awful Adolescence?

An adolescent boy is an exquisitely sensitive plant. Parents may be excused if they sometimes forget this when faced with an over-critical, arrogant, self-centered youth! Such unattractive behavior is a defense mechanism to hide the flaws the boy perceives in himself. Mood-swings, often put down to hormones, are more usually fears of an unacceptable body image and low self esteem.

Spurning parental advice and criticizing their lifestyle are part of the natural search for autonomy. Denial of adult values is a youthfull attempt to find his own. There is no excuse for obnoxious behavior; avoid tolerating it. But a boy's struggles for independence are a critical factor in his becoming mature.

If serious conflicts erupt, consider whether adult reins are appropriate for his age group. If so, be certain they are consistently held. Reins which are too lax one day, and too rigid the next, result in a boy taking tremendous risks, in case he has the right day! The flooding of his system with testosterone is partly responsible for the risk-taking nature of youth.

If the early parent/child relationship was satisfactory, this stormy stage soon passes — and without too much pain. If the relationship was unsatisfactory, parents should not hesitate to seek professional help. Unconsciously, the boy is seeking revenge, he wants to hurt the world now he is big enough to repay the pain of his childhood. A large angry youth, unaware of his motives, is a danger to himself, his family — anyone in his path.

Moral values aside, early sexual activity is inadvisable. It involves high levels of anxiety: lack of time, space, privacy, comfort, fear of failure, discovery, disease, pregnancy, heart break. Such anxiety is thought to be a major cause of ejaculation distress. Not all early love-making ends in disaster. But teen marriage due to unwanted pregnancy blights many a promising young career.

Dads taking sons for initiation at the local whorehouse is a male fantasy of dubious intent. It assaults the boy's privacy, denies his autonomy and keeps the reins of power firmly in dad's hands. Records of the experience found in fiction spell out the son's (secret) rage at the father's intent.

Adolescents see issues in terms of black and white. There is rarely, if ever, an acceptance of grey. They lack the skills of maturity to accept people, especially parents, as mixtures of frailty and strengths. Yet teens and parents both are learning new roles. They are equally capable of mistakes.

Share this with a growing boy. Admit to frailties. Avoid power boasting of strengths. Above all, keep the lines of communication open.

# CHAPTER 12

# Potency Problems

## Mind or Body?

*Potency* can be defined as the psychological desire for, and the successful completion of, the act of sexual intercourse. Whether a man ejaculates or not, he is potent if he desires to make love and can do so when the opportunity occurs.

*Impotence* can be defined as failure to erect in one fourth of attempts. It has two causes:

1. The body is handicapped in some way due to organic disease. This is *physical impotence*.

2. The psychologic desire is weak or absent. This is *psychogenic impotence*. Also called non-specific impotence.

The psychiatrist Sigmund Freud called impotence "the most prevalent failure of human life." Estimates in the U.S. alone suggest 15 to 20 million men suffer — one in eight males. In Freud's day, almost all cases were diagnosed as psychogenic. This is now known to be hopelessly inaccurate. Cynics say the reason for the wrong diagnosis was physicians did not know how to help!

It is now estimated 70 percent of cases are physical in origin; there is some organic disorder. Keep in mind even minor health problems rarely act in isolation but interact with other systems. So impotence can be perceived as a valuable health warning.

The four main organic disorders in their order of occurrence are:

1. *Diabetes*, or pre-diabetes, which has not yet been diagnosed.

2. *Blood flow disorders* which interfere with erections: hardening of the arteries, high blood pressure and heart disease.

3 *Nerve disorders* which prevent the messages to erect from getting through. These are neurological conditions.

4. *Low testosterone* reduces the sex drive. Hormone dysfunction is the least common cause of physical impotence.

5. *Psychogenic impotence* is due to stress factors (often in the unconscious) which inhibit the erection process.

Whether physical or psychogenic, impotence feels much the same — calamitous. Once it starts, it is almost impossible for a man not to suffer distress. Behavior may become cranky and it can be difficult to unravel a physical cause from a psychogenic one. Because mind and body are not separate, *physical impotence causes psychologic distress and the other way around*.

Some men can erect, but not stay erect. They can "have" but not "hold." This may seem a needlessly fine distinction but in issues of distress, fine distinctions matter. A man who perceives himself as impotent may become extremely upset. If he perceives himself as having a slight *maintenance problem*, he can stay on a more even keel.

Age is an important factor to consider. As a rule of thumb: At age 40, 80 percent is *psychogenic* in origin, and 20 percent physical. At age 80, 80 percent is *physical*, and 20 percent psychogenic. Whatever the cause of impotence, all men should know *both kinds can be successfully treated or managed in about 95 percent of cases*.

The next paragraphs include investigative self help to work out if the problem is physical or psychogenic; also, behaviors to avoid, and those which may be appropriate. Diabetes is the number one cause of potency loss. It is essential for health to first consult with a physician to rule this out.

# Avoid Humiliation

At age 53, Stan was having erection problems. His health was OK, so he feared the problem was psychogenic — "all in the mind." The idea of seeking professional help gave him the shudders. He intensely disliked what he called "embarrassing psycho-babble." He reckoned his aversion was a natural and healthy response. Stan longed for something to be physically wrong because it is easier to accept problems in terms of poor health. Eventually, this longing grew overwhelmingly acute. It encouraged the secret hypochondriac lurking in all of us. Stan seized upon every snuffle, sneeze or chest pain to prove to himself he was really ill. (Which he was, of course, but in a different sense.)

When Stan finally went to the physician, he exaggerated his symptoms. He invented a few others to make sure he sounded ill. He did not realize physicians are familiar with this syndrome. He was treated with barely-concealed contempt and told to see a psychiatrist as the problem was "all in the mind." This added humiliation was the final blow to Stan's already diminished self-esteem. Like Stan, some men never recover. Others have an uncanny awareness of what to expect, and avoid medical help. Many physicians are not trained in erection problems. Yet all potency loss deserves the best of professional help. Whatever the cause, it can seriously reduce the quality of life. Consult a urologist who specializes in erectile disorders; not all do. Or work through the next articles.

# Rigidity Check

The following self help involves solitary masturbation:

· Abstain from trying to erect for a week, if possible.
· Banish all thoughts of erection problems during this period.
· Then, masturbate the penis to the pre-emission stage. Stop.
· Check rigidity. Compare it with erections from the past.
· Allow the erection to collapse, then stimulate it again.
· Check rigidity. How does it compare with the first erection?
· The result should be pleasing. A minor rigidity loss does not signify impotence, and can be treated.

If this does not work, obtain a massager. The appropriate kind is fairly heavy duty, not a light buzz. It should give a moderate to somewhat relentless massage. Repeat the above steps. Are things OK?

Assume a base line for rigidity of 100 percent. An erection of 70 percent rigidity can be sufficient for penetration. Use lubrication to help. With 70 percent to 50 percent rigidity, what urologists call "stuffing"is possible. Once safely in, the penis generally hardens. A 70 percent rigidity is not unusual in older men. With less than 50 percent rigidity, penetration is not possible; it produces what urologists call the "buckling effect."

If the checks work, the problem may be due to stress. Relax. Keep in mind erections are not essential for satisfaction. Take sexual pleasures in other ways for a while. If both checks fail, something is amiss. Consult the urologist or physician. The cause might be a heart problem requiring speedy therapy. Avoid delay.

## The Forbidden Solo Act

Obviously, many men will have tried the above checks many times. But others have not, due to entrenched fears of masturbation. It may seem strange to promote the act, but a few men avoid it like the plague. If masturbation fears prevent self-help, consider the following true tale:

"Mr. Grave had no problems with erections. But he suffered prostate congestion. The inflammation and pain made his life a misery. His physician said therapy was to ejaculate regularly four to five times weekly to relieve the congestion.

Mr. Grave called a medical phone-in station complaining the therapy was inappropriate because his wife worked at nights. He worked days, so they could only get together on weekends. Now, certain topics may not be discussed on the airways. And masturbation is one of them. So the phone-in physician had the tricky task of trying to persuade Mr. Grave it was not only perfectly reasonable, but critical for his sexual health, that he masturbate when his wife was absent during the week.

Mr. Grave responded with a shocked, "No, I couldn't do that!" He rang the station a month later, saying he had to endure weekly prostate massage to relieve the congestion. He loathed the procedure. He would do anything to avoid it, apart from handling himself. What else could the physician suggest? This occurred in 1989. It holds a message for men with concerns over masturbation.

# The Stamp Test

This is a self-help check which avoids masturbation. It tests for the presence of NPT. It can be done in privacy at home. It does not require a partner's help. It is not 100 percent accurate, but may be useful as a first step towards investigative self-help.

Buy a perforated sheet of stamps large enough to fit snugly around the relaxed penis. At bedtime, wrap the stamp sheet closely around the base of the shaft. Secure the ends firmly with tape to prevent it slipping during the night. If the problem is physical, NPT will be absent, and the stamp sheet will be in place the next morning.

If the problem is psychogenic, the penis erects during REM sleep. The engorging shaft exerts pressure on the stamp sheet. Because the tape holds it firmly in place, this pressure breaks the stamps along the perforated edges. In the morning, there are crumpled bits of stamps scattered throughout the bed.

The stamp test cannot check full rigidity. It can interfere with REM sleep and give a false result.

A ring called the Snap Gauge measures penile rigidity. It consists of three colored bands. One of each will break at three pre-chosen erection pressures: minimal, moderate and maximum. The Snap Gauge measures rigidity only at one moment in time, and there are other measurements it cannot take. Even so, maybe it should be freely available to the public as a useful self-help.

# The Sleep Laboratory

The sleep laboratory is popular in some areas. In others, it is not, partly due to the high expense. A healthy sexually-active man may have five separate erections during the night. The average number is three to five, depending upon how often the sleeper enters dream sleep.

In a sleep laboratory, sleep cycles and NPT are monitored on a device called a Rigiscan. Two silicone rings filled with mercury act as "strain gauges." They are put around the corona and the shaft base. Each takes a separate recording calibrated to measure width increase in millimeters. This is called penile plethysmography.

Normal erectile capacity as girth increase is in the range of 10 to 15 mm at the corona, and 12 to 20 mm at the base.

Rigidity is tested in the same way. The readings are recorded as millimeters of deflection. These are converted by calibration to the grams force needed to buckle an erect shaft. A force in excess of 1500 must never be applied. Normal tonicity challenge is in excess of 500 grams force. (Penile plethysmography is also used for sex criminals who deny their desires. Pictures of a woman being attacked and of naked children of both genders are shown when he is awake. If the plethysmograph records tumescence, he is shown the print-out and can accept his deviancy. And the psychologist learns in which area to apply aversion therapy techniques.)

Other measurements include: two leads on the outer area of the eyelids to record separate eye movements; two EEG leads on the head to record brain activity on the electro-encephalograph; and various other leads to record involuntary muscle movement, heart and respiratory rate, and skin activity. There should be at least one full erection lasting at least five minutes without any fluctuation in width increase and rigidity.

It may be necessary to spend three nights in the laboratory. Night 1 is for getting used to strange surroundings, and learning to sleep while wired up (painlessly) to machines. On Night 2, sleep is usually better quality, allowing more REM sleep and more NPT. Recordings of these two nights are collated and become data base for assessing maximum NPT rigidity, number, endurance time.

On Night 3, the man is awakened during REM sleep and asked to observe his erection, and comment on rigidity, width and angle. A polaroid photograph is taken so he can rate the quality with those before trouble started. If the problem is psychogenic, they are much the same.

If the problem is physical, other factors to note are:

· Partial engorgement only.
· Frequent short-endurance erections.
· Very few short-endurance erections.
· Uneven ratio of width increase between the corona and base.

## At the Urologist

In Western countries, some men go directly to the urologist. A medical history is taken, with special reference to any family background of diabetes. Blood pressure, pulse and respiratory rate are checked. The presence, or absence, of secondary sexual characteristics is noted. The genitals are examined for scars from trauma or surgery. The penis is checked for plaques denoting Peyronie's disease. The testicles are palpated for size and consistency. A urine analysis checks kidney function, together with fasting blood sugar tests for diabetes.

The following is a composite of questionnaires which may be used by a urologist or sex behavior therapist. It begins by collecting the usual data: name, age, relationship and employment status. Some of the next questions include:

1. How would you define the quality of your relationship with your wife or primary sex partner: good, fair or poor?

2. How would you define the quality of your sexual relationship: good, fair or poor?

3. Do you think your partner contributes to your sexual problems? If so, give details in which respects.

4. Would you describe yourself as an anxious or depressed person? Do you consider your sex drive abnormally high, very low, just right for your age?

5. Is the attitude of your wife or primary sex partner to your problem indifferent, upset, relieved or understanding? Or is no partner available?

6. Have you consulted with another physician or a sex behavior therapist before?

7. Describe your sexual problem and how it affects your life. Fill in the blank pages attached if there is a particular problem which has not been addressed.

8. Complete details of your medical history by putting checks in the following 40 appropriate boxes.

The following helps to estimate whether erection loss is more likely to be physical or psychogenic in origin. Place a check against those which are appropriate:

*Acute Onset*: Did the problem start suddenly?

*Selectivity*: With one particular partner only?

*Periodicity*: Does it remit every now and then?

*Masturbation*: Are rigidity and endurance time unchanged?

*Sensations*: Are there sensations in the testicles?

*Investigation*: Does it remit with a different partner?

*Sweet Dreams*: Do erections occur during sleep, NPT?

With two or more checks, the potency loss may be psychogenic; it may be due to stress. This does not rule out physical illness or mental depression. The following are a series of investigative tests which may, or may not, be undertaken.

# Blood Flow Checks

## Medication

There are drugs which, when injected into the penis, cause an erection within three to fifteen minutes. If engorgement is partial only, the problem may be clogged arteries. The *inflow* of blood to the penis, or within the penis itself, is blocked by *plaque*. These are fatty deposits in the blood which harden and become attached to the artery walls.

If the erection lacks rigidity, or lasts for less than fifteen minutes, the problem may be leaking veins. The extra blood is not trapped inside the penis. Blood *outflow* does not slow down, and the erection cannot be maintained. This is called *venous leakage*.

## Blood Pressure

Penile blood pressure is measured rather like arm blood pressure. A special small three cm wide cuff is wrapped round the base of the shaft. The cuff is inflated above systolic pressure. A Doppler stethoscope using ultrasound is placed over the two upper tubes (corpora) in turn. As the pressure in the cuff slowly deflates, the point at which sound is heard is recorded as the systolic penile blood pressure.

This procedure is repeated after exercising on a treadmill to check for a rare problem called pelvic steal. During deep thrusting, blood can get shunted from the penile arteries to those of the buttocks or legs. The ratio of penile blood pressure to arm blood pressure should be greater than 70 percent.

## Temperature

A thermometer placed in the urethra measures penile temperature. A lower than average reading may indicate poor blood flow from the penile arteries. Penile temperature of 1.6 Fahrenheit or more below normal body temperature may indicate a blockage in the arteries.

*Thermography* is a color map" of penile core temperature; average increase is two percent. An area with less color may be blocked.

*Cavernosometry* checks the exact sites of faulty blood flow. It measures the pressure in the cavernosa, the two upper tubes. An erection is induced by drugs or saline infusion into one tube at a time. An X-ray dye is then injected into a vein; the amount of radioactivity is tiny, and harmless. A Geiger counter maps the flow. Areas with poor blood flow will have less dye.

*Cavernosography* is an X-ray check for venous leakage at erection.

Hardening of the arteries is the main cause of faulty blood flow. It is more common with high blood pressure, hypertension or heart disease. *Reduce all fats in the diet as they contribute to plaque build-up.* Faulty flow is more common in overweight men, and smokers. Sickle cell anemia can restrict blood flow; it alters the structure of blood cells and scar tissue may build up.

# Drug Checks

Certain medications impair penile blood or nerve supply. The prescribed drugs include tranquilizers, muscle relaxants and those which control ulcers and raised blood pressure. It may be appropriate to change the medication, or lower the dosage.

Certain non-prescription drugs for colds, sore throats and sinus, those containing antihistamines, weight loss pills and diuretics, can interfere with blood flow. Consult a physician before using them. Marijuana, cocaine and amphetamines affect the central nervous system, and should be avoided.

Heavy long-term alcohol abuse hardens the arteries, damages the nerves and destroys liver function. In certain liver diseases, a substance is made which binds with testosterone and stops it from working. For this reason, some drugs to treat impotence are inappropriate for alcoholic men.

Tobacco tars, nicotine, carbon monoxide and other cigarette pollutants do not of themselves cause impotence. But they are *vasoconstrictors*. They reduce blood vessel size which aggravates any tendency to potency loss. A 1989 U.S. study found 80 percent of impotent men were heavy smokers. Even the slightest strain on the tiny penile arteries can pinch them off.

*Bikers beware!* Avoid testicle vasoconstriction by making sure your bike seat is comfortable and the appropriate height. If there is a tendency to potency loss, avoid prolonged journeys.

## Nerve Conduction Checks

1. Check for the knee-jerk reflex. Sit in a hard chair. Cross one leg loosely over the other at the knee. Tap smartly just below the patella (knee bone). The crossed limb will automatically (reflexively) kick out. Repeat with other leg. Are things OK?

2. Squeeze the head of the penis. Does the anus contract? If not, try again, moving the fingers until the appropriate place on the glans is found. There should be a fairly obvious sensation of a definite contraction within the rectum.

3. Palpate down the length of the shaft. There should be a fairly obvious sensation in response to the squeezing. Repeat for the scrotum. There should be an equally noticeable response here.

The signal to erect comes from the pudendal nerves in the lower spine. To check the main pudendal nerve, the urologist stimulates the penis by mild electric current. As in erotic stimulation, this causes the muscles of the anus to contract. The length of time between stimulation and contraction is a measure of *pudendal nerve conduction time*.

One-third of penile fractures cause impotence. Parkinsons, kidney disease, alcoholism, strokes, cerebral palsy and multiple sclerosis (not muscular dystrophy) affect erections only if the nerve or blood supply is destroyed. With spinal cord injury, if the nerves are severed above the nerve center, reflex erections may be possible but not emotionally stimulated ones.

## Hormone Level Checks

*RIA* stands for radio immunoassay. It measures the levels of serum or plasma testosterone concentrations (hormones circulating in the blood.) If the levels seem low, the sex drive may be reduced, and this may be causing the problem. Radio immunoassay is done in the morning when serum testosterone levels are highest. Three blood samples are taken 20 minutes apart, and then pooled to get an accurate result.

The endocrinologist may wish to check for other problems. There may be excess production of *prolactin* or *estrogen*. These female hormones can lower testosterone production. It is thought that large numbers of fat cells in obese men can increase estrogen.

Other areas of the endocrine system may be checked. Certain kidney and liver diseases can upset the normal hormone balance. Discussion of these further tests is outside the parameters of this book. However, keep in mind that low testosterone production or other hormonal disorders are the least likely reasons for potency loss.

## Diabetes

Diabetes mellitus is the number one cause of physical impotence. It is a disorder in which carbohydrates are not properly used by the body. Normally, the digested sugars in food are removed from the blood and converted to glycogen by the liver. The hormone insulin, made in the pancreas, controls the blood sugar level.

With diabetes, sugars for energy are not oxidized due to lack of insulin. So the sugar level in the blood remains too high. The condition is called hyperglycemia. The excess sugar is filtered out by the kidneys, and appears in the urine. The tests for diabetes are by blood and urinalysis.

Over the years, the damage done by diabetes to most body organs is considerable. It affects the nerves, the large arteries and tiny blood vessels within the penis. As erections depend upon a healthy nerve and blood supply, *diabetic impotence* can set in. There is nothing wrong with the man's testosterone output or his sex drive, but his penis cannot erect.

Mild symptoms of diabetes include tiredness, blurring of the vision or increase in appetite without any weight increase. More severe symptoms include excessive urination, thirst, hunger, and pruritis (itchy anus). Any man with these symptoms should seek medical help promptly.

# A Lean Machine

At age 45, Rudi was fighting for his career. In his high profile business, the knives were out. Junior staff got pink slips. In Rudi's age group, there was talk of "cutting the fat" by early retirement. The new corporate image was for a lean mean machine.

Rudi was becoming lean and mean. He was highly irritable, always tired, yet unable to sleep. His erections produced the "buckling effect." He moved out of the marriage bed into the guest room. He did the stamp test to check for NPT. In his impatience, he bungled the attempt. The wretched thing slid off in the night. He felt a fool. Yet he could not, and would not, believe the problem was psychogenic.

The physician diagnosed Rudi as a "borderline" diabetic.

"I'm not thirsty," Rudi objected. It was all he knew of the symptoms. "My — er, impotence? Is it from borderline diabetes?"

"You are not impotent," the physician was firm. "When a man is in reduced physical health; when he is under mental stress at work; when his erections are less than satisfactory and give concern — we don't categorize causes. It's probably some of each. We will find out, once you begin therapy."

He continued, "In borderline diabetes, blood-sugar levels can be controlled by diet and exercise programs. Medication may be required to stimulate your own production of insulin. *You must take your condition seriously.* If you neglect only one aspect, the slow yet lethal effects of uncontrolled diabetes may kill you; they will almost certainly destroy your potency."

"Fortunately, you came at the primary stage. Early therapy prevents heart disease, stroke, blindness, gangrene, kidney failure. . . I don't wish to alarm you but some men get careless once their energy level returns. They neglect the diet and exercise programs. Avoid this."

"You've got me hooked," Rudi spoke with fervor. "Is this thing inherited. What about my son?"

"There is a predisposition in families, yes. However, Type 1 diabetes is different. It occurs in childhood up to about age 25. It is called *juvenile* or *sudden onset diabetes* because it happens very suddenly and the symptoms are unmistakable. You have Type 2 diabetes. It occurs mainly in older men. At age 45, you are rather young. The symptoms often go unnoticed because they progress slowly. They start with a slight decline in rigidity but if penetration is possible, this is put down to the aging process. By 18 months, however, the decline is noticeable. Ejaculation occurs, but not every time. If orgasm feels good, the sex drive remains high. If the doctor is consulted about the decline, the man may mention he feels tired or irritable. All the symptoms of diabetes are present, but have gone unrecognized."

Rudi reckoned he had been saved from a fate worse than death. For that is how he perceived his potency loss. He decided to take early retirement, invest his savings in real estate, and paint. He had always wanted to paint.

## Diabetes Self Help

Diabetes is a fairly common disorder worldwide. Some two million U.S. men suffer from it, and over 50 percent have diabetic impotence. The greater the age, the higher the risk. Estimates suggest that at age 50 plus, there is a 50-75 percent chance of impotence. At ages 20 to 49, there is a 25-30 percent chance. Diabetes occurs more often in minority and low-income groups. It also favors obese men with diets rich in sugars and fats.

*From a potency aspect alone, whether diabetic or not, any overweight man should improve his diet, increase his level of exercise and reduce his weight.*

When diabetes is first diagnosed, especially for a younger man, the shock can be shattering. Believe that this shock can be absorbed. Keep in mind diabetes is not a stable condition. It can remit, then relapse, then remit again. Potency can return at varying times. If love-making stops, these times are missed.

Expect to experience rage and pain at the damage to sexual manhood. This is a natural response. Yet try to avoid empowering these negative emotions to block arousal. Increase and enhance other love-making skills. If desired, seek counseling for further techniques. Above all, avoid despair; do not give up hope. There is too much at stake.

A diabetic man does not produce less testosterone. Nor is his sex drive impaired, unless the diabetes makes him feel ill. Sexually speaking, there is nothing wrong with him. He would be potent if it were not for the disorder. For this reason, there is no need to feel less masculine, less virile, in any way less of a man. In many cases, a penile implant puts things right.

Before the discovery of insulin, diabetes was fatal. And there is no cure as yet; the "yet" denotes there is reason for hope. When medical science turns its mighty weight and resources on a disorder, all sufferers everywhere have reason for hope. Apart from self help, consider social help. A local diabetic club needs help with its support programs. For example, a small boy gains enormously in courage, endurance and self-esteem when shown how to manage his insulin shots by an adult male with the same disorder, one who really understands how he feels.

If this is inappropriate, consider the deployment of other skills. Help organize publicity campaigns to raise much-needed research funds. The more a community knows of diabetes, the more generously it will give of its funds. And the more funds for research, the sooner the chance a cure may be found.

## A Rose by Another Name. . .

There are various names for erection problems, most of which are inappropriate. Many men are not truly impotent, but have a minor problem which can be sorted out. Yet the word implies a total absence of erections. *Temporary secondary impotence* shows the problem is recent; erections were satisfactory until now. *Erectile dysfunction* suggests a more serious problem. Perhaps the one term which should be forever banned is *erectile incompetence*. Who wants to be told they are incompetent in bed?

The problem with the label "impotence" is that it sounds so terminal. It undermines sexual confidence, a crucial factor in the erection process. And the label can act as a self-fulfilling prophesy. The more a man perceives his organ as dysfunctional, the more likely it becomes so.

And *stress impotence* is more appropriate than psychogenic because the word "stress" highlights the close relationship between the erection process and the mental state. It underlines the way body and mind work together, not as separate units. Another term just coming into use is *non-specific impotence*. This implies no physical cause has been found as yet.

Avoid thinking in terms of labels. A potency problem from

whatever cause is just a health issue which needs to be resolved. When Shakespeare wrote, "A rose by another name would smell as sweet," he was not referring to problems which cause distress. It can be perceived that crushing labels such as "sexual dysfunction" are unhelpful for the average sensitive man.

# CHAPTER 13

# Power Maintenance

## The Placebo Effect

This chapter contains information on the medical therapies now available. The next chapter contains information on self-help and sex behavior therapy. Keep in mind that medical therapies for both physical and psychogenic impotence can be much the same.

Research shows the placebo effect works. In one study, patients with raised blood pressure were divided into three groups. Group A went to faith healers who "laid on hands." Group B did the same, but the faith healers did not touch them. Group C were the control. They were fully aware of this. They knew they had raised blood pressure and were not to receive any treatment.

When the blood pressure dropped, it did so evenly for all three groups. And it dropped equally by 30 percent. The reasons why it dropped in Group A and B are open to debate. Why it dropped in the control Group C is even more of a mystery. The physicians who monitored the study could only suggest the satisfactory results were due to the placebo effect.

The power of the imagination is stronger than the power of facts. In control group C, participating in the study and just having blood pressure regularly monitored was enough to produce the desired effect. In marginal cases, the placebo effect of just seeking a urologist's help has been known to restore the ability to erect. It might be worth giving the placebo effect of the consultation a chance to work before opting for therapy. Or, if embarking on therapy, become strongly motivated to believe in its success.

## Who's for Medical Therapy?

The answer would seem to be any man with a problem. Yet this is not always so. Like women, men have different levels of sexual need. Some are relieved to be free of the "turbulent demands of the flesh." No man should feel pressured by social values or other obligations to undergo therapy unless he himself is strongly motivated to do so.

The following groups may opt for medical therapy:

1. Men who suffer physical impotence, including diabetes.

2. Men whose impotence is due solely to the aging process — the erection lacks enough rigidity for penetration.

3. Young men whose psychogenic (stress) impotence has lasted over two years. They may not respond to self-help because they no longer believe they can sort out their unresolved conflicts.

4. Men over age 50 with stress impotence who may feel too angry or defeated to believe they can be helped.

There are many different choices of therapy, some of which may seem totally unacceptable. They lack aesthetic appeal, or sound fiddly and unlikely to work. Try to avoid rejecting one without a trial. Keep an open mind.

## The Challenge

Some men with physical impotence withdraw into themselves. They refuse to acknowledge what is happening and become isolated with their grief. The damage to their psychosocial well-being can be profound. In effect, they "turn their face to the wall." This seems so sad, especially as the problem can usually be resolved.

*Psychogenic (stress) impotence often follows physical impotence.*

It is natural to feel anxious, angry or depressed. Accept these painful emotions, rather than denying them. Denial directs valuable energy away from erection goals, and increases stress. Stress damages the cardiovascular system, which makes erection problems worse. For these reasons, all men with even minor potency loss can benefit from reading Chapter 14.

It may be necessary to try different therapies before satisfactory erections occur. From long experience, the urologist may short-list the options, suggesting only one type. A man with potency loss can feel he has lost control in other areas of life. He may go along with this advice, which could be the opposite of how he would normally act. Try to avoid loss of choice. As far as possible, be your own physician.

Regard an erection problem as a gauntlet thrown down. There are only two choices: pick it up, or leave it alone. Why not pick up the gauntlet? What is there to lose? An erection problem may be the greatest challenge a man can face and overcome.

## A Little of What You Fancy. . . ?

For mild to moderate impotence, and with no contraindications, the drug *papaverine* may work. It was first used to relieve spasms in the arteries of the brain, heart and limbs. It acts as a penile neurosmitter by relaxing smooth muscles without paralyzing them. This widens the arteries and increases penile blood flow. It may now be used in combination with *phentolamine*, a drug with similar effects. Or *prostaglandins* may be used instead.

The medication is injected into the base of the shaft with an ultra-fine needle (26 gauge or less). There should be no pain, apart from a brief needle sting as there are no pain fibers in the *corpora*. It produces an erection within 3 to 15 minutes which can last 30 minutes, or more. Better results are gained by solo masturbation to obtain a reflex erection and by use of fantasy.

Possible problems include:

- Numbing or tingling sensation in the penis.
- Discoloration of the penile skin.
- Pain at the injection site.
- Lumps forming at the injection site.
- Infections from the needle.
- Scar tissue forming inside the penis, with risk of chordee.

These problems are due to mismanagement of the shots. Be fully trained in the correct self-injecting techniques. While the erection lasts, there is a gradual decline in rigidity. Keep a log of endurance times. Note and report any unusual results.

In the U.S., the use of medication to induce erections has not yet been F.D.A.-approved. A signed and formal consent may be required. In Europe, both shots and patches are available by prescription. However, recent studies seem to suggest the patches may adversely affect the vagina.

A very dangerous side effect is "lock up" (or priapism). If detumescence does not occur within four hours, an antidote must be injected into the penis. Drugs which reverse the effects are epinephrine and ephedrine. The urologist gives warnings and pre-directions to cover this.

Another possible side effect is a rise in liver enzymes. The complication rate is thought to be 8 to 10 percent. For this reason, regular visits to the urologist for checks on health, and liver function tests, are recommended. However, any pain, swelling or other problem must be reported immediately.

Shots of medication are usually successful if potency loss is due solely to the aging process. They can be self-administered in privacy at home. The time for love-making can be freely chosen. Because of side effects, they must not be used more than twice a week.

A study of elderly couples who had stopped making love found loss of interest on the man's part was the main reason given by both partners. In each case, it was the man who felt responsible and guilty. But how can he be blamed for the aging process? Why should he perceive himself "at fault"? No matter what age, *men do not lose interest in the ability to erect*.

For men with psychologic (stress) potency loss, these shots can break up the damaging cycle of low self-image and self-esteem which increases fear of failure:

· Which results in further potency loss.
· So the pain of failing stops further attempts.
· Which results in psychogenic (stress) impotence.

For young men, the shots can be a transitional stage back to full potency. Once the damaging cycle of fear of failure is broken, the shots are no longer required. A different problem can arise from the relief experienced at regaining erections. There is a risk a few men will over-inject the medication and it will become another drug of abuse. The urologist has to decide if the man will use it responsibly, e.g., one who injects his organ with expoxy glue, or inserts objects in the urethra, would be a high risk candidate for this kind of drug abuse.

So shots to enduce erections are not quite the wonder cure they first seemed. They are *contra-indicated* with leukemia, sickle cell,

Peyronie's disease, a tendency to priapism, bleeding or large leaks from penile veins. Some urologists dislike inducing erections by medication. They do not help the man regain his own erectile powers.

*Phentolamine* pills are now undergoing clinical trials. In one small U.S. study of 16 impotent men, half were able to gain erections by simply swallowing the pill. If, after exhaustive tests, phentolamine proves to be safe in tablet form, it is hoped an otherwise healthy man can be given a prescription. The pills carry ten times the amount of the injected dose. Yet there seem to be almost no side effects. A few men experienced slightly stuffy noses. But this is not unusual with unaided erections.

Once disease is ruled out, a man with potency problems will simply ask for the pills. He will avoid medical tests, the inconvenience of injections, and questions about his personal life. It is taken 1 to 3 hours before use. The effect is at its height when taken 1 1/2 hours before. Other drugs are also undergoing clinical tests. There are high hopes they will be effective without dangerous side effects. In the meantime. . . .

If the impotence is mild to moderate, as in the early stages of diabetes, *yohimbine* may help. This drug is extracted from the bark of evergreen trees. It acts as a neurotransmitter. It enhances the release of nor-adrenaline by the nerve endings. This increases blood pressure and flow, and slows down the heart rate.

The effects of yohimbine are cumulative. The drug must build up in the body before it can work. Be patient; erections should improve within three to five weeks. Some urologists dismiss yohimbine as of limited use. Yet it might be worth a try. Due to side effects, it is not recommended with heart disease or high blood pressure.

# Erection Devices

There are a variety of external management devices for mild to moderate impotence. They used to be sold in pornography shops and so gained a dubious reputation. However, they have been restyled and raised above the level of quackery. They are now considered legitimate erection aids.

The main type is a cylinder pulled over the relaxed penis. It creates a controlled vacuum worked by a hand pump. Blood is drawn into the penis, which engorges and erects. The cylinder is removed and an entrapment ring put at the base of the shaft. The ring maintains the erection by stopping blood outflow leakage. *Trapped penile blood is dangerous and causes priapism.* Avoid leaving the entrapment ring on for longer than directed, usually 30 minutes. Follow all directions to the letter.

Each device involves some paraphernalia, and none of it is cheap. Some men complain their erection is less rigid than they wish. Others rejoice in the pump because full penetration is regained. The devices are non-invasive, and their use can be discontinued when the man wishes. Perhaps their greatest appeal is that the man always stays in control.

The U.S vacuum pump was designed by an autoparts salesman, or so the story goes. In 1974, at age 72, he had been told by his physician that he must put up with his impotence. The autoparts salesman set about manufacturing the pump, then marketing it himself. He did this by showing a grainy old film loop on which he could be seen pumping up the device, waiting a few minutes, then showing a full erection. Not a pretty sight perhaps, but one of benefit to older men. Who says American initiative is dead?

## Mismanagement

Mr. X asked his urologist for an erection maintenance device. On learning the paraphernalia cost $500, he changed his mind. He visited the mean streets downtown and entered a pornography shop. Here he bargained successfully for a cut-price device. He left clutching his precious package, and with $400 change. He spent some of this on a bottle of gin.

At home, Mr. X discovered the directions were written in Eastern hieroglyphics. Nothing daunted, he considered any fool could operate the device. After two attempts, he gained the erection he desired. It felt so good he decided to finish the gin and repeat the attempt. He dampened the entrapment ring, which was nothing more than twine, with gin and tied it tight. At some time, he drifted into a deep alcoholic sleep. He did not feel the twine dry out, shrink, and finally bite deep.

Fortunately, Mr. X was a diligent employee and obeyed the summons of an early call. The discoloration and badly swollen appearance of his organ sent him in panic to the emergency room. Damage was widespread, though not life threatening. The penis had to be irrigated of the sludged blood which had collected. Fortunately, there was no gangrene, but this mismanagement narrowed his therapy options. The only choice left was penile implant surgery, or he could opt for permanent impotency.

# MEGS

The signal to erect comes from the pudendal nerves in the lower spine. To check the main pudendal nerve, the urologist stimulates the penis by mild electric current. As in erotic stimulation, this causes the muscles of the anus to contract. The length of time between stimulation and contraction is a measure of *pudendal nerve conduction time*.

MEGS is the acronym for Male Electronic Genital Stimulator. It is a small self-contained device which is battery operated. It is put into the man's anus before making love. MEGS creates an erection by electrically stimulating the pudendal nerves. It is operated externally, so the man stays in control. The current is low; there should be no discomfort. The urologist checks the device for acceptability and effectiveness in the office.

MEGS is not appropriate with blood flow disorders. It works well with certain kinds of nerve disease. It is relatively non-invasive, and can be removed at any time. These factors afford it strong appeal to some men. MEGS is now in the trial stage as a successful therapy for stress impotence.

# Testosterone Replacement Therapy

All medication has side effects. Testosterone replacement therapy (TRT) is no different. With long-term use, and incorrect dosage, it can be toxic. In pubertal boys, it can halt bone growth. In adult males, TRT halts the production of natural testosterone from the testes due to the feedback control in the brain.

In large doses, TRT slows down sperm production, speeds up hair loss, promotes gynecomastia (male breasts), increases the risk of jaundice, liver cancer and heart disease. It can increase prostate size, with an ensuing loss of bladder control. It is linked to prostate cancer. In extreme cases, the testicles shrink and become atrophied.

These side effects may sound alarming. But the dosage is worked out for maximum effectiveness and minimum side effects. As with all medication, it is an issue of options, of weighing the benefits against the risks. A man with malfunctioning testes may decide the benefits of a restored sex drive and satisfactory erections outweigh the health risks. Keep to the prescribed dosage. Avoid taking an extra dose for an extra boost. Consult with the physician regularly for close checks on health.

Testosterone is a steroid and, if used by others, may come under the heading of steroid abuse. In homes with young aspiring athletes, it may be appropriate to keep the medication under lock and key. It is estimated half a million children under age 18 are taking steroids to improve their sporting performance.

Parents can explain the symptoms of steroid abuse which are most likely to impress a growing boy: skeletal muscle grows faster than cartilage and connective tissue, and this uneven development can cause pain. Even more impressive is the fact that steroids speed up the maturation process, closing off the ends of growing bones before they have fully developed. This results in shorter stature, a permanently shorter height.

Parents also need to explain that taking steroids illegally does not affect all teenagers in the same way, i.e., not all suffer symptoms, not all get caught.

(For further information on TRT, see Chapter 14).

# Vascular Surgery

The blood supply to the corpora (tubes) is separate. The upper two corpora share a connecting channel through which blood flows. If this is blocked, the surgeon has several options. Restoring blood flow to one side only may be enough to restore erections.

*Balloon Angioplasty*: A deflated balloon is inserted by catheter along the artery to the blockage. The balloon is inflated, and compresses and flattens the plaque against the artery wall. This usually opens a wide enough passage for satisfactory blood flow.

*Bypass*: If the artery is in poor repair, or the blockage is large or difficult to reach, the surgeon may close it off and choose another vein or artery to bypass the obstruction.

*Revascularization*: An artery is taken from the stomach and re-routed to the penis. It is a new and more lengthy operation.

If erections are satisfactory, but not maintained, the veins of blood outflow can be tied off. When venous leakage stops, erection maintenance is restored. If leakage occurs in the body of the shaft deep inside the pelvis, surgery is more difficult.

Vascular surgery is new, and some surgeons lack sufficient skills. It is not appropriate with diabetes or certain kinds of blood vessel disorders. The younger the man, the more successful the outcome. Like other surgical options, it carries a risk of short-term success only or failure. Long-term success rates will improve considerably with more advanced techniques.

# Penile Implants

There are different kinds of implants, and all require surgery. Some cause fairly severe pain afterwards. Swelling and mild pain may last for several weeks. But pain relief is readily available. And tranquilizing drugs prevent spontaneous erections during the healing process. A man who is strongly motivated to regain powers of penetration can accept these drawbacks.

There are certain criteria to be an implant candidate. They include the presence of some sensation in the penis; some ability to achieve orgasm; no urinary, prostate or other health problems which might affect the proper working of the device. Other factors may include past sexual history, the presence of a loving and supportive mate, a strong desire by the man to satisfy himself and his partner.

# Types of Implant

*The semi-rigid implant* is made of two thin sponge-filled silicone rods. They are designed to be compatible in length and width width the man's normal erectile capacity. They are implanted in the corpora cavernosa, the two upper tubes in the penis. The soft yet firm rods are strong enough for penetration.

The main disadvantage is being in a permanent half-erect state. During the day, the penis is placed up against the abdomen wall, and held there with jockey shorts. Another disadvantage is the risk of the implant shifting out of place. This causes pain or discomfort. If left unchecked, it could damage the urethra.

Compared to other prostheses, the semi-rigid device is the simplest to implant, and the least costly. There is less swelling and pain, and quicker recovery time after surgery. There are no moving parts which can break down. Love-making can resume in four to six weeks.

*The flexi-rod implant* is a variation of the semi-rigid one. The silicone rods are hinged so they can be moved by hand to give the penis an upright stance. When unerect, the penis hangs normally. It is not as successful as the semi-rigid implant. During the daytime, boxer shorts keep the penis flat against the abdomen. The pressure from jockey shorts can cause prolonged pain.

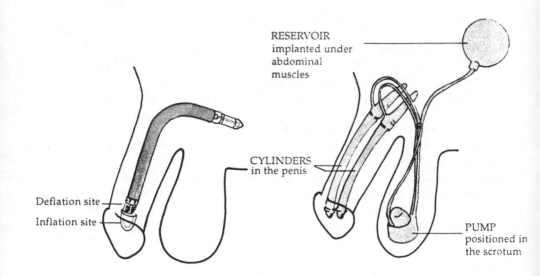

RESERVOIR implanted under abdominal muscles

CYLINDERS in the penis

Deflation site

Inflation site

PUMP positioned in the scrotum

## The Inflatable Implant

The inflatable device is more complex. Two hollow silicone rods fill up with fluid to simulate a normal erection. Once all the parts of the device are in place, none can be seen externally. The device requires different implant sites:

- The rods are inserted into the penis.
- The pump is inserted into the scrotum.
- The reservoir bag of fluid is inserted in the lower abdomen.
- Each of the above has to be connected by silicone tubing.

When an erection is desired, the small pump in the scrotum is squeezed. The pressure travels along the connecting tubing to the abdomen and pumps the fluid out of the reservoir bag. The fluid travels along more connecting tubing into the two hollow penile rods. These fill, and the penis erects. A one-way valve keeps the fluid inside the implant for as long as is desired. When love-making is over, a release valve on the scrotal pump is squeezed. The fluid drains out of the penile rods and back into the reservoir until next time. The inflatable implant has many advantages. It is the devise which most closely resembles a naturally erect and relaxed penis. It can be operated without the partner noticing. To some extent, rigidity can be increased or decreased at will. There is less risk of the rods shifting and damaging the urethra. The disadvantages include the much greater extent of surgery involved. The operation takes longer, and so does the healing process. There is a greater degree of pain, with a higher risk of post-operative infection. Because of the many mechanical parts, there is more chance of one section breaking down. There is also a higher medical bill.

## The Self-Contained Implant

In this type, the fluid is contained within the prosthesis. The pump and deflation valve are at the tips of the device, where the glans joins the shaft. The implant becomes firm by squeezing the inflation site with mild steady pressure. This brings the fluid from the back of the prosthesis into the rods, and erection occurs. After love-making, the deflation valve is squeezed to transfer the fluid back to the reservoir.

It takes time to learn to use the self-contained prosthesis. The advantages of this device include ease of implant, with a shorter surgery time. It can be done on an out-patient basis. The disadvantages include having mechanical parts which can break down; in particular, the part which inflates and deflates can go wrong. But if re-implantation is required, it is less difficult than with the fully inflatable type and causes less pain.

## To Implant, or Not?

The use of mechanical prostheses has been strongly criticized in recent months. By no means is there unanimous support. Indeed, many good long-term studies find, with time, the mechanical penis is not used and the surgery is regretted. More often than not, the relationship was the problem, not the penis. In some clinics, an implant is the first choice on offer for many kinds of impotence. It may be strongly recommended by the urologist. Yet there can be infection after surgery — check the latest figures. Antibiotics destroy the germs, but this may not happen until the implant sites are severely damaged. Keep in mind if the prosthesis fails, it has to be removed. Erection ability is then forever lost. Re-implantation is the next procedure to consider. The wound is washed with antibiotic solution and a new device is re-implanted within the next few days. Not all men get post-operative infection, but some do. There is no guarantee the second one will not get infected. It is a very big risk, and a very difficult decision to make.

Penile implants are subject to much the same problems as breast implants. There is a risk of shifting, texture changes and so on. On top of which, they have to function in a way a breast implant does not. Consider carefully before opting for the knife. Yet the news is not all dark. Just as breast implants can be successful, men with successful penile implants absolutely swear by them. They insist their quality of life has greatly improved. Find a local support group, and learn from their comments. If this is inappropriate, ask to speak with both a satisfied and a dissatisfied client. A thorough research of all the issues can greatly help in deciding whether to opt for an implant or not.

For men at certain stages of diabetic impotence, these prostheses have been described as a "heaven-sent boon." For other men, it might be appropriate to consider this therapy option as a final resort.

# An Overview

By now, the reader may be bemused by all the different tests and therapies. And many urologists will not tackle many of the procedures. This is because some results are unreliable, and others are too difficult to interpret. Keep in mind research into potency problems is recent. Each year brings new experiments, new techniques, more clinical trials to be tested. As fast as one procedure becomes popular, another falls out of favor.

It is possible for a man with erection problems to feel like a rat being experimented upon. This cannot always be helped. Urologists, like other specialists, learn by trial and error. They constantly devise brilliant new techniques which may, or may not, work in the long term. It is important to understand that these techniques have to be tested out by clinical trials. Part of the problem is due to the complex nature of the erection process. Keep in mind the shaft lies deep within the pelvis, so the arteries and nerves are not easily accessible. And men who embark on these trials may not be always reliable in their reports. They are often confused with the problem, or have mixed feelings about the therapy, or drop out of the program at the first sign of a hitch.

Nevertheless, and in spite of these drawbacks, potency loss can be successfully treated or managed in the vast majority of cases. There are numerous books devoted solely to the topic of restoring potency which the reader may find of further benefit.

## Different Folks/ Different Strokes

Not all men desire to regain erection ability. Great care must be taken not to confuse an erection with sexual desire. All lovers can have truly joyful times without penetration. Indeed, many other methods and techniques for sexual satisfaction are readily available and often preferred. No man has to seek therapy for any reason whatsoever. But the fact he now has the option can be a great comfort.

However, for the man who does want therapy, there may come a period of intense doubt. There may be dreary feelings including a certain squeamishness and a sense of despair. In part, they are due to the variety of choices which, paradoxically, can create an aura of defeat. All therapies do involve a degree of indignity. Yet, this can be born by a man who is highly motivated to achieve satisfactory erections again. It is neither ridiculous nor self-indulgent to opt for power maintenance.

*For everything that lives is holy. Life delights in life.*

CHAPTER 14

# Stress Management

## Stress

*Stress is defined as an emotional state which affects the body.* During a challenge, the adrenal glands produce stress hormones, adrenaline and noradrenaline. Stress hormones speed up the heart and breathing rate so more oxygen is rushed to the muscles. Extra fats and sugar enter the blood to fuel the muscles. The mouth dries, the pupils dilate, sweating ceases. All systems not required to face the challenge shut down, including the erection process.

Body and mind are in a state of emergency; they are on Red Alert. This is the "flight or fight" syndrome. In everyday life it is helpful. The extra energy produced by the stress hormones helps either to win the challenge, or avoid an inappropriate one.

But with erection challenge, this help is meaningless. Fight does not work: fighting for an erection produces the buckling effect. Flight ignores the problem. It would seem a man must accept flight, and this adds humiliation, which undermines his sense of self-worth. Sexual confidence ebbs and stress impotence sets in, often at a later and unexpected date.

The good(!) news about stress impotence is that it affects the nicest of men. The more subtle and perceptive the psyche, the more it suffers from inappropriate challenge. There may be some small, though cold, comfort in this.

# The Man Who Came to Dinner

Grant's father came to visit. This extended to four months. Grant and Fran live in an open plan house. At night, every sound echoes throughout the home. Each time they make love, Grant's father has a coughing fit. The sound freezes Grant in his tracks. He cannot maintain his erection knowing his father is awake.

At first, he and Fran laugh off the situation. Then Grant develops vertigo and strange aches and pains. He imagines his father is still trying to control him as he did so often and so painfully in youth.

Finally, he asks Fran to tell his father to leave. Fran says that is his job. But at age 33, Grant cannot communicate with his father on anything except a bluff hearty level. So Fran tactfully does the deed. As the front door closes, Grant falls upon Fran in a frenzy of desire and gratitude. Only then does he realize he still cannot maintain his erection.

Grant puts this down to his vertigo and other aches and pains. Fran suggests he see a psychiatrist. This panics Grant and he spends night after night trying to maintain his erection. The more he tries, the more he fails, the more he drives them both frantic. Eventually, he is unable to start an erection. To his horror, Grant realizes he is becoming impotent.

# Gremlins in the Works

*Situational impotence* means just what it says. The psychologic desire to make love is present but erections stop, or cannot be maintained, because something in the situation is amiss. The problem may be immediate, e.g., the couple have argued and not resolved their conflict. Situational impotence is common, short-lived and nothing to be concerned about.

But, and there are many "buts" in the erection process, if the gremlin in the works is not removed, the unconscious starts to respond. It begins to make links between the immediate potency loss and long-term loss of erectile ability. Memory patterns for failure start to be laid down. For men like Grant, they loom so large that stress impotence sets in.

Situational impotence rarely develops overnight. This kind of unconscious learning occurs over a prolonged period of time. The erection process can be affected by stress more than is (consciously) realized. In situational impotence, the challenge to erect is inap-

propriate because the stress hormones are in control. Avoid prolonged stress. Give the erection process the consideration it deserves.

# A Philosophy of Erection

One of the main confusions comes from an unenlightened attitude, a perception that the proof of manhood is to be rampantly
erect. To quote from *The Joy of Sex* by Dr. Alex Comfort: "The
conventional male fantasy of being able to perform anytime, anywhere, is wholly neurotic and impractical. Only the totally insensitive are all-time f*** machines like a stud bull, and even stud bulls
have their off days."

Many men no longer have such (neurotic) fantasies. But some
still do. The author Ernest Hemingway may leave his mark on the
youth of countless generations to come with his "a man is a man is
a man," whatever that means. He eulogized the cult of machismo,
which terrorizes growing boys with fears of being a wimp. As girls
are also avid readers of his books, they too are affected by sexually
inappropriate expectations.

The cult of machismo denies a man his spirit, his soul. In sexual
matters, it insists he is a performing machine. It denies him human
vulnerability, human sweetness, human love. It focuses on his
primitive state, his brutish undeveloped lusts. Sexual machismo
is the worm eating away at the heart of sexual truth.

The belief that erection is essential for satisfaction is a social
phenomenon, not a biologic one. (Keep in mind orgasm can occur
independent of erection.) It is related to a similar belief that sexual
love is for reproduction, hence the ban on all forms of birth control.

Nowadays, most couples believe in sexual pleasure, and use
birth control. Yet the old belief that erection is essential for satisfaction dies hard. Of course, individuals are free to choose their
own beliefs, but this is an unhappy choice if it results in the sexual
power game.

The sexual power game revolves around the erection process.
The penis becomes a psychologic weapon either partner can use.
The man can withhold erection to punish the woman and make her
feel undesired. The woman can manipulate him, emotionally
and/or physically, to taunt erection success, and then destroy it.

Carried to excess, this power game is vicious, destructive. As in
all such games, there is a winner and a loser. Control of power may
eventually belong to one partner alone. And who uses power

wisely, let alone humanely, appropriately? The game can be played only by partners who insist that erection is essential. It is surprising how many still do.

A man becomes unsure of his potency when he is uncertain of the demands on him and has invested emotionally in their outcome. These demands include work, family, religion, battle, health and so on. Stress impotence can reflect his under or non-performance in any area of life, including the sexual one. It can reflect his success as well, if he does not perceive it as such. Women have no such easy give-away of their emotional state.

## Paralysis by Analysis?

There is a school of thought which believes if you study things too closely, they stop working. Men raised under the cult of machismo tend to believe this of their erections. But do they believe it of their car engines? Computers? Voyages to the moon?

*Psychogenic (stress) impotence is an unconscious device to keep a man safe from harm.* Some psychiatrists believe stress impotence is rooted in anxiety. Others think it is due to repressed rage. Before dismissing these concepts as mere psycho-babble, consider the following: Impotence is defined as "having no power, not in control, ineffective." But is there not something extremely powerful, highly controlling and very effective about an organ which refuses to erect?

· Anxiety is the major cause of stress impotence.
· Anger is a common cause of stress impotence.
· Anxiety is fear of pain in the future (failure to erect).
· Anger is holding on to pain from the past (repressed rage).

Just think how sensible the penis is! Why should it erect if something is amiss? Why would it pretend everything in the garden is lovely if its owner is suffering in some aspect of life? Or why erect for a partner who is manipulative or emasculating? The penis has thrown down the gauntlet. By showing what real paralysis is, it calls for an analysis of the situation.

## Slings and Arrows

Stress impotence can attack suddenly in youth as a delayed

response to a frightening or hurtful sexual experience. These can include: a cruelly broken heart, a narrow escape from unwanted pregnancy, hasty sex with fear of discovery, penile infections, over-boisterous sex with glans damage resulting in circumcision, sleazy encounters with a prostitute (or destructive girlfriend) which undermine human dignity and destroy romantic dreams.

Negative sexual experiences can seem like punishment, and not only in youth. The painful feedback sets up an (unconscious) belief that partner sex is full of danger and strife. So partner impotence is the psyche's natural response. It is an unconscious device to protect the man, and keep him safe from harm.

Check values and goals. Are they being betrayed by sexual greed, by an over-ambitious sex drive? Studies show Western cultures are more afraid of intimacy than of sex. In a perceptive young man, the unconscious teaches him otherwise. It shows the close relationship between erection and desire for intimacy. Sex which betrays personal values rarely fulfills the need for love. As success breeds success, so failure breeds failure. This is especially so in potency loss. It is very important to avoid the vicious circle of trying to erect, failing, trying again, failing again. Accept the protective messages the unconscious is sending out. Avoid partner sex. Allow time for the wounds from the "slings and arrows" of outrageous (sexual) fortune to heal.

## Self Help for Younger Men

Check erection ability by solitary masturbation:

- Is the penis firm and fully-engorged?
- Is endurance time satisfactory?
- Is the orgasm pleasing?
- In other respects, is life *reasonably* happy and fulfilling?

If the answers are no, there may be physical disease or mental depression. Consult with a physician promptly because they can be treated and cured. If the answers are mainly yes, the problem may be due to stress.

Go slow on future relationships. Avoid pressure from self or a partner to make love. That can be a betrayal of values which the unconscious immediately recognizes. The real challenge is not to erect with a partner, but to find a partner whom the unconscious

217

trusts, one with similar values and needs. Give this challenge a best shot. Wait until then.

Regard stress impotence as a challenge, not a curse. Avoid self-pity which can increase stress. If necessary, masturbate to relieve sexual tension. Regard this as temporary. Avoid letting it replace the real thing with the risk of isolation. It can reduce the desire to seek the wider pleasures of partner love.

If self help does not work, seek a sex behavior therapist. Above all, continue the search for a compatible mate.

## All That Jazz

Is stress impotence due to poor parenting? What of psychotherapy, psycho-babble, all that jazz? The majority of men under stress do not want to delve into their past. They feel they have enough to cope with in their present state. Sex behavior therapy is no longer mainly concerned with investigating childhood trauma. It tackles the immediate problem of restoring potency, and fast. The following check list is only for those men interested in unresolved conflicts. Was suffering caused in youth by:

· Strict over-moralistic rearing?
· Sex for procreation only?
· Guilts over masturbation?
· Homosexual anxieties?
· Religious/cultural taboos?
· Domineering/manipulative mother?
· Weak/passive/brutal or absent father?
· Childhood sexual abuse?

Any of the above can traumatize a sensitive child. The critical word here is "sensitive." In a family of boys, brothers who receive equally poor parenting are not equally affected. It is the sensitive son with highly developed perceptive powers who may develop potency problems in adult life.

## Stress and Testosterone

Testosterone has been called the winner hormone because the blood levels rise when a problem is solved, a battle won. The euphoric mood which follows winning shuts down the production of stress hormones, which results in a natural surge of testosterone.

It can be seen that these hormones work in opposition. Once a battle is won, testosterone converts the extra fats and sugar for flight or fight back into stored energy. This does not happen if the battle is lost and/or the man remains stressed. He stays wired for action. Nor does he gain that natural surge of testosterone. Some men thrive on stress; others do not. In the latter group, even if the battle is won, they cannot relax. They remain tense, anxious and uptight. It is now thought the production of testosterone may be blocked with prolonged stress. And that it is the ravages from those unabated stress hormones which speed up the aging process. By staying on Red Alert for fight or flight, the health problems which ensue go something like this:

- The stress hormones keep putting fats and sugar into the blood.
- These cause an unhealthy build-up of sugar and cholesterol, with an increased risk of the formation of plaque. Plaque speeds up the aging of the cardiovascular system, with hardened arteries, high blood pressure and heart disease.
- This can turn a minor problem of stress impotence into major physical impotence because penile blood flow is also impaired. Keep in mind: *Stress is the enemy of the erection process.*

## Regaining Testosterone

A few scientists now believe older men under prolonged stress should take regular testosterone therapy, TRT. They think it may help maintain a more youthful and healthy cardiovascular system, and reduce the risk of impotency. They also think TRT puts back that slightly lost winner edge in everyday life.

This theory is highly controversial. It may be dangerous for health because testosterone is implicated in prostate cancer and, paradoxically, early heart disease, the two top killers of men. Nor is there proof TRT stops the damaging effects of stress, let alone improves the quality of life by putting back that winner edge. If TRT ever does become a viable option, it may cause as many health concerns as estrogens for women at the menopause.

*Avoid empowering stress to speed up the aging process and so damaging the erection process.*

Natural relaxation and the euphoria which follows is the healthy option. For men under stress, achieve that winner edge by testing out the body's physical strengths. Go for the high. Learn to experience euphoria by winning at tennis or exercising in a gymnasium. Even climbing stairs can produce euphoria, when the number which can be tackled increases. The natural surge of testosterone these activities produce may be a real incentive for men who are reluctant to reduce stress.

## Older Men: The Challenge

A heart attack shows a man his life is on the wrong track. It warns him that if he does not change track, he will soon die. It forces him to admit something is wrong with his values or goals because they have made him ill. He gets the chance to mend or end them, according to his circumstances and needs.

Stress impotence can be compared to a heart attack. It warns a man his life is on the wrong track. He may secretly fear his partner; his penis demands he resolve this. He may dislike his lifestyle or goals; his penis tells him he is right. Or he may have painful sexual memories from so long ago it seems unlikely they still count. But they do. And his penis insists he resolve them, or it will continue to die on him.

Beware altruistic counter-arguments from the conscious mind. They go like this: A real man has duties and obligations, people to support, ends to meet. How can he change goals, relationships or lifestyle in mid-life? And since when has making love become a top priority of existence? Oh, no! What nonsense! A real man ignores impotence and simply soldiers on. . . .

Other counter-arguments go like this: I did it my way. It was bad luck that my dreams went wrong. Now I feel like a loser. I don't mind being impotent. Who gives a toss?

*Denying a problem its value is an avoidance technique.*

## The Quality of Mercy

Imagine holding a newborn babe in your arms. Let feelings of tenderness invade the mind. Now imagine that babe is in danger of harm. Let strong protective feelings mingle with the tenderness. Now imagine you have made that baby safe. Let the pleasure which comes from having put things right totally occupy the mind.

The heroes of antiquity were honored for such virtues as stoicism, fortitude in adversity and self-sacrifice. Today's heroes, often unsung, are much the same. The majority of men are natural protectors. They direct their lives at unpleasant tasks to provide for their offspring. They readily engage in stressful lifestyles or goals rather than evade their protective role.

Such men are too busy as providers to care for the child within themselves. By ignoring their own nurture needs, they suffer potency loss. When the stress becomes overwhelming, or eats away at moral strengths, they face the crushing blow of impotence, rapidly followed by that horrendous syndrome known as "shame and blame."

Men do not suffer stress impotence unless something is wrong. Instead of putting things right, manly virtue demands they accept shame and blame. They simply "soldier on." Though these are admirable virtues in battle, they are sadly misplaced in issues of health.

Consider the quality of mercy; in this case, self-mercy. It is not strained, but drops on everyone alike. Try being merciful on yourself. Eschew shame and blame. Get in touch with the child within, whose needs have been ignored for so long. Learn to parent that child by protecting it from the pain of further impotence. Discover the pleasure of putting things right again.

## Self-Help: Older Men

First, accept the problem. Like the alcoholic who wants to stop drinking, the greatest breakthrough comes when the truth is known. And as with the alcoholic, this truth can produce sudden tears. Let them flow. They are healing tears. They bathe and heal the wounds of life, so long denied, so long endured.

Releasing tears stops the bitter bile of rage. If held back, the bitterness will emerge in spiteful, destructive ways. Keep the grieving short. Prolonged sadness can cause depression, a condition in which interest in life itself is lost. If depression has set in, consult with a physician. But the very act of reading this book suggests a healthy interest in life, in sexual love.

It can feel very threatening to admit relationships or goals have been damaging. A whole life has been based on them. Can a whole life be awry? Yet it is likely these tracks were not freely chosen in youth. They came from an unconscious need to fit in, to meet the expectations of other people. Options were not freely available

221

because the need to please childhood authority figures — parents, teachers, preachers — was too strong.

It is never too late to stop living other people's lives. For that is what is happening when a life is on the wrong track. Let the dead bury the dead! Dump the need to overachieve. Or dump the illusion of being a loser. Where did these stressors come from in the first place?

If this is too painful or inappropriate, find a really good sex behavior therapist. Consult with a valued physician over whom to choose. Studies show the match between therapist and client is more important for a successful outcome than any number of skills or credentials. Though some therapists are excellent, some are useless or worse. Leave one who does not suit.

The function of the sex therapist is to help mend or end behavior which is damaging the erection process. All energy is focused on achieving and maintaining a high level of sexual satisfaction. It is now a medically accepted fact that a good therapist can resolve 90 to 95 percent of cases of stress impotence.

Is therapy too embarrassing to contemplate? Try self-help. Examine a committed relationship. Is it warm? loving? supportive? Is real friendship there? Or is there now a mutual feedback of pain which is so deeply ingrained that both partners are equally toxic to the relationship? Be honest and fair. Anger at a partner comes from power struggles, lack of trust, fear of communication. Was the impotence first intended to punish the partner, and now has become ingrained?

If there is no committed relationship, consider why not. Widowhood is tragic, but so is loneliness and protracted grief. On average, men die five years younger than women; it is not clear why. This leaves many single women needing love and companionship from whom to choose.

Perhaps, just perhaps, men die younger because they abandon sexual love at an inappropriate age. If they live with anxiety or repressed rage, this could be the one act of denial which hastens an early grave. For if a man abandons what is central to himself — if he denies his masculinity, his deepest concerns — what is left at the heart of him? Where is that all-enriching, life-enhancing renewal of sexual joy?

True strength lies in the willingness to face a challenge, not deny its value. Give top priority to emotional needs. If the relationship is unhappy, decide to mend or end it. Concentrate on mending first, there is no guarantee a new partner will work. If single, seek to give rather than take love. There tends to be an increase in self-preoccupation in later life. Try to avoid this.

Self-help is much the same for inappropriate lifestyles. Ask a simple question: What is the point of staying on the wrong track? At this life stage, it is an "all-lose" situation. Unhappy men suffer more health problems, age more quickly, die younger. When a life is back on track, the immediate reward is a huge increase in self-worth. So the function of impotence, that unconscious device to keep a man safe from harm, is gone. And — Hey Presto — the erection process is freed from its chains!

Reach for happiness. Give it a best shot. The following jingle may help, or put the teeth on edge:

If you always do
What you've always done
Then what you'll get
Is what you've always got.

The following articles are some further observations concerning potency which may be worth consideration.

# Mate Selection

Men are handsome, homely or plain. They are tall, medium or short. Their sex drives are as individual as their looks or their height. In the strength of the sex drive, men are more like women than they are like one another. As far as the libido goes, the genders are much the same.

There are natural extremes at each end of the spectrum. A few men do have very high levels of sexual need. Others are the "tried it once, didn't like it, gave it up" type. Neither extreme is good or bad; neither is positive or negative. They are perfectly normal examples of perfectly natural human variation.

A recent mate selection study asked some 10,000 people of 37 cultures and 33 countries to rate 31 desirable characteristics in a mate. Kindness and intelligence were the most sought-after traits by both genders. But worldwide, men placed more value on young and physically attractive mates. Women preferred somewhat older mates with good financial prospects who were industrious and ambitious.

During evolution, young and attractive females signified the likelihood of high fertility. Older industrious males signified the ability to provide during the child-bearing years. Perhaps these characteristics are programmed in the unconscious because youth and beauty are still potent attractions for men, as power and success are magnets for women.

Yet first attractions are based (unconsciously) on sexual compatibility, equal libido strengths. Other considerations come later. If an older man chooses youth and beauty, is he really opting for fatherhood? If his sex drive is less than his mate's, after the first flush of desire, there is a risk he suffers from stress impotence. Keep sexual compatibility in mind when selecting a mate.

## Saints or Sluts?

Some men (unconsciously) still divide women into two groups. The Madonna is the saintly mother, the virgin — she does not really enjoy sex. The Magdalene is the wicked woman, the temptress — she is always hot for sex. The Madonna fits his public life. Her rewards are his name, status, home, children. Magdalenes fit his fantasy life. Her rewards are money, usually sporadic, and little else.

The Madonna/Magdalene complex is not necessarily religion-related. It can be due to the profoundly close ties a baby boy has with his mother. He imprints on her smell, her soft skin, her gentle comforting ways. As he grows he learns, often with pain, that women-as-mothers are sexually taboo. Though not all mothers are loving, indeed a few are destructive with their sons, even poor role models do not seem to affect this early imprinting.

## Call Me Madam

A man with the Madonna/ Magdalene complex needs his woman to be sexually active or passive, not both. In his unconscious, she is saint or slut and must not step out of her role. If a Madonna, he will be appalled at her attempts to seduce him. He will find her actions so disturbing, so sluttish, that he fails to erect. If a Magdalene, she must always be hot for him. He can make joyous love, providing she does not change her status.

But how can a Magdalene remain a saint? She is a woman, and women become pregnant, raise children, enter menopause, undergo gynecologic surgery and so on. Any of these life events can change her role in his unconscious. Magdalenes, after all, do not raise children, need operations, grow old!

She then becomes a Madonna in the man's psyche. And once a saint, she is unsuitable for his "animal lusts." She is a mother; too pure, too frail or too old for his desires. With his conscious mind, he cannot understand what is wrong when he cannot erect.

# Heartbreak Hotel

Elvis Presley was a classic example of this unconscious taboo. Once his young and pretty wife bore his child, his psyche refused to "see" her as a woman to be desired. Instead of trying to find out what was wrong, he helped himself to other young girls. This brought his marriage and family life to an end. The heartbreak may have been responsible for his drug addiction and early death.

A few men find desire ebbs when a partner is pregnant. This is not necessarily the Madonna taboo. More often it is loving concern for her health or an uncanny sensation the unborn babe is watching him from the womb. If the latter, he can overcome these fears by knowing he is including his child in their love.

There is no need to suspect the Madonna/Magdalene complex unless desire does not return after the baby is born.

# Femaphobia

One cause of stress impotence has its roots in childhood rearing. Small boys are taught not to cry, to deny their feelings. They are trained to be fearless, tough-minded, outward-looking. Their "female" side is routinely repressed.

This repression comes from misguided fears of homosexuality. Often the fears are unconscious, having been learned by adults in their own childhood. It is a precept of psychiatry that *denial can create more problems than it avoids*. Having to deny the female side of his nature can make a boy fearful of "all things womanly."

If the denial is mild, he may nurture an unconscious grudge against women. His psyche thinks they have it easy, in sexual terms. All they have to do is lie back and pretend. And because potency is not a female issue, women enjoy talking about it. They make matters worse by spelling out exactly what is wrong. . . .

If the denial is severe, it can have the opposite of the intended effect. A sensitive perceptive boy may be driven so far that he avoids "all things womanly." As he matures, no matter how hard he tries, he cannot be comfortable with women. Parents need to understand a boy has no choice over this. He is then driven to seek affection and sexual love in the arms of men. If he retains a high degree of fear/fascination of women, he apes their dress and mannerisms as a homosexual man.

# The Lonesome Trail

Even without a trace of femaphobia, all men (unconsciously) recognize the "challenge of the vagina." It produces a degree of camaraderie, of simpatico, with other males. For it is always the man who must be the penetrator, never the woman. It is he who must get into the appropriate mindset to allow for erection. No matter how much help he may get from a partner, on the bottom line, erection is his responsibility, and his alone.

It can be perceived that erection is a position of singular isolation. And that this isolation is sometimes overlooked in the mutuality which love seeks. At different times it makes a man feel very differently: joyous, victorious, powerful, vulnerable, anxious, threatened, wretched, alone. . . .

Whatever he feels, a man cannot hide this awareness. It shows in his actions, his behavior and bearing towards women. It shows in his speech, the words and tone of voice he uses to and about them. A man who consistently "puts down" or "elevates" women may be giving off signals of femaphobia. Avoid doing this. Consider what is going wrong.

# Modern Times

In recent times, a new buzz term has been coined: "inhibited sexual desire," ISD. Various magazine articles warn women that ISD is on the increase. However, sexologists agree this is a philosophic concept, not a biologic one. If a man does not wish to make love, it does not necessarily signify inhibited desire.

One theory suggests that the roots of ISD lie in female emancipation. Some men now feel under real pressure to "perform."The very word offends. Others feel uncomfortable with the general depreciation of the male role. Still others suffer from a type of female assertiveness which shows little understanding of, and less sympathy for, the complex nature of the erection process.

A man can feel coerced into unwanted intercourse. Due to the stereotype of men-as-strong, he finds it difficult to refuse a partner's demands. But men are weak too. Like women, they desire to be popular. Like women, they can be altruistic; they do not want

a partner to feel rejected. Men-as-weak is not a common perception of sex role expectation. It might help some women to be aware
the phenomenon exists.

# Divorce Is Difficult

*You can take a horse to water,*
*But you cannot make him drink.*

A new value can be quickly accepted. But it takes longer to reject
older values passed down over the centuries. When today's men
make love, many still hold yesterday's values. They feel adrift
with the free-wheeling, money-earning, sex-demanding lifestyles
of the women displayed in the glossy magazines.

Yet the average woman is still more reluctant to become sexually
involved than a man. In an uncommitted relationship, she is still
more at risk than he. Some methods of birth control carry risks to
her health, as does pregnancy and childbirth. Due to her different
anatomy, she is more likely to catch AIDS than pass it on. Her
slighter build adds a further risk of violence and rape.

So perhaps it is natural the man is usually expected to take the
sexual initiative. Most men delight in the role of the hunter, and
why not? Yet what of the man who does not wish to hunt with
today's assertive woman? He can limit his search to partners who
prefer yesterday's values and courtship ways.

The human mind strives to be whole, to be in harmony with
itself. When the conscious and unconscious are split, one part is
likely to sulk. A man who perceives himself as superior and in
control of women, yet seeks today's uncommitted relationships,
can suffer stress impotence. His values do not fit the reality. His
unconscious recognizes this more quickly than he does.

Divorce is difficult! Decide which values fit, yesterday's or
today's — perhaps a little of both — and act accordingly.

# Take a Pair of Sparkling Eyes

A man separated from his beloved may gaze at her sweet photograph and find it a most erotic "object." To some degree, male
erection does depend upon visual stimulation. Consider the use
of erotica for stress impotence; it may prove of value. It is certainly
not to be condemned, or to be ashamed of. (Whether visual stimulation is more critical for male than female erection is not yet

known.) Is he a tit man? Is he a leg man? Some men do stereotype themselves this way. And though it is crass, it works, but not at all times. Keep in mind the erection process can be more sensitive than speech! Some men pay good money for the huge breasts or shapely legs of a prostitute only to find they still cannot erect.

A man who depends solely on object stimulation is depending on past history of erection success; he stays with what he knows will work. The responsibility for his potency can be (often unconsciously) transferred onto the object. If he fails to erect, it is because the object has in some way failed. In this way, he protects himself from the challenge of becoming erect.

There are more men like this than is sometimes thought. It is an unhappy conceit, which is further encouraged by the sexual hype. It is in Western cultures, where it is acceptable to use the female form to sell everything from mousetraps to machinery, that male lack of desire is on the increase.

## How Much Is Enough?

A Western man cannot help seeing women as objects. He is as much a product of his social environment as she. The persistent and blatant use of women's bodies as objects can keep him slightly over-charged about sex. He believes he is not getting enough from the act. He thinks love-making should not be what it has become — a satisfying, comforting, ordinary part of life. He seeks the over-excitement of the sexual hype every time.

To quote again from Dr. Alex Comfort: "The conventional male fantasy of being able to perform anytime, anywhere, is *wholly neurotic*. . . like a stud bull." Wholly neurotic, eh? Well, a man who was a stud bull in youth can suffer potency loss in mid-life because he has ignored the complex nature of desire. He remains sexually greedy, gross, boring and finally dead in bed.

How much is enough? For the record: Married couples aged 18 to 24 engage in sexual activity 3.25 times a week. For couples aged 25 to 34, the median is 2.55. This can be non-stop on holiday, to weekends during the working year, to any combination of times whatsoever. But data of this type are not really helpful. Men (and their partners) are too individual, and real-life situations too varied, for such categories to fit.

As sex is such an intriguing subject, there tends to be more talk than action. Whether this creates male feelings of personal dissatisfaction is not yet known. But keep it in mind if such feelings arise when listening to locker-room (tall?) stories. Nevertheless, one study came up with an interesting finding: many men would prefer to make love more often than they do. Whatever the reasons for this, at least it is a very healthy sign.

# A Clear Perspective

There is a curious condition called Koro, in which a man becomes preoccupied with thoughts of death. It is directly related to fears of impotence. Koro begins when one man wakes at night with deep chills and premonitions of death. To warm and comfort himself, he handles his penis. To his horror, he imagines it is shrinking in size. Even worse, he imagines pressure from his abdomen is trying to suck it back inside his body.

His shouts of terror wake up the entire community. Soon other men are infected by the same fear. Panic sweeps through the village. No penis is safe from retraction. Wives and other adult females are enlisted to help pull each penis out, or to stop the retraction before it starts.

Over the centuries, epidemics of Koro break out in various countries. They are more common in China and other Eastern lands, but have occurred in Belgium and Britain. Whole communities of men believe death is imminent and "turn their face to the wall." Yet in no single case has the penis been observed to shrink, let alone retract into the abdomen. But these observations were made by strangers: anthropologists, physicians, nurses, people who do not belong. How can such strangers be expected to understand the community's concerns?

Another form of Koro is imagining the tongue is being pulled back into the throat. It is not gender-specific. Real and severe gagging follows in both men and women. Perhaps seeking a physical cause for psychogenic (stress) impotence is rather like Koro. It is the power of the imagination over the power of facts.

# CHAPTER 15

# Sexually Transmitted Disease

## Close Encounters

If a man has a cold, his partner can catch the virus. If his partner has fleas, he may soon begin to itch. Naked flesh, hot and sweating in motion, is ideal for the exchange of infections. In close encounters of the sexual kind, the human body is highly vulnerable to the transmission of disease.

The act of penetration is ideal for the exchange of infected fluids. Any disease in the penis is directly "injected" into the vagina. During thrusting, infected fluids in the vagina are forced into the meatus. Lovers share infections as well as affections. Is this what is meant by the "give and take" of love?

## The Hidden Epidemic

The most common STDs are gonorrhea, chlamydia, NGU, herpes, and condyloma. In 1988, one U.S. report estimated there were 38,000 new STDs each day! It is not possible to get precise data because many cases go unreported. The media concentrate on AIDS, and the community forgets there is a raging epidemic of all other STDs.

When AIDS was first diagnosed in the early 80s, certain individuals considered it to be the "wrath of God." The disease was seen as a fitting punishment not only for male homosexuals, but for heterosexuals who did not lead monogamous lives. The barbarism behind this wishful thinking would have wiped out most of the adult population because only one sexual partner in life is no longer the norm. Fortunately, the hysteria which provoked such cruel thinking has since died down.

Health professionals hoped the fear of AIDS would encourage all sexually active people to turn to monogamy. And data from STD clinics show the majority of male homosexuals have. But the number of heterosexuals attending STD clinics has not changed in the last decade. In spite of fear of AIDS, other STDs remain at epidemic proportions. It is estimated most adults will get a sexual infection, other than AIDS, at some life stage.

## Silent Reservoirs

When a man has an STD, he is usually knows he is infected. He has symptoms of disease soon after catching it. He can see the chancre (sore) of syphilis on his penis, or the drip of pus from gonorrhea. He can feel the stinging pain of NGU or chlamydia when he urinates. One survey suggests only 5 percent to 15 percent of men with STD are asymptomatic, have no symptoms at all.

The opposite holds true for women. Some 50 to 80 percent with gonorrhea or chlamydia are asymptomatic in the early stages of infection; 25 percent with syphilis are unaware because the chancre is hidden from view on the cervix. By the time they realize something is wrong, the disease may have caused havoc in their reproductive system. Until such unlucky women find out they are infected, it is they who act as "silent reservoirs" for the spread of STD.

## Strangers in the Night

Prostitutes, overseas business travelers and tourists are often blamed for the spread of STD. Yet the facts prove otherwise. There is now evidence neither prostitutes, travelers nor tourists are the main sources of infection. Young people between the ages of 15 and 30 are the top transmitters of STD.

A young man is more at risk of infection from a casual girlfriend than from a prostitute. The reasons are the "silent reservoir" syndrome and because young men are still reluctant to use condoms. While condom protection against STD is accepted by travelers and prostitutes, young women in the community find it difficult to persuade their partners to take protective measures.

Within each community is a pool of STD infection. If young women are the silent reservoirs, how did they contract STD in the first place? Which man in the community, young or old, married or single, preacher or atheist, passed it on? To focus on only one group is to ignore *STD as multi-linked* throughout a community.

If therapy is sought at the first signs of disease, most STD can be quickly cured. Men have early and obvious symptoms, so it is they who have the chance to reduce the pool of infection in their community. They can:

· Stop partner sex at once.
· Seek prompt medical help.
· Inform their partners.

Women have no such choices. They require a health check at each new sexual encounter to find out if they have been infected. Contrary to popular adage, all is not fair in love and war.

## The Repeaters

The repeaters are young men who keep catching, and passing on STD. They regard the "clap" or "drip" as little more bothersome than the common cold. Indeed, some of the cruder ones boast of how often they have been infected, and cured. Ironically, it is the efficiency of modern antibiotics which has given rise to this "don't care" attitude.

## Familiarity Breeds Contempt

And it breeds STD! Some repeaters take a course of antibiotics each time they change partners. They do not consider it is their responsibility to warn the partner to take a course as well. They often do not bother to complete the course, or they use the wrong antibiotic, or they take a dose which is too low to be effective. The symptoms vanish, but they remain infectious. They eschew condoms; what is the point when antibiotics work so well?

Self-medication with antibiotics (for any reason) can cause serious medical and social problems. With repeated use, bacteria have time to develop resistance and eventually the drugs lose their effect. In 1988, the U.S. Surgeon General reported a 75 percent increase in penicillin-resistant gonorrhea and syphilis from 1987; one year alone in which the killer AIDS was rampant.

In countries such as Thailand, which men visit for "sex holidays," antibiotics are costly. Prostitutes may be given such low doses that they, and so their clients, develop penicillin-resistant STD. Travelers from remote areas bring back new strains against which antibiotics do not work. To date, not enough is known about the wide variety of organisms which cause STDs.

Antibiotics cannot destroy viruses. They are powerless against AIDS, herpes and condyloma, all of which may be linked to cancer. Both AIDS and cancer can be fatal. Other STD viruses can cause birth defects, sterility, joint disease and progressive, permanent health problems. The repeater appears blithely unaware of the risks he takes. He also seems unaware of the damage he is doing to his partner.

# Hope Springs Eternal. . .

There are minor STDs, and there are major ones. There are very rare infections, and very common ones. It is not possible to self-diagnose from a book. Only an expert in the field, with the use of the latest medical technology, can diagnose a particular strain of STD. In recent years, more men are becoming silent reservoirs of sexual disease; it is not known why. But it may be related to the delaying tactic known as "hope springs eternal in the human breast."

For the average person, the slightest sign of an STD causes anxiety. Though the worst may be feared, there is hope against hope for the best. And while the hope lasts, there is a "waiting to see what happens, to see if the symptoms disappear." The fearful moment when a sexual infection must be acknowledged and accepted is delayed.

This is natural behavior. Unhappily, it can have dire results. The time lapse between hoping and going to the clinic gives the infection a chance to spread further inside the reproductive system. One major factor in successful STD therapy is *the earlier the treatment, the quicker and easier the cure.*

# No Shame?

To encourage early therapy and avoid delay, the public has been told there is no shame attached to STD. This is more easily said than believed! The average person does feel very upset. Not only is there physical disgust at the symptoms. There is often a far more complex interaction of extremely painful emotions:

- Natural anxiety about the infection.
- Fear of consequences of own behavior.
- Rage and pain at a partner's infidelity.
- Insecurity within the relationship.
- Sense of betrayal and threatened trust.
- Desperate need to blame outside agency.
- Shame, lies, secrecy, guilt, remorse and so on.

When one person is infected, any other partner is a contact. They must also be treated even though there are no symptoms of disease. For obvious reasons, one partner in a relationship may be reluctant to inform the other. With casual sex, the name of the partner may not even be known.

The "ping pong" effect occurs when one partner alone knows of the infection and receives therapy. It could be the man, as his symptoms are obvious and painful. It could be the woman, un aware the man is a silent reservoir of her vaginal itch. After therapy, the cured person is re-infected, has more treatment, is re-infected and so on. The disease travels back and forth between the couple, creating what is known as the ping pong effect.

Partners may regard infidelity as a minor peccadillo. Or they may consider it a major breach of trust. Whatever the moral stance, silence is the coward's way to make the disease worse. Silence puts at risk the health, perhaps the reproductive life, of a partner. Contact tracing is essential to reduce the pool of infection within a community. Yet many STD sufferers are not willing to assist the health professionals in their task.

Medical specialists in STD are called *venereologists*. The name comes from Venus, the Goddess of Love. In 1970, a U.S. venereologist spoke of the vast amount of public funds available for research into a poliomyelitis vaccine. Yet polio, dreadful as it is, cripples and kills far fewer people than STDs. If the same funds were available for STD research, he reckoned it was almost certain vaccines would soon be found.

That was 20 years ago. Today, there are still no vaccines. Is lack of funds for STD research where real shame lies?

## Sexual Behavior

High risk sexual behavior includes:

· Sex which is paid for.
· Multiple heterosexual partners.
· Male sex (anal homosexual intercourse).
· Unprotected sex with a new partner.
· Heterosexual anal and oral unprotected sex.
· Boisterous sex which causes minor lesions, bruises or bleeding.

The HIV virus for AIDS is transmitted in infected blood, semen and vaginal fluids. It is transmitted in skin sores, and genital lesions too microscopic to be seen. Infected blood and semen contain the highest concentration of the HIV virus. Vaginal fluids have a lesser concentration. The virus may be present in tears, saliva and sweat, but the concentrations are usually too weak for there to be any risk. STD infections can be transmitted in very low concentrations; one germ may be enough.

Recent medical studies suggest syphilis and genital herpes are a significant risk factor in the transmission of the HIV virus. The sores of syphilis and herpes are not only on the genitals. They can be on the mouth and inside the rectum as well. In a recent study of men who tested positive for both syphilis and herpes, 86 percent carried the HIV virus. But only 44 percent who were negative for syphilis and herpes were positive for HIV.

In another male study, the AIDS infection was associated with a history of syphilis and/or a positive test for syphilis. Among women, the HIV infection was associated with a history of genital warts. Though genital warts do not usually form ulcer sores, they may be associated with inflammation or secondary infection. It seems likely STD which disrupt epithelial (skin) surfaces may be important factors in the transmission of HIV.Appropriate ways to avoid infection are to avoid being in direct contact with a partner's blood, semen, vaginal fluids or sores anywhere on the skin. If abstinence or monogamy are unacceptable, condoms provide some protection.

# Anal Sex

Anal sex carries specific health risks for everyone, whether heterosexual or homosexual. Feces (waste from the bowel) contain highly infectious matter. If the penis is not washed immediately after anal sex, these germs may be directly thrust into the vagina. (Repeated attacks of vaginal monilia, a yeast infection, can occur this way). For obvious reasons, male sex carries a greater risk of transmitting diseases such as salmonella food poisoning, hepatitis, amoebic dysentery and lupus.

The walls of both vagina and rectum have a rich supply of blood. But unlike the vagina, the walls of the rectum are only a few cells thick. They are not designed to resist the pressure of a thrusting penis. Herein lies the main danger of anal sex for both heterosexuals and homosexuals. The thin walls of the rectum tear and bleed easily. Infected blood, semen or feces can then pass directly into the blood system.

The second danger lies in the skin of the penis. At erection it becomes very stretched, taut and fine. During normal vaginal thrusting, it is common for invisible lesions (microscopic breaks) to occur in penile skin. These lesions are more common in anal sex due to added resistance from the rectum walls.

The third danger also involves the fine skin of the penis. It becomes super absorbent when stretched taut at erection. This was first realized when women were given estrogen creams as vaginal lubricants. Their partners began to develop male breasts. The problem with using estrogen creams has since been resolved. It is related here to remind all men how super absorbent the erect penis is to any substance, including infections.

Whatever the moral stance, hygiene is top priority. The penis should never enter the vagina or mouth straight from the bowel. Hands, particularly finger nails, are an added factor in transmission of disease. They must be washed! In today's AIDS climate, it is advised condoms always be used during anal sex.

# Oral Sex

It is thought the practice of oral sex has increased in the past 40 years. Its skills have been widely promoted in sex manuals, erotic books and magazines. Indeed, oro-genital sex is now considered a normal activity in certain cultures. For a few men, it has replaced penetration. During an epidemic of disease, it is appropriate to be aware of the health risks.

Specific micro-organisms inhabit the mouth, just as they inhabit other orifices of the body. They do not cause problems within their natural habitat. But if they are transmitted to other orifices, they can cause an infection. One typical example is a harmless bacteria of the mouth which, if transmitted to the penis, can cause male urethritis.

Add to which, the membranes lining the mouth are naturally subject to microscopic lesions. It is estimated there is gum bleeding after cleaning the teeth in at least one-third of any given population. Small ulcers can be present at the sides of the mouth. The tongue may be sore for a variety of reasons. All these factors can make the mouth an "unsafe" place for sex.

Diseases known to be transmitted by oro-genital infection include AIDS, gonorrhea of the throat, the syphilis chancre on the lips, the herpes virus cold sore and yeast infections. To date, two cases of AIDS have been contracted this way. There are no data on the frequency of STD transmitted by oro-genital sex.

It would seem unlikely there is a strong desire to kiss a partner sporting a sore on the mouth. But keep in mind the time factor for incubation of disease. There is always a time lapse between the time of catching an infection and when the first symptoms appear. Incubation periods vary widely with different STDs, they can be some years for AIDS.

Also keep in mind that with some STD, both genders can be asymptomatic. There are no signs of disease to help remind lovers oral sex can be dangerous. Avoid direct mouth contact with semen, where there is high risk sexual activity, or any reason for doubt. One option is to completely avoid oro-genital sex. If this is inappropriate, wait until both partners are tested and known to be infection-free.

# Safe Sex?

In April 1987, the U.S. Food and Drugs Administration wrote to the manufacturers of condoms. They explained that due to the AIDS epidemic: "it has become very important that users be fully aware that latex condoms provide protection, but do not guarantee it, and that protection is lost if condoms are not used properly."

Since the 1960s, the FDA has conducted random unannounced tests of sample condoms from domestic and foreign manufacturers. If more than 4 out of 100 are found defective, the entire batch is rejected. During year ending April 1988, 41 out of 204 batches of latex condoms failed to meet government standards, just over 20 percent. And just under a third of them were made in the U.S.

Condoms are tested for tensile strength and water leakage, possible pinholes or tears. But the FDA tests take place under pre-set laboratory conditions. There are no data for the failure rate when used in real-life situations. Real life has a habit of not conforming to pre-set and carefully monitored conditions. It is likely the results would be very different from FDA tests.Health professionals promote the use of condoms as "safe sex." In an epidemic of STD and AIDS, this is understandable. Any method which offers protection should be made known. Yet a condom may not be put on properly. It may break. It may not be worn from the beginning to the end of sexual activity. And whether it is used properly or not, a defective one is worse than useless.

The high failure rate of the laboratory tests highlights the fact that condoms do not provide 100 percent protection. Consider what health professionals know only too well: that condoms do not ensure total protection against AIDS, STD, pregnancy or anything else.

## Condom Care

Latex condoms are sturdier than natural skin. Spermicides are sperm killers. They provide increased protection because they inactivate many of the organisms which cause STDs. There are now spermidical condoms for increased protection. Or, a condom can be used with a spermicide cream or a contraceptive sponge.

Condoms are often used in conjunction with lubricants. A recent survey by UCLA in America estimated between 50 percent and 90 percent of condom users may be relying on lubricants which cause condom failure less than 60 seconds after application.Of nearly 13,000 men, 61 percent used Vaseline Care lotion. Baby oil was used by more than half the men in a similar British study. Both these products contain mineral oil, and it is mineral oil which weakens latex and causes the condom to break. Two other products containing mineral oil which are used as lubricants are Nivea hand cream and Vaseline petroleum jelly.

Vegetable oils were also used as lubricants. They include Mazzola and Wesson oils, olive oil, safflower oil and Crisco. Keep in mind any oil-based lubricant will damage latex. In fact, all of the above products are inappropriate. They can upset the ecological balance of vaginal flora, and cause a yeast infection. Check the use of lubricants. Read the contents list before purchase. KY Jelly, any water-based lubricant will do. There are many on the market. Ask the pharmacist to recommend one.

If short of funds, avoid the temptation to use a condom more than once. Find a clinic which supplies them free, or at a reduced price. If buying a large batch by mail order to minimize costs, take care to check they are not factory rejects.

When donning a condom, watch out for rings and snagged or sharp fingernails which can tear the fine latex.

Unroll the condom onto the penis as soon as erection occurs. Be sure to hold the closed end between finger and thumb so no air bubble is trapped inside which would cause the condom to burst.

As soon as erection ceases, slide the condom off holding the rim firmly between finger and thumb to prevent the contents from spilling out.

Condoms provide some protection, but it is not total. There is, in fact, only one certain way to avoid STD. Dr. Catterall, an eminent British venereologist, wrote in the IPPF Medical Publications: "The most important fact about sexually transmitted diseases is that they are not contracted by people who have only one sexual partner."

How dangerous are public rest rooms? What is the risk of catching AIDS or STD from infected toilet seats, faucets, towels and so on? The twist in the answer goes: "Of course you can catch AIDS or STD in a public rest room. But it is an undignified and unromantic place to make love."

## Symptoms of Disease

The symptoms of AIDS and STD vary. Visit the physician or clinic if any of the following appear. They may not signify STD, but they show something is wrong which needs to be put right. If there is a recent change of partner, or other high risk behavior, it may be an infection. The sooner an STD is diagnosed, the more easy it is to treat and cure.

·  Abnormal discharge or unusual fluid from the penis.
·  Pain, burning or frequency at urination.
·  Any itching on the genitals or around the anus.

- Sores, blisters, or bumps on genital skin or the anal area which may or may not be painful.
- Enlarged lymph glands in the groin area.
- Pain during intercourse.

# The STD Clinic

Some clinics are free. Others charge for their services. Some are walk in, others require an appointment to be made. Some STD are notifiable. They must be reported to the health authorities by law. The notifiable ones vary from area to area, and from time to time. Some STDs are anonymous; a number instead of name is used. Others are confidential; name, address and telephone number are kept in secret files. Again, it varies with the area and time. Some STDs have more than one name. Others change their names when more is discovered about them. They then get placed in their own special category because they no longer belong to the group they were originally put in. In much the same way, therapies and medications change from clinic to clinic, from time to time. All this may seem confusing. Yet it shows medical knowledge in venereology is advancing. Keep in mind a specific therapy at one clinic may be different from another. There are likely to be sound reasons for this, such as local environmental conditions, the endemic nature of the disease in one particular area.

In towns and cities, there are hot lines to call for help, advice and information. There are telephone tapes which help. In isolated areas, look for notices in public places such as town halls, libraries, wash rooms. Consult the phone book. The entries may be under "V" for venereal disease or "S" for STD. Above all, *AVOID DELAY*.

(The following three articles are about infestations, not infections).

# Little Visitors

These include fleas, mites, ticks, jiggers, bedbugs, scabies and pubic lice. They are all parasites and blood suckers. They have mouth parts adapted into special tubes. One tube injects saliva directly under the host's skin. The saliva contains a substance to prevent blood clotting. This allows the other tube to suck up the blood while it is still liquid. It is the anti-blood clotting factor which causes the tell-tale itching of little visitors.

241

These parasites are *infestations*, not sexual diseases. Most are passed by contact with infested animals. However, scabies and pubic lice are usually transmitted sexually. The main symptoms of infestation are red, swollen, itchy bumps. If the genitals are infested, avoid scratching. Heavy or persistent scratching breaks open the skin, which opens a pathway to more serious *secondary infections*, such as STD.

Genital infestation carries a risk of secondary infection. A few unlucky people are unaware they have gonorrhea or syphilis until they experience the tell-tale itching of scabies or lice. Infestations can be cured by self-help. However, a medical check is advisable because of the risk of secondary infection.

## Scabies

These are highly contagious mites passed by close physical contact. Children playing together can catch them. For adults, the most usual way is by direct sexual touch. They can be caught from infested bed linen, towels or clothing, though this is less usual. Any fabric or material in shared use can be regarded as a source of infestation.

The male lives on the surface of the skin. The female burrows beneath it. She may burrow anywhere, but usually chooses places where the skin is thin, damp and folded. Hence scabies are seen as tiny spores on finger and toe webs, wrists, elbows, belt line, thighs, under breasts and on the genitals of both genders.

The female lays her eggs at the end of the small burrows she makes. These can be seen from the surface as thin dark lines. The eggs hatch in a few days. The mites crawl out and begin feeding. They then mate with the males on the surface of the skin, and so large areas of the body can become infested.

SYMPTOMS: Intense itching, especially at night. Scabies is best diagnosed by a physician. Therapy is by applying Kwell in cream or lotion form. It is a prescription drug in some countries. In others, it can be bought over-the-counter. It contains 1 percent gamma benzene hexachloride, gamma BHC, or malathion. WARNING! People with sensitive skins, or any kind of allergy, should not attempt self-therapy. EXTRA EXTRA WARNING! Pregnant women must not use gamma BHC as it can be absorbed into the blood and appear later in breast milk. Both groups should consult with the physician.

- Begin with a hot bath or shower, and a brisk body scrub.
- Rinse, and dry the skin thoroughly.
- Paint gamma BHC on lower trunk, genitals and down to lower legs.
- Leave for 12 to 24 hours, then bathe to remove medication.
- Place all suspect clothing in an airtight polythene bag.
- Smother with gamma BHC. Leave for one week. Wash or dry clean.

One application of the scabicide should be enough. Itching may continue for several days after therapy. This is normal, and does not mean there is reinfection. Avoid the temptation to apply more gamma BHC; this can be dangerous. If re-infection does occur, repeat the self-help program, or consult the physician.

A few people with no previous history of allergy develop an allergic sensitivity to the scabies mites, their eggs and waste products. Unfortunately, the allergic reaction does not begin until some weeks after the original infestation. At night, the itching can become so acute it is not unknown for some men to actually tear the skin of the penis by scratching. Wear gloves in bed; if necessary, boxing gloves! Consult with the physician.

## *Pubic Lice*

These are so common they are nicknamed "crabs" or "crab lice." They live on the hair of the genitals, crawling from partner to partner in close sexual contact. They fasten onto the new host by sinking their mouth parts firmly in the skin and gripping a pubic hair with their curved claws. They can be caught from infested bed linen, towels or clothing, though this is not usual.

The female louse lays 8-10 nits (eggs) each and every day. She cements the nits to the hair shaft with glue from her body. This makes them difficult to dislodge. They hatch within 10 days. The lice spread and begin feeding, at which stage itching becomes intense. The person is usually unaware of infestation until this stage is reached. On close inspection, the tiny live crabs can be seen. They are dark grey or pink in color. The nits (eggs) on the pubic hair are dark brown.

Gamma BHC destroys pubic lice. The same warnings for its use in scabies elimination applies to the treatment of lice. Pubic lice can also be destroyed by non-prescription medication such as A-200, XXX and RID. These can be bought at the drug store. Check the infested area thoroughly. Pubic lice can migrate to body hair. In rare cases, they reach the beard and eyebrows. If infestation is local only:

· Begin with hot bath or shower, and wash and dry thoroughly.
· Shampoo entire hair of genitals with medication for 5 minutes.
· Rinse and repeat one week later.

If the trunk and legs are very hairy:

· Begin with hot bath or shower, wash and dry thoroughly.
· Apply lotion over the trunk, genitals and legs.
· Leave for 24 hours, then thoroughly rinse lotion off.
· Repeat treatment after one full week.

Some men shave off their body hair before self-help therapy for both pubic lice and scabies. It is not necessary, but it instantly removes lice and their eggs, and gives a better view of the areas of infestation.

Medication can change with new therapies. Whatever type is used, READ AND FOLLOW THE DIRECTIONS CAREFULLY. Wash all infested clothing and bed linen. A spray for cleaning the mattress and furniture can be obtained from the drug store. Clean the home thoroughly. Vacuum carpets and then throw away the bag.

But with any infestation, it is preferable to consult with the physician at once. Self help is an issue of choice.

# Genital Warts

## *Condyloma*

Genital warts are caused by the *human papilloma virus*, also called *condylomata acuminata*, condyloma for short. It is a wart virus specific to the genital area and is transmitted by direct sexual contact with a partner who already has them. To date, 56 different types of the virus have been identified, and 12 more are waiting identification. Condyloma is linked with cancer of the cervix, but this relationship is not 100 percent proven.

The virus appears on the penis as genital warts. The warts can be single. More often, they grow in clusters like grapes. With their raised bumpy tops, they look like baby cauliflowers. They may be on the glans, at the meatus and the corona. They can appear on the testicles, and in and around the anus.

The warts generally appear 1 to 3 months after infection. But the incubation period can be as long as 8 months. They are usually painless, but can be irritated by rubbing, and sometimes they itch. If there has been anal sex, the warts may be inside the rectum and around the anus. More rarely with oral sex, they can infect the membrane linings of the mouth. Without treatment, condyloma can spread rapidly and cover the shaft. They enter the urethra, and set up a colony of warts there. In some cases, this causes burning pain on urination, with frequency, urgency, bleeding and discharge. However, many men are asymptomatic because condyloma lesions can be invisible to the naked eye. These men have no idea they are passing on disease.

If condyloma warts set up a breeding colony on a woman's cervix, the disease may not be found until she has a Pap smear, or problems with fertility. Her partner may be asymptomatic; the warts are not visible on his genitals. Yet the "ping pong" effect means he is likely to be infected as well. For self-help: put the penis in a cup of hot water. It may be possible to see the invisible lesions of condyloma.

When condyloma is diagnosed in a woman, and her partner is asymptomatic, he is tested in the following manner. The genitals and surrounding area are painted with dilute acetic acid (white vinegar) and wrapped in layers of gauze. The acetic acid turns the tiny lesions white so they can be seen. A biopsy is taken of any suspect area. The inside of the urethra may be examined. Venereologists report "some men resist this." If small, the warts can be chemically treated by the drug podophyllin. It is painted on with great care, as it can damage the surrounding tissue. It stays on for 2 to 6 hours to allow sufficient time to destroy the viruses. The medication is thoroughly washed off, or it can burn the skin. It takes 3 to 4 weekly treatments for the warts to dry up, and finally drop off.

If warts are inside the urethra, a podophyllin suppository may be inserted through the meatus. The penis is covered with gauze and an athletic support worn for the next 2 to 6 hours to keep the medication in, and allow sufficient time for the drug to destroy the viruses.

Larger warts in men, and internal warts in women, may be

245

vaporized with a carbon dioxide laser. But it can be difficult to know if they are all destroyed. Repeat treatments are needed if they flare up again. This can seem exasperating, but avoid losing patience as laser therapy usually works in the end. It takes 6 weeks for the healing process to be complete. Other therapies include burning the warts by electric cautery, or freezing them with dry-ice. The physician may then snip off the warts.

In 1989, condyloma was officially diagnosed in 6 percent of U.S. men and women. Research suggests the undiagnosed number is nearer 30 percent. It is thought the incidence is rising rapidly because many lesions are invisible to the naked eye. Check after high risk unprotected sex. In Europe, the peak age group for condyloma is 25- to 35-year-olds. In America, the peak ages are 15 to 25.

## Simple Warts

*Molluscum Contagiosum* are simple warts, the same kind which appear on the hands. They can be transmitted to the penis, pubic area and inner thighs. Simple warts are small, dimpled *papules*. They look like spots with a pearly fluid inside. The virus enters the skin through invisible lesions which occur during sexual activity. The warts appear some 30 days after infection.

Simple warts are highly contagious, as their Latin name suggests. They can be self-transmitted from warts on the hands or elsewhere. This is called *auto-inoculation*. Inform a partner. Simple warts appear most frequently in teenagers and the 20 to 30 age group. Check general and genital hygiene.

Like simple warts on the hands, self therapy is possible but not advisable. It consists of pricking the wart with a sterile needle, squeezing the fluid out and dabbing the area with phenol. Thoroughly clean the hands and infected area first. Keep in mind the risk of secondary infection. Be sure the area is clean during the healing process and avoid sexual activity until all the warts have disappeared. If not, the warts will spread further.

Beware! Simple warts can be confused with genital warts or other STD. Self-help is for those who, for reasons of distance, cannot get professional medical help.

# Blood Diseases
## *AIDS*

*AIDS* stands for Acquired Immune Deficiency Syndrome. *Acquired*: it is not inherited, but passed on in some way. *Immunodeficiency*: the body's defense system becomes destroyed. *Syndrome*: a group of symptoms where the cause is unknown.

However, the cause, HIV virus, is now known. But the word AIDS is still used to avoid confusion. The HIV virus damages the immune system, leaving it vulnerable to rare infections and cancers which are life threatening. The infections and cancers are *opportunistic*. They are not caused by the virus. They attack because the immune system has lost its power to destroy them.

HIV virus is not transmitted by casual contact. It appears to flourish in semen and is transmitted by anal sex; homosexual women rarely get AIDS. It is also transmitted by infected vaginal fluids, infected needles of drug users, transfusions of infected blood and blood products, and from infected breast milk given by an infected mother.

At first, the disease is silent. There may be no symptoms for months, sometimes years. The HIV virus works as follows:

*Virus Infection*: The virus enters the body and starts infecting the cells. The person feels fine, and does not have AIDS.

*Illness*: There is a mild illness like mononucleosis. Some people miss this stage and go straight to the next.

*Antibody Presence*: Antibodies are made to fight off HIV infection (seroconversion), usually one or two months after infection.

*AIDS Related Complex*: ARC is a serious illness, which shows the immune system is now very weakened. This stage may be missed.

*AIDS Diagnosis*: A rare cancer or infection attacks, and a clear diagnosis of AIDS is made. From now, life expectancy is one year.

*Death*: There are repeated bouts of very serious illness, from one of which the person is now too weak to recover.

The symptoms of AIDS include:

· Unexplained and persistent fatigue.
· Unexplained fever, shaking chills, or drenching night sweats lasting for longer than several weeks.
· Unexplained weight loss greater than 10 pounds or 10 percent of bodyweight in one or two months.
· Unexplained swollen glands in the neck, armpit or groin which last more than two months.
· Pink, purple or brown, flat or raised blotches or bumps which feel harder than nearby skin, like bruises which do not disappear on or under the skin, inside the nose, mouth, eyelids or rectum.
· Persistent white spots or unusual blemishes in the mouth.
· Persistent diarrhea.
· Persistent dry cough, especially with shortness of breath.

But most of these symptoms occur in less serious illness. They do not necessarily signify AIDS. But if there has been high risk sexual behavior, or any reason to suspect exposure to HIV infection, avoid waiting for the symptoms to appear. It takes a minimum of one month for HIV antibodies to develop in the blood, so a test immediately after exposure will not give a true result. Most clinics offer free testing after two months. If the results are negative, it is advisable to be re-tested in six months, just in case it takes longer for the HIV antibodies to appear.

If the result is positive, join a local support group. The counselor at the STD clinic will have the names and addresses. Support groups have done a marvelous job at mobilizing their own resources. They have far more knowledge of the disease and skills of compassion than those of an over-worked medical profession. They help with housing, financial support, nursing facilities and company. Avoid facing the future alone.

AIDS is a horrifying disease, destroying many bright young lives. To date, there is no vaccine against the virus, nor is there a cure. Various medications are available. AZT slows down its progress. Medical research continues to seek better ways to prevent, diagnose and treat the HIV infection. Until a vaccine or a cure is found, the only sure protection for homosexual men is monogamy or abstinence. And the data show a real reduction in their promiscuous behavior. But some young men now consider AIDS an "old man's disease." They believe they are safe if they choose partners only in the under 25 age group, and only practice oral sex. But two cases of full-blown AIDS have been reported as the result of this mistaken notion. It seems young men will have to be monogamous too.

A serious problem for heterosexuals is that they have not reduced promiscuous behavior, and this is having dire results in the spread of AIDS. In 1982, ten women and two men were reported having heterosexual AIDS. In 1989, 749 women and 386 men were reported with heterosexual AIDS. The only sure protection for the whole community is to restrict sexual activity to a monogamous partner. Condoms give some protection but are not entirely safe.

Hospitals are now scrupulous at monitoring blood and blood products. Blood donating and transfusions are considered safe. But drug addicts still share infected needles, and AIDS is increasing in this group. The disease is also breaking out among teenagers in schools and on college campus.

By December 31, 1988, a total of 83,764 AIDS cases had been reported; 90 percent were males. The mean age at diagnosis was 37.0 years; 61.0 percent were white, 23.7 percent black and 14.5 percent Hispanic. Some 68 percent of men had histories of homosexual/bisexual activity and no IV-drug use; 17 percent had IV-drug use; 2 percent had a history of blood transfusion; 1 percent had hemophilia or other blood clotting disorders.

By the same date, 6983 American women had AIDS. The mean age was 35.7 years; 51.6 percent were black, 27.9 percent white and 19.5 percent Hispanic. There is a wide variation in HIV virus transmission to women. Some acquire it from an infected partner after a few encounters. Others are free of infection after hundreds. A study of women married to HIV positive hemophiliacs found 15 percent were infected; 22 who did not use condoms were infected; 14 using condoms were not.

By December 1988, 1346 American children had AIDS; 82 percent were under age five. Of these, 40 percent were under one year old. Racial distribution was the same as for women.

By December 1988, 56 percent of all AIDS patients and 85 percent of those diagnosed before 1986 had died. AIDS deaths were 9 percent of all deaths in the 25-34 age group, and 7 percent of all deaths in the 34-44 age group.

When the U.S. epidemic was first recognized in 1981, almost all cases were among white middle-class homosexual men and blood transfusion recipients. By 1989, more than 11 percent of all new AIDS patients were female; 23 percent were intravenous drug users and 43 percent were blacks or Hispanics.

As the AIDS epidemic enters the 90s, there is a shift in the groups of Americans who are at risk. Due to increased drug use, the virus in the second decade is being spread heterosexually and women are more at risk. It is afflicting whole families, especially among poor blacks, but no one group will be completely spared.

According to the Center for Disease Control: 1 to 1.5 million American citizens are infected with the human immunodeficiency virus. By the end of 1992, 1 million Americans will have AIDS. These tragic and appalling data speak for themselves.

In July 1990, new reports from Britain stated that a vaccine may have been found. However, it will take some while before the clinical trials prove that the vaccine is both safe and effective.

## Hepatitis

Hepatitis A and B are caused by virus infection of the liver, and by such diseases as amoebic dysentery and lupus. The virus breeds in feces, and is common where there is poor sanitation. It is passed in contaminated food and drink. Less usually, it is passed by sexual contact; very rarely, by transfusions of infected blood. When in areas of poor sanitation, observe strict personal hygiene. *Avoid anal and oral sex.* Hepatitis is on the increase, probably due to more foreign travel.

Symptoms of hepatitis A begin 15 to 40 days after infection. There is mild fever, nausea, headache, tiredness, loss of appetite and chills. *Jaundice,* a yellow tinge to the skin, fingernails and whites of the eyes, starts a week later and lasts about 3 weeks. Urine may be dark in color; stools almost whitish. A few people are asymptomatic. The defense system builds immunity to the virus, but it remains in the blood and can be transmitted. They are *asymptomatic carriers* of the disease.

The symptoms of hepatitis B are the same as A. But they are severe, and start suddenly 1 to 6 months after infection. If the liver is very damaged, death occurs in 5 to 20 percent of cases. For others, recovery can be very slow, with a 1 in 5 chance of permanent liver damage and cirrhosis. A new drug, cholchecine, seems hopeful. It is at the clinical trial stage.

Hepatitis B (HBV) is transmitted in blood and blood products such as semen, saliva and feces during sexual contact. It is now classified as a sexually transmitted disease. It is also passed by IV drug users sharing infected needles. The incidence of HBV is rapidly increasing, perhaps due to the rapid increase in foreign travel and IV-drug use. Male homosexuals, heterosexuals with multiple partners, travelers and drug addicts are high risk groups.

In the U.S., there are some 300,000 HBV cases yearly, mostly in young adults. 25 percent will develop jaundice; more than 100,000 will need to be hospitalized. Between 350 to 400 people die each year from severe acute Hepatitis B. HBV carriers are more likely to get cancer of the liver. It is estimated 4000 persons die from hepatitis B-related cirrhosis yearly, and more than 1000 die from hepatitis B-related liver cancer.

After high risk sexual behavior, or any cause for concern, get tested immediately. Seek medical help at the first symptoms of disease. When nursing an HBV patient, observe strict hygiene. Precautions include keeping family utensils separate. Any object in intimate contact with the patient — soaps, towels, razors and so on — can be highly infectious and must not be shared.

Gamma globulin shots give effective protection for up to 5 years. The vaccine is given on Day 1, 1 month later, and 6 months after Day 1. The full course of 3 shots is critical to build up enough protection. Homosexual men require regular blood tests to check for immunity and against being asymptomatic carriers. *Avoid anal and oral sex* unless or until a partner is protected by the hepatitis B vaccine.

# Vaginal Infections

The vagina is not a germ-free environment. Many harmless flora live there, as they do in the male urethra. Yeasts, protozoas and bacteria flourish without any trouble. Under certain conditions, they flare up and cause vaginal infections. These include *monilia* (yeast or thrush), *trichomonas* (protozoa), *bacterial vaginitis* (mixed bacteria) and *non-specific vaginitis* (gardnerella). The symptoms are soreness, itching, swelling, stinging on urination and unpleasant-smelling discharge.

A vaginal infection may not be sexual disease. Antibiotics or a change in diet can upset the natural ecological balance of flora and allow a yeast infection to spread. They used to be thought "women only" conditions. But trichomonas and gardnerella can cause male urethritis. A few men are affected by the fungus of monilia. The glans feels sore and itchy, and small skin ulcers appear a few days after infection.

Such infections breed in stale smegma. *Check genital hygiene.* Less usually, they lurk inside the urethra or prostate. The man is unaware of a problem; he is asymptomatic. So he acts as a silent reservoir of vaginal infection for his partner. If she has therapy, he should involved. If not, she suffers repeated re-infection from the "ping pong" effect.

# Urinary Tract Infections

## Gonorrhea

Gonorrhea is an infection of the mucus membranes which line the male urethra. The disease usually stays localized; it rarely becomes systemic. The symptoms start two to five days after sexual contact with an infected partner. They can start the next day, or two weeks later. If there has been oral or anal sex, gonorrhea can infect the throat or rectum. It is estimated 20 percent of men can have "silent" gonorrhea: they are *asymptomatic* for the disease.

The first symptom is a tingling sensation in the urethra, followed by the urge to urinate frequently. Then, a creamy stringy discharge starts to drip from the meatus. It thickens, turns yellowy-brown and smells unpleasant. The meatus looks red, sore and swollen with an everted rim, its "lips," turn outwards. There is burning discomfort on urination.

With oral gonorrhea, there may be excessive mucus and a mild sore throat. With anal gonorrhea, there may be discharge or an itchy rectum. But gonorrhea of both throat and rectum is usually silent, i.e., asymptomatic.

Gonorrhea is caused by the gonococci bacteria. On average, bacteria reproduce by dividing in two every 20 minutes. A single bacterium becomes 100 million, million, million in one day. Avoid delay. Visit the clinic at the first symptoms. A culture of the discharge is analyzed for gonococci bacteria. A positive result takes 2 days; a negative result, 4 to 6 days. Blood may be taken to test for syphilis, as it can be present in silent form.

Penicillin is both speedy and highly effective therapy. If a person is allergic, tetracycline is given for seven days, or other antibiotics may be used. A return visit is critical to re-check the cultures and ensure all the bacteria are destroyed. In most cases, there are no complications and the cure is complete.

There is a penicillin-resistant gonorrhea called PPNG. The antibiotic, Trobicin, is given for PPNG. With delayed therapy, or inappropriate self-medication, gonococci can cause urethral stricture, prostatitis and epididymitis. More rare complications include endocarditis (infection of heart lining and muscle), arthritis (joint infection) and sterility. Sterility is due to the scarring which creates blockages.

Some 50 percent of men develop urethritis after gonorrhea is cured. This is due to another STD present at the time but taking longer to appear. U.S. health professionals estimate up to two million gonorrhea cases go unreported each year. Avoid self-medication. Seek medical help to become free of gonorrhea and its complications.

## Chlamydia

Chlamydia is another urinary tract infection. The symptoms are similar to gonorrhea but appear later, some two weeks after exposure. There is mild burning on urination near the tip of the penis. Discharge may be absent, or scanty and only in the early morning. A microscopic test called Gram's stain is done while the patient waits. Until recently, chlamydia was just considered one of a large number of organisms which cause urethritis. It was a "male only" problem, irritating but rarely serious.

It is now known untreated chlamydia can cause infection of the eye lining, conjunctivitis. Arthritis is another complication which appears much later with painful swellings of the larger joints: hip, shoulder, knee and wrist. The arthritis gets better but chlamydia returns to plague the victim now and then. Repeated attacks can cause permanent joint damage.

Undiagnosed chlamydia is especially damaging for women, as it can infect the oviducts, and causes infertility. Unfortunately, many men are asymptomatic carriers and act as silent reservoirs of the disease. It is estimated there are between 3 to 10 million U.S. new cases yearly. In Britain, the estimate is 75,000 per year. Fortunately, chlamydia responds well to tetracycline. Chlamydia is more common than gonorrhea in Caucasian men; in those with higher incomes, fewer partners and above average education. Men with hypospadias are more at risk because vaginal germs can be scooped into the meatus due to the penile curve. In older men, it is linked to prostatitis. Urinary tract infections from all causes are higher in homosexuals because anal sex exposes them to rectal bacteria.

## Urethritis (NSU)

Urethritis is the generic name for any urinary tract infection. It is specific when the cause is known, when the germs are identified. It is non-specific when no germs are found, or those found are of unknown origin. With specific urethritis, there is often discharge. Chlamydia or gonococci bacteria are present, and the disease is specific.

Non-specific (or non-gonococcal) urethritis is NSU or NGU. The symptoms are similar to gonorrhea and chlamydia. If the infection reaches the bladder, the pain of cystitis may be felt in the pelvis. There may be fever, with a slight rise in body temperature. It is now known the cause of 30 percent to 60 percent of NSU cases is chlamydia. It is thought the rest are caused by the herpes virus, or trichomonas, but this is not proven. Men who dislike dosing themselves sometimes stop taking the medication when the pain stops. This is dire. Keep in mind *it is the toughest germs which take the longest to destroy*. If the course is not finished, those tough germs start breeding again and there is another flare-up. Another course of medication is required. But over-use of antibiotics gives germs time to develop resistance. If this occurs, the infection can become progressive, and difficult to dislodge.

Cystitis is inflammation of the bladder. It is more common in women who have a short urethra, so the invading bacteria have less far to travel. The symptoms and therapy for cystitis and urethritis are much the same.

# Genital Ulcer Diseases

## Syphilis

The cork-screw shaped bacteria of syphilis penetrate the skin of the penis and within 30 minutes reach the glands in the groin. Some 36 hours after infection, the bacteria have doubled in number. They then double again every 30 hours. It takes an average three weeks (10 to 50 days) for the first symptom to appear. By then, there may be countless bacteria in the blood stream.

The first symptom is a *chancre* (ulcer) on the penis. It starts as a red pimple and develops into an open sore with a hard rim two days after infection. The *chancre* does not hurt, and may be small enough to go unnoticed. It heals slowly and disappears. But the infection remains highly contagious because the bacteria continue to multiply and cause damage inside the body.

The chancre usually appears on the glans. But it can appear on the meatus, shaft, scrotum, anus or pubic area. It can be on the finger, lip or tongue, wherever it was first caught. If it is small, or inside the rectum or urethra, it is possible to have syphilis without seeing the chancre. Have a blood test after high risk sexual activity.

The secondary stage of syphilis starts two to six weeks after the chancre heals. The symptoms vary from a skin rash over the body, swollen glands to a flulike condition. If untreated, they disappear. But syphilis continues to wreak its havoc in the vital organs. The tertiary (third) stage is devastating: heart and brain disorders, joint inflammations and early death.

Early therapy at stage one results in a speedy recovery. Antibiotics destroy the bacteria of syphilis. Complete the full course or series of injections. Regular blood tests checking for lingering infection may be necessary for two years. Keep all follow-up appointments to ensure the disease has finally gone.

In recent years, syphilis is on the increase again. In 1987, the number of U.S. cases rose by 25 percent. Syphilis is three times more common in men than women, and rare in female homosexuals. Because it can be passed to the fetus after the 20th week of pregnancy, a syphilis blood test is a routine part of prenatal care.

## Genital Herpes

The first attack of genital herpes is the worst. Within two to 20 days after infection, there is a tingling or throbbing sensation on the penis, with an itchy area on the shaft. This develops into one or more clear fluid-filled painful blisters in the next few days. There may be pain on urination, with swollen lymph nodes in the groin area. In some cases, the whole body reacts to the virus with flu-like symptoms: fever, headache and chills.

The blisters burst quickly, shedding the highly contagious viruses everywhere. The burst blisters turn into shallow painful ulcers. In some cases, the ulcers join together to form large open sores. A watery unpleasant-smelling discharge drips from the penis. The ulcers form crusts and heal spontaneously within one to five weeks. But some cases of herpes can be asymptomatic, or show only as discharge from the urethra, and be mistaken for NSU. Visit the physician or clinic on the first or second day after the symptoms appear. A diagnosis can then be made by viewing the symptoms and taking a personal history. The cost of a culture test from the blisters is very expensive. At the early stage, the diagnosis can be made by sight alone. At least five types of herpes virus are known to affect humans. Two cause infectious mononucleosis (glandular fever). These are the Epstein Barr virus and cytomegalovirus. The varicella virus causes chicken pox in children and shingles in adults. There are two types of *herpes simplex viruses.* HSV 1 causes cold sores (also called fever blisters) on the lips or nose. HSV 2 causes genital ulcers, or herpes.

By adulthood, most people have been infected with the cold sore virus HSV 1. They have developed antibodies against it, and only a few actually get cold sores. Fewer adults have HSV 2 antibodies because the virus is spread by sexual contact. The results of a recent study estimate 3 percent of nuns, 29 percent of women in a committed relationship and 99 percent of prostitutes have HSV 2 antibodies in their blood.

About half the adults infected with HSV 2 have no symptoms. The other half develop symptoms within three to seven days after sexual contact with an infected partner. The recent increase in genital herpes is thought to be due to the increase in oro-genital sex because both HSV 1 and HSV 2 can cause genital herpes.

Not all viruses die after the active phase of herpes ends. The virus coats itself with the man's own protein substance, and retreats from the penis along the nerve ending. It lies dormant in the large nerve ganglion along the spinal column. It stays inactive for varying periods of time.

The virus usually returns to the same place on the penis. Recurring attacks can be virulent and painful, or very mild. If mild, the man may be unaware he is shedding viruses and is highly contagious. As yet, there is no medication which kills the virus. Each active phase will heal on its own by keeping the area dry and clean. Acyclovir is a prescription drug taken orally. It helps reduce the pain and irritation of an attack. In some cases, it controls and reduces the number of attacks. HSV-2 is linked to cancer of the cervix. It can cause miscarriage in the first trimester of pregnancy. If the virus is shed during birth, one in two babies will be infected. Two out of three will die. Half the others suffer brain damage or visual defects. Birth is by caesarian section. The baby is lifted from the uterus to avoid contact with the virus. Inform a partner before making love to allow freedom of choice over the health risks involved.

## Herpes Self-Help

Because herpes recurs, medical opinion is divided on how long the contagious period lasts. Some doctors think it is only during the active phase and for seven days after. Others believe there is a permanent risk of transmitting the disease. An infected person cannot be free of this worry. Though it is a miserable condition, ignore scare tactics by the media. The over-hype of genital herpes has actually caused some people to take their lives.

There is disagreement over when it is safe to be sexually active. During the dormant phase, if there is virus shedding, it may not be enough to infect a partner. Focus on health. Learn to recognize the warning signs of the onset of an active phase: penile itching, tingling, throbbing sensations, usually at the site of the first attack. Keep a record of the frequency of outbreaks. Avoid all sexual activity during an active phase.

A recurrent active phase can be stimulated by any factor which upsets the balance of the body. Possible causes include:

*Becoming Ill*: Try to keep healthy and fit. Having to cope with another infection can over-load the immune system so that it can no longer hold the herpes virus in the dormant phase.

*High Levels of Stress*: Learn to cope with emotional problems. Avoid over-reacting to stress. Practice meditation to stay calm when faced with happy, sad, or difficult problems in life.

*Poor Nutrition*: Boost the immune system with a healthy diet. Lysine tablets taken when an active phase starts may reduce its duration. Nuts and chocolate which produce the amino acid, orginine, may trigger an active phase.

*Irritation*: Take care with sexual activity. Over-boisterous sex can acutely irritate the areas where the herpes sore previously appeared. Use extra lubrication to avoid this.

*Sunlight*: For men with cold sores, *avoid exposing the genitals to the sun*. Sunbathing can actually bring about an active phase of genital herpes. (It is always unwise to try to tan the penis).

During an attack:

1. Avoid scratching the blisters. Wear loose clothing.

2. Keep the sores as clean and dry as possible. Wash hands after touching the area and applying medication. If the virus is transferred to the face, it can damage the eyes.

3. If it hurts to urinate, pour warm water over the genitals, or urinate in the shower or bath. Drink plenty of water to dilute urine.

4. Sitz baths bring soothing relief. Immerse the buttocks and abdomen in warm water (92-97) for 5 to 10 minutes. Pat herpes lesions dry with a clean soft paper or cloth towel.

5. If the pain is acute, obtain a prescription for topical (local) anesthesia to reduce the discomfort.

All this may sound depressing. Yet herpes is much less dangerous than many other STDs. A calm attitude of mind is all-important. Practice meditation to reduce stress. Think positive. Many people with herpes live happy and fulfilled lives.

## Safe Sex

- The condom does act as a barrier, however incomplete, but only if it is put on before genital contact.
- Always use a condom for high risk sexual activity.
- Always use a condom from the beginning to the very end.
- Urinating after sex helps very slightly to flush out organisms.
- Always have a check-up after high risk sexual activity. It is possible to have asymptomatic STD and be highly contagious.
- The earlier the therapy, the easier the cure.
- Always complete the full course of medication.
- Return for all check-ups after therapy. The lurking nature of STD organisms make this imperative to prevent further attacks.

- One attack of STD gives no immunity against further infection.
- Avoid sexual activity during the infectious stage. If this is not possible, inform a partner of the health risks.
- Avoid auto-inoculation; scratching a herpes ulcer can transmit the virus to the eye.
- Take extra care with hygiene. Face cloths, towels, bed linen and clothing are for personal use only.
- Help reduce the pool of infection in the community by assisting the health professionals in contact tracing.
- Strict hygiene before and after sex can avoid infestation.

The above are merely tips. There is, in fact, only one way to avoid STD. Dr. Catterall, an eminent British venereologist, wrote in the IPPF Medical Publications: "The most important fact of sexually transmitted diseases is that they are not contracted by people who have only one sexual partner."

# Index